LOVE RULES

Other titles in the

True-to-Life Series from Hamilton High

by Marilyn Reynolds:

If You Loved Me

Baby Help

Too Soon For Jeff

Detour for Emmy

Telling

Beyond Dreams

But What About Me?

LOVE RULES

True-to-Life Series
from Hamilton High

By Marilyn Reynolds

Morning Glory Press

Buena Park, California

Library of Congress Cataloging-in-Publication Data

Reynolds, Marilyn, 1935-
    Love Rules / by Marilyn Reynolds.
        p.   cm. -- (True-to-life series from Hamilton High)
    Summary: Seventeen-year-old Lynn experiences surprise,
discomfort, and a new awareness of prejudices and
stereotyping when her best friend Kit comes out as a lesbian.
    ISBN 978-1-885356-75-8 (1-885356-75-7) (hc.)
        ISBN 978-1-885356-76-5 (1-885356-76-5) (pbk.)
    [1. Lesbians--Fiction. 2. Homosexuality--Fiction. 3.
Prejudices--Fiction. 4. Best friends--Fiction. 5. Friendship--
Fiction. 6. High schools--Fiction. 7. Schools--Fiction.]
I. Title.

    PZ7.R3373 Lo 2001
    [Fix]--dc21

                                                2001030645

MORNING GLORY PRESS, INC.
6595 San Haroldo Way   Buena Park, CA 90620-3748
714.828.1998, 1.888.612.8254   FAX 714.828.2049
e-mail: info@morningglorypress.com
Web site: www.morningglorypress.com

"Do you think being in San Francisco turned you into a lesbian?"

"Nothing *turned* me into a lesbian. I just *am* a lesbian!"

"You don't have to get all hostile about it!"

"I'm not *hostile*! I'm trying to tell you this is me! Your sister-friend for life! I didn't just *turn* into a lesbian, any more than you just turned straight. You *are* straight. I *am* lesbian. That's just so how it is! Believe it!"

I take a deep breath and count to ten. What I most want to do is grab my backpack and run home, where everything feels safe and predictable.

ACKNOWLEDGMENTS

For help along the way, I wish to thank:

The students of Calvine High School, especially
Joseph Perez, Janis Gannaway, Patricia Damian,
Robin Petersen, Xenia Echevarria, and students
in Shawn Hamilton's classroom.

Also — Mimi Avocada, Barry Barmore, Corry Dodson,
Dale Dodson, Margaret Dodson, Judy Laird,
Cassandra Lewis, Karyn Mazo-Calf, Matthew Reynolds,
Mike Reynolds, Sharon Reynolds-Kyle, Anne Scott,
Albert Sotelo, and Geoffrey Winder.

Like Marilyn Reynolds' other novels,
Love Rules is part
of the **True-to-Life Series from Hamilton High.**
Hamilton High is a fictional, urban, ethnically mixed
high school somewhere in Southern California.
Characters in the stories are imaginary
and do not represent specific people or places.

To Geoffrey Winder
and the many other young people
who are working to make school campuses
safe and accepting places for all students.

CHAPTER

1

I'm Lynn Wright, seventeen, a senior at Hamilton High. It's Wednesday afternoon, the first week of school. My best friend, Kit Dandridge, and I are on our way home. Her real name is Katherine but no one except her parents ever calls her that.

Kit spent the summer working at her aunt's bookstore in San Francisco, and I worked at a Girl Scout camp up near Big Bear Lake. Usually, whenever one of us goes away, we keep in touch by e-mail. But the one ancient computer at camp wasn't even connected to the Internet. Besides that major block to communications, there was no time of the day or night when kids weren't lined up to use the one pay phone. Even when I could get to the phone, it didn't make for relaxed conversation to have twenty homesick girls behind me, clamoring for me to hurry up. So Kit and I have a lot of catching up to do.

"You have something important to tell me?" I ask, remembering last night's phone conversation.

"I do," she says. "But I want to wait until you come over this evening. I'll tell you when we're under the tree."

"Why the mystery?"

Kit's the type that always blurts out what she's thinking, wherever and whenever.

"I want us to be under our tree when I tell you — like old times," she says. "That's all."

She looks serious, the way she looks when she's talking about some psychological theory, or doing a play-by-play analysis of a lost volleyball game. What could be so important that she's waiting for a special time and place to tell me? Any other girl being all secretive like that, I'd wonder if she was pregnant. But not Kit. She trips hard on the tragedy of teen pregnancy every time she sees a pregnant girl on campus. Not that she's rude, or disrespectful, but Kit has definite, well thought out opinions. So did Jessica Rand, though, and her baby's due any day now. I wonder . . .

"You're not pregnant are you?"

Her look tells me I've asked an eleven on the one to ten scale of stupid questions.

"Well, what am I supposed to think?" I ask.

"Think we're going to sit under our tree, and talk, like we've always done, and I'm going to tell you something I've been wanting to tell you for a long time."

I hope you won't mind the interruption here, but there are some things you should know before we go any further.

Kit and I have been best friends since we were eleven, when she and her parents moved into my neighborhood. By the time the Dandridges' moving van was unloaded, Kit and I were already friends. That day, we went back and forth between our two backyards so many times, my mom joked that we'd soon wear out the hinges on the gate.

Neither Kit nor I have any brothers or sisters — "The Only Child" is how magazine articles refer to people like us. On the very first day we met, we decided we were tired of being "The Only Child," and that we'd be sisters. Not that our birth certificates show we have the same parents or anything, and we definitely don't look alike. Our personalities are different, too. Once Kit gets focused on something, she *stays* focused.

Me, I have a wandering mind. I focus on something for a while, and then some unruly thought intrudes and my brain follows it down a crooked path of more unruly thoughts and pretty soon I'm so far off the subject . . . like now. I started giving you some basic background on me and Kit, and now I'm telling you about the inner workings of my wandering mind. Sorry. Back to necessary information.

There's a huge, ancient walnut tree in Kit's yard, tall and broad and graceful — a magical tree. The summer Kit moved in, we used to sneak copies of the *World Weekly News* from my mom's hidden stash. We'd spend afternoons under the tree, backs resting against its rough trunk, reading outrageous story after outrageous story. We were particularly interested in kidnappings by aliens, but the German shepherd who gave birth to a half-dog, half-child creature, and the one about the face of Jesus appearing on a tortilla also entertained and amazed us.

The *World Weekly News* was Mom's secret addiction. She was ashamed to read "trash" and she thought I didn't know of her collection. Talk about someone not having a clue! I was a very curious eleven and I often had the house to myself. There was not one thing in our house that I'd not examined. I even found an old, sugary love letter from some guy Mom knew before she married my dad. It was on U.S. Army stationery and . . . Oh, no. I'm not going to follow *another* unruly thought.

At first the sister thing was sort of a joke. But the more Kit and I got to know one another, the more we felt like we truly were sisters. Kit believed that even though we were way different on the outside, our spirits rose from the same source. That made sense to me.

We wanted to make the sister thing be official, like maybe doing that blood sister thing. As a potential nurse, though, I didn't think we should share blood.

Here's what we did. The day before school started, Kit and I met under the tree, after dark. I brought a whole stack of *World Weekly News* and a small pitcher of water. Kit brought eight big fat candles, a smaller, heart-shaped candle, a book of matches, and a battery operated fan.

We arranged the candles in a half-circle around the neatly piled papers. We placed our right hands side by side, on top of the paper that claimed Marilyn Monroe's ghost had increased the bust size of a flat-chested woman who visited her Hollywood grave. Then we began our chant.

"We are sisters. Kit Dandridge. Lynn Wright. Sisters for life. Spirit sisters . . . "

We repeated those words over and over again, chanting in a hypnotic rhythm. After about the twentieth "spirit sisters" phrase, we removed our hands from the *World Weekly News* papers.

"Sisters of flame," Kit said, as she lit the candles.

I picked up a handful of dirt and let it fall slowly over the ghostly image of Marilyn Monroe.

"Sisters of earth," I said.

Kit pointed the fan upward and turned it on, causing a slight stirring of leaves on the branch directly above us.

"Sisters of wind," she said.

I dribbled water first over Kit's right hand, then over mine. We grasped one another's dampened hands.

"Sisters of water," I said.

"Spirit sisters forever," we promised.

We sat for a while, watching the flickering candles, then blew them out. We faced one another, gripping each other's hands.

"Goodnight, spirit sister," Kit said.

"Goodnight, spirit sister," I responded.

And that's how we became official spirit sisters. For life.

All through middle school we half-believed in a fantasy world of elves and trolls and leprechauns. To us the walnuts that lay on the ground around the tree were like little brains, and their brainpower refueled our own brains. We'd sit resting against the trunk every morning before school, refueling. I guess it worked, because we both always got good grades back then, even though we hardly ever studied.

In high school we got out of the habit of refueling our brains with walnut brainpower, but we often would sit out under the tree in the evenings, talking about the day, who said what at school, complaining about our parents, or dreaming about the future. We always met there, on Friday evenings, before settling down to junk food and a video at one house or the other. I guess you could say the walnut tree has been a friendship tree for us. Maybe that's why Kit wants to save her big news for a "tree-talk."

So . . . now that you know some of our history together, and you know you have to put up with my unruly wandering mind, we can get on with it. Remember? Kit and I are on our way home, Wednesday afternoon, our first week as seniors at Hamilton High. Are you with me?

Kit is telling me about her summer in San Francisco.

"I really liked working in Aunt Bernie's bookstore. It's a cool place," she says.

"What'd you do there?"

"Worked in the back room, unloading books from boxes and arranging them onto rolling carts, so Bernie could move them out into the store. I packaged orders for UPS pick-ups, answered the phone — you know, the usual no-brainer stuff."

"Sounds better than summer camp."

"Sometimes Bernie had me arrange window displays. That was more of a challenge."

I laugh. "My biggest challenge this summer was staying sane while the little Scout squirts sang us to sleep with 'A Hundred Bottles of Beer on the Wall.' Only they started with a thousand."

"You're in good shape for volleyball, though — all that swimming and aerobics classes with the kids. Except for walking the hilly streets of San Francisco, I got no exercise. The muscles in my arms are mush."

"Coach Terry'll get you back in shape in no time," I say, flexing my biceps.

Kit groans. Terry's a fiend for conditioning. We've already had two practice sessions that left me with aching muscles, and I'm the one in good shape. Kit spent both evenings after practice with her feet elevated on the couch and large packages of frozen peas on each knee. I don't think I'll ever eat peas at her house again, seeing the packages all squished up and dripping. I prefer not to eat anything that's already been used for medicinal purposes.

"How come you're not in PC this semester?" Kit asks. (PC is short for Peer Communications, my favorite class.)

"I am, just not the same period as you."

"Holly and Nicole are in my class," Kit says. They're our friends from middle school days, and they're also on the volleyball team.

"Eric Weiss is in my class," I say.

"Lucky you," Kit says, all sarcastic.

Eric was my boyfriend for a while last year.

"There's this new guy, Conan, who sits behind me. He's nice," I say.

"Football player?"

"Yeah. I guess."

"Robert told me about him," Kit says. "Coach Ruggles thinks Brian Marsters and the new guy are unbeatable . . ."

When Kit says "Brian Marsters," she wrinkles her nose, like she's just smelled something nasty. I'll wait and tell you more about that later, though.

" . . . and the state championship's a sure thing for us this year, with this new Conan the Barbarian guy."

"He hates being called the Barbarian. His dad actually named him after Conan the Barbarian. That's how he's raised him, too. His dad used to set up fights with the neighborhood kids to make Conan prove how strong and tough he was. That's sick, if you ask me."

"How do you know all that stuff?"

"You know. PC. The first day of class Ms. Woods asked us to tell about how we got our names. Didn't you do that in your class?"

"No. She had us tell which animal we'd most like to be, and why."

"What did you choose?"

"A tiger. Because they're strong, and fast, and nobody messes with them."

"So you're changing from a Kitty to Tiger?"

Kit laughs. "I hadn't thought of it that way, but yeah, maybe . . . Did you tell how you were named after that Redgrave actress?"

"No. How embarrassing! I didn't want to say I'm named after some old movie star!"

"So, what did you say?"

"I said I didn't know how I got my name. But Conan, who seems like kind of a shy guy, went on and on about how he hates the whole barbarian thing. Just 'cause he's big and black and plays football, people think he's mean. He's not . . . "

I stop, realizing I've been *totally* breaking PC confidentiality.

Kit knows exactly why I stopped talking.

"I won't say anything."

I know she won't. But in PC we all sign promises to keep whatever goes on in the room absolutely confidential. I'm not the kind of person who goes back on promises.

"I'm sorry I blabbed about Conan's name. That's all."

Kit gives me a long, searching look.

"So are you in love with this guy Conan or something?"

I feel my face warming into a blush, and look away. One of the spirit sister things I'm *not* so wild about is that sometimes Kit knows what I'm feeling even before I do.

"I barely know him."

Kit laughs.

"Well, something's going on. The back of your neck is red as can be, and if I could see your face . . . "

Kit jumps in front of me, pointing and laughing. I laugh, too, feeling my face get even hotter. I wish I didn't blush at all the worst times.

My mom always tells me I should be happy I have such a beautiful, light complexion, and that showing a blush can be quite attractive. I don't think so. I wish I were dark, like Kit. Her mom's part Cherokee, and Kit inherited her dark eyes and nutmeg skin. Kit has her mom's hair, too — thick and black and shiny. It comes down past her shoulders and no matter what she does with it, it looks good.

Mostly she wears it loose, but for volleyball she braids it in one long, single braid. I'd trade my thin, wiry, drab brown hair for hair like Kit's in an instant.

When Kit finishes laughing at me, she gets right back to the subject. Like I told you earlier, Kit's the type that stays focused. She wants to be a psychologist. She'll probably be good at it. She's always practicing.

Me, I'm going to be a pediatric nurse. When I was nine, I had an emergency appendectomy and ended up staying a week in the hospital. That's when I realized how important nurses are. Also, I'm pretty sure it's a job that'll never get boring. I'm good at science, and I like little kids, so even though I decided on a career at the age of nine, it still seems like a good decision.

Kit gestures toward a non-existent couch, and in a fake accent says, "Lie down, relax, and tell Dr. Kit all about Mr. Conan."

"Well, doctor," I say, going along with a familiar game, "I notice when he walks into the room. I'm aware of him."

"Hmmmm. Very interesting. Could it be because he weighs two hundred and thirty pounds?"

"It's more than that."

"More than two hundred and thirty pounds? Ach mein goodness!"

"No, I mean I'm aware of him for other reasons. Not just his size."

"Explain," she says, raising an eyebrow.

"Well . . . sometimes, in class, he'll lean forward and tap me on my shoulder, to ask a question or something. All day long the place where he touched me feels warm, like maybe it's glowing."

"Like your face right now," Kit says, dropping the doctor accent and laughing.

"I just think he's a nice person, and I'd like to get to know him better."

"Well . . . I think your glowing shoulder is a good sign. It means you're over that butthead Eric."

"Yeah," I agree. "Now I wonder how I could ever have liked him.

He says some really stupid stuff in class."

"No surprise," Kit says. "He's got the emotional maturity of a two-year-old."

"Woodsy's already sent him and Brian out of class once."

"Brian's in there, too? I could puke just thinking about him," Kit says, looking like she really *could* puke . . .

So I guess now's the time to tell you about Kit's aversion to Eric's friend, Brian Marsters, and the New Year's Eve party. That was back when I was all excited about Eric. He was cute, in a blond jock kind of way. Lots of girls liked him. That always makes a guy seem even cuter. I could pursue a whole stream of unruly Eric thoughts here, but since I said I'd tell you about Kit and Brian, I'll force my wandering mind to focus.

CHAPTER

2

Here goes. The background on Kit and Brian.

Knowing Kit and I were best friends, Brian asked Eric to set him up with her. It was funny, because Brian always had a bunch of girls hanging around him, especially the cheerleader/drill team types. It's that football player thing. But he'd told Eric that if Kit wouldn't go to the New Year's Eve party with him, he wasn't going. When I asked why, Eric said it had something to do with Brian wanting to experience the passion of a half-breed. What an idiot, I'd said. I'm not setting my best friend up with someone like that.

But then Eric said no, it was only a joke, and that Brian had liked Kit for a long time but he was too shy to do anything about it. Oh, right, Brian Marsters is shy, I'd said, all sarcastic. But Eric said Brian was shy with girls he really likes, he didn't mean the half-breed thing, blah, blah, blah, so I talked Kit into going to the party with Brian. The four of us went together in what our moms referred to as a double date.

Kit and I were more into sports than boys, so we weren't used to the party scene. This one was supposed to be fancy, because of New Year's Eve, and our moms took us shopping for "evening wear," as the store clerks called it. Kit's mom tried to talk her into buying high heels to go with her fancy dress.

"Sorry, Mom. I only wear shoes I can walk in," Kit said.

They compromised on something sort of dressy, but flat. Not me. Eric had said he liked the look of women in heels, so that's what I got.

I hobbled around at the party at first, feeling awkward and out of balance, but then I got sort of used to the unnatural act of standing on my toes with my body pitched forward.

Eric and I danced and talked and hung out with friends. Really, Eric and I had some good times together for a while. Then I sort of got tired of him. Like with his jokes. They were funny the first time, but then it was like constant replay. I think there's something dumb about a guy who laughs so hard at his own jokes he doesn't notice that no one *else* . . . oops. There went my wandering mind again.

Back to Kit and Brian and the New Year's Eve party. All the time Eric and I were enjoying ourselves, I kept noticing Brian and Kit, standing off to the side. Brian had his arm around Kit, but neither of them was smiling and it didn't look like they were talking, either.

At midnight the lights went out and, except for Kit and Brian, everyone kissed the New Year in. Kit told me later that Brian grabbed her and tried to kiss her, but she pushed him away. He tried again, more forcefully, managing to get his mouth pressed against hers. She twisted loose and ran to the restroom, where she rinsed her mouth out, over and over. I thought she was being extreme. It's not like Brian had some dread disease, or toilet breath, or anything like that. I mean, really, what's a New Year's kiss?

For months after the party, Brian kept calling Kit, asking her to meet him at the mall, or go to some party with him, or go for a ride, or whatever. Eric told me that Brian always got whatever girl he wanted and Kit was a challenge. Brian was a pest as far as Kit was concerned — someone with the brains of a beetle and the personality of a rock, she'd said. He finally gave up, but not before Kit pretended to get a whiff of something bad every time she heard his name.

So now you know.

Back to the present.

As we wait at the signal to cross Main, I tell Kit, "We were only juniors in the Brian and Eric phase. We didn't know anything! Our senior year is going to be soooo cool."

"Or, different at least."

"No, really. Everyone says your senior year is the best. That's how this year's going to be!"

"Maybe," Kit says, obviously not overcome with enthusiasm for my prediction.

We cross the street and stand counting our money in front of Barb 'n Edie's. My mom remembers the grand opening of this place, back in the seventies, when the red leather booths were new, and Barb and Edie were young. Hard to imagine. Mom says this place is the quintessential greasy spoon, whatever that means.

Kit and I have enough money for two sodas and a large order of fries. They've definitely got the best fries in town and their garbage-burgers are practically world famous. We don't have enough money for one of those. Besides, a garbageburger's a feast, not a snack.

Barb 'n Edie's is jammed, but the wait is worth it. McDonalds' fries, or Barb 'n Edie's? It's like the difference between a pile of sawdust and a hot fudge sundae. We carry our fries and sodas to a table near the back. The faded red leather on one of the seats is held together with duct tape, as is the back of the opposite seat. The formica tabletop is gouged and scratched with hundreds of initials of previous diners. Well, we're here for the food, not the decor.

I go to the counter for packets of catsup and see Rosie, the librarian's daughter, sitting on a stool near the kitchen, drawing on a paper placemat.

Here's another interruption, but you'll need to know a little something about Rosie and her mom.

Last year, when I was a junior, I was an aide in the library. I got to know Rosie's mom, Mrs. Saunders, really well. Only it wasn't Mrs. Saunders then. It was Ms. Morrison. She got married last summer. I guess it's a second marriage or something, because she's got Rosie.

Every day, after school, Rosie came to the library and worked on her homework in her mom's office. When I was finished shelving books, sometimes I would practice math facts with Rosie. She's really smart, but she still had to count on her fingers to add numbers. And subtraction? Not a clue.

Sometimes I baby-sat for Rosie, when Emmy and Mr. Saunders went out. After a while, Emmy told me, "Ms. Morrison sounds too formal. I'd rather you just call me Emmy."

So that's how it's been. Anyway, back to Barb 'n Edie's.

"**H**ey, Rosie-Posey, how's third grade?"

"Look!" she says, showing me her picture. "It's Mom's library."

"Wow! Good job!" I tell her, amazed by how much better this picture is than the ones she drew last year, in second grade.

"See, here are the books, and the computers are over there . . ."

"I can tell," I say. "How's math?"

"Okay," she says, carefully outlining the computers in black. I think she doesn't want to talk about math.

Barb, of Barb 'n Edie's, pauses on her way back to the kitchen. She smiles at Rosie. I notice that, because a smile on the face of Barb is a rarity.

"Doin' okay there, Kiddo?"

Rosie smiles back. "Can I have another Coke, Grams?"

"You bet, Sweetie. Comin' right up."

"See ya," I say, and go back to our table.

"Is that Mrs. Saunders' daughter you were talking to?" Kit asks, opening a catsup packet and dripping it out, dot by dot, over two fries.

I nod.

"What's she doing in here by herself?"

"She's not by herself. She's with her grandmother — Barb."

"Hold on. *Barb* is that little girl's grandmother?"

"Yeah."

"So does that mean that *Barb* is the librarian's mother?"

"Clever deduction, Dr. Dandridge."

"No way!"

"Yes, way. I'll bet Emmy doesn't know Gramma Barb is supplying Rosie with caffeine filled colas, though."

"Mrs. Emily Saunders's mom is *Barb*? Are you sure?"

"I'm sure! Barb was at their house one night when I baby-sat Rosie. Emmy called Barb 'Mom.' Okay?"

"How did Mrs. Saunders ever get to be so nice with a mom like Barb?"

"You tell me, Dr. Kit. You're the big psychologist."

"Well, you're the big library aide pet."

"Just because I call her Emmy doesn't mean I know her whole history. Besides, I'm not an aide anymore."

"Why not? I thought you liked being an aide."

"I couldn't fit it into my schedule."

"Oh, look! There's your friend Conan!" Kit says, looking toward the door.

I turn quickly, but there is no two hundred and thirty pound hunk anywhere to be seen. Kit laughs.

"Made you look!"

"You can be as irritating as a singing Scout," I tell her.

"Made you blush!" she says, laughing harder.

I take a long, cool drink of my soda.

"Seriously," Kit says. "I'm glad you're in love."

"I'm telling you, I don't even know him!"

"But face it. Dr. Kit knows that when you blush at a name, you're entering the department of l-o-v-e."

"Yeah . . . whatever," I say.

My wandering mind goes to Conan. What if Kit's right, and I'm interested? What's wrong with that? He's got a great smile. And when he looks at me, when we're talking, it's not like he's half-looking, or half-listening. Most guys are constantly on the lookout for who else is around, or they're thinking about what they're going to say next, everything but listening. That's how Eric was during the three months we were doing the boyfriend/girlfriend thing. Conan's different. And his eyes . . .

When I've conquered unruly thoughts and come back to reality, I ask Kit, "What about you? Is there anyone you might blush over, if I could see you blush?"

"Not really," she says.

"How about Robert? You're always talking with him."

"He's a friend."

"I think he likes you."

"Yeah, well . . . he doesn't increase my pulse rate."

"Who does?" I ask.

We sit, slowly munching our fries in silence, watching other Hamilton High students come and go.

"Is that what you want to tell me under the tree? You met a guy in San Francisco and you're in love? Is that it?"

I'm smiling in anticipation. That *must* be what she wants to tell me. Why didn't I guess that before?

Kit shakes her head.

"Well, what then?" I ask, frustrated. "What's the big news?"

"It's not exactly news," Kit says.

"Well??? What *is* it then?"

Kit is quiet for what seems like a long time, dipping and re-dipping a now limp fry into a mound of catsup. Finally she says, "We tell each other everything, right?"

"Right."

"Straight out. Spirit sisters. For life. Right?"

"Right," I say.

"Well . . . It would be better to talk under the tree," she says.

I sigh. "Just tell me."

Kit looks around the cafe, which is quieter now, and less crowded. She takes a deep breath, like she's getting ready to dive from the high board and knows she'll need all the breath she can get before she surfaces.

"It can wait."

"Kit!"

Pause. Long pause. We may as well leave. Let her tell it her way, under the tree. I'm reaching for my backpack, ready to go, when Kit starts talking. "Remember that time with Brian?"

"How could I forget?"

"It wasn't only Brian."

"What do you mean?"

"Well, Brian is a jerk all right. But I realized something that night that I'd not been wanting to think about, even though deep down inside I knew I *had* to think about it."

"Think about *what?*"

"Think about how it wasn't only Brian I didn't want kissing me. I didn't want *any* boy to kiss me. Ever."

I don't understand what she's saying. "So?" I ask.

"So...I don't like boys 'that way,'" she says. "I don't want a boy touching me 'that way.'"

She fiddles with another limp, grease-laden fry, not looking up. Finally she says, softly, still not looking at me, "I like girls."

"You like girls?"

"That's how I am," she says.

It's my turn, now, to play with a french fry, mulling over what I hope I didn't just hear.

"I like girls, too. Some of my best friends are girls," I say, trying to force a joke. But this is Kit. The one with focus.

"You don't like girls the way I do. I like girls the way you like boys."

Follow your breath. I heard that on some stress reduction tape my mom was listening to. How stupid, I'd thought. But right now, I'll just sit here and breathe. In. Out. In. Out.

"That's it. That's what I had to tell you. I'm tired of secrets."

So okay. I live near the second largest city in the United States. I watch TV. I read the newspaper. I know there are people who like people of the same sex, "that way." But Kit? I don't know what to say. I don't even know what to think.

Kit watches me, looking for a reaction. I'm stunned. Shocked. We've told each other some strange stuff over the years, but I never expected to hear anything like *this*. I mean, I have nothing against women who love women, or men who love men — homosexuals. I'm not a bigot. I watch all of the "Will and Grace" reruns. But Kit? Maybe she's joking? Kit wouldn't joke around about something this important, though. I'm confused. No, I'm **CONFUSED!**

"How long?" I ask.

"How long what?"

"How long have you liked girls, instead of boys?" Kit makes figure eights on her napkin, using her catsup tipped French fry as if it were a paintbrush.

"Always, I guess. But I really started thinking maybe I was . . . different . . . sometime in seventh grade. You know, it was like one day we were a bunch of girls, only interested in soccer and volleyball, everyone hanging out by my tree, and the next day you and all of our friends could only talk about Ken's so cute, and Steve likes Crystal, and doesn't Brian have the sexiest eyes you've ever seen, and isn't Freddie Prinze, Jr. just the finest thing ever on screen. And I didn't get it. All that boy talk bored me."

"It did?"

"It wasn't only that I was bored by it, either. It made me mad. I felt like we were losing something important, and no one else noticed. Not even you."

"*What* didn't I notice?"

"We had our circle of friends. That's all we cared about or needed. Remember? Holly, Nicole, Tina. We had sports, jokes, silly songs, going to the beach on the beach bus. We were tight. And then it ended. Just like that. And I'm the only one who cared."

Kit's voice is shaky now, like when her mom changed the locks on their doors and wouldn't let her dad come in. He was locked out for a week, and all that time, Kit's voice was shaky.

"But we were all friends," I say. "We're still friends, except for Tina, and that's just because she moved away."

"It wasn't the same. We weren't a *circle* of friends anymore, looking across at one another, laughing with one another."

Pause.

"You know those pottery candle holder things you see in trendy shops up in Old Town?"

I shake my head no.

"I know you've seen them. Maybe not exactly pottery, maybe that terra cotta stuff. There're five women, arms locked, forming a circle, facing inward . . ."

"Oh, yeah. I know what you mean. My Aunt Grace has one on her mantle."

"Okay. So that's how we were, that circle of friends thing. Only we were kids."

"Right. And the problem was . . .?"

Kit sighs. "The circle broke apart. It became more like a line, so it was easier to look across at the boys. Girls watching boys watching girls. At least four of you were watching boys. I didn't care about the boys. But our circle was gone."

Kit gazes out the window. Sadness permeates the space between us. I want to say something.

"But . . ." But what? I don't know *what* to say. I'm looking across the table at Kit, and I'm thinking, do I know you? Is this conversation really happening?

"There was all that other stuff, too," she says, shifting her gaze away from the window and back to me.

"What other stuff?"

"Stuff that made me think I wasn't like the rest of you."

I wait for Kit to continue, aware of a growing dimness inside the cafe, aware of the scent of a few cold fries on the table between us, aware that nothing is as it has always seemed.

Kit is watching a couple, college age maybe, who are waiting at the counter for their order to come up. I, too, watch, wondering why Kit is so interested. The two are smiling, leaning into one another, obviously enjoying the moment. Kit sighs. She takes our few remaining fries, dirty napkins and paper containers from the table and carries them to the trash.

"Okay, other stuff," she says, sliding back onto the seat across from me.

"While you and the rest of our friends were fantasizing about your romantic heroes, I was fantasizing about Miss Hughes," Kit says, her voice back to its usual strength.

"You were fantasizing about our choir teacher?"

"Remember that old Carpenters' song we did for the spring concert?" She sings, softly, "Love, look at the two of us . . ."

I join in with the alto part . . . "strangers in every way . . ."

"Right. She'd look my way, and I was certain there was a special, hidden meaning in her look, and that she loved me in the same way I loved her."

"Oh my God!"

"Gosh," Kit corrects me.

I can't believe she's doing this, right in the middle of the most intense conversation we've ever had. My mom has this thing about not using "God" in a slang way. She says it's disrespectful to toss God's name around like that. Kit agrees, and I sort of do, too. I don't know if there even *is* a god but it's probably good to be respectful, just in case. But I really don't think *now* is the time for Kit to correct my speech patterns, while she's confessing her bizarre love for Miss Hughes!

Like any good psychologist would, Kit knows I'm steamed.

"Sorry," she says.

"*Gosh* forgives you," I tell her. We laugh. Which helps.

"So anyway, after class I'd always walk up to Miss Hughes and stand close, just for an instant, to breathe the same air she was breathing."

"Weird," I say.

"But *I* couldn't help thinking about *her*, anymore than *you* could help thinking about *Freddy Prinze, Jr*. I mean, how many times did we have to rent that stupid video, 'I Know What You Did Last Summer,' just so you could drool over Freddy?"

"I thought you liked that movie."

"I liked Jennifer Love Hewitt."

"Weird."

"Would you please stop saying that?" Kit says, her voice sort of quivery again.

"What?"

"Weird. Stop saying weird. I know it sounds weird. It's not easy to tell you this. I thought about writing it all in an e-mail, while I was away this summer. I'd click send and it'd be waiting for you when you got back from camp. You'd read it before I even saw you . . . so I wouldn't have to see your face . . ."

Tears run down her cheeks. She turns away.

"I just want to be sure I understand," I tell her. "You're saying you're . . . a . . . homosexual. Right?"

"Right."

"You're sure?"

"Yeah. I am. Sure and scared," she says, in a whisper. "What will my parents do when they find out? And I'm afraid you won't believe we're spirit sisters anymore. I can't keep pretending I'm like everybody else, though, especially not to you . . . We are still sisters in spirit, aren't we?"

Are we, I wonder? We've always been there for each other. When Kit's family life was a mess, she'd stay at my house and we'd talk and talk until she felt better. And back when I was thirteen, my mom and I were constantly fighting. In those days, Kit's mom was perfect and mine was a witch — with a capital B. Even then, Kit would be the psychologist and I would spill my guts. Not just about Mom, either. I was way worried that I'd never grow boobs. Kit was already a 34B cup, and I was still in the saucer stage. She never made fun of me, though, or told me I was stupid to worry. She even looked up stuff about hormones on the Internet for me. We'd talk for hours, and end up laughing so hard I'd forget my problems. She's always done that for me.

"A question hangs in the air," Kit says. She gazes out the window, as if the answer doesn't matter. "Still spirit sisters?"

"Spirit sisters," I say, giving her a high five. "For life."

"For life," she says, smiling, returning the gesture with enthusiasm. "I was sure I could count on you . . . pretty sure, anyway."

We laugh. The tension melts away. Again I am at ease with Kit.

The lights are on in the cafe now, and my butt is numb from sitting here so long. On the walk home, I keep sneaking looks at Kit, the way she walks, her hands, her thick black hair framing her dark, high-cheekboned face. It's the same old Kit, isn't it? But then why does everything feel so strange?

CHAPTER

3

Friday night. It's been two days since Kit confessed to me that she likes girls. I was supposed to spend the night at her house tonight, getting back to our usual Friday night sleep over routine, but at the last minute I backed out. I was a sneak about it, too. I called at a time when I knew she'd be gone, and left a message on her machine.

"Kit? Listen, my mom already had plans for us to visit Aunt Grace tonight, so I can't sleep over. Sorry."

Aunt Grace's not my real aunt, that's just what I've always called her. She's one of my mom's friends from a long time ago. Kit knows we do visit her sometimes, so maybe she'll believe my story.

I've never, ever lied to Kit before. I feel like trash. I'm not even sure why I did it, except that it just seemed too creepy to spend the night with her, and sleep in the same bed, knowing what I know now.

Just after I've left the lying message on Kit's machine, Mom comes in from her job at Microdyne Technology.

"I'm surprised you're home. I thought you'd be at Kit's by now."

"She had to do something with her parents," I say, not looking Mom in the eye.

"Really?" Mom sounds doubtful.

"Yeah."

"Well . . . Roberta and I have plans to go to dinner and see a movie. Do you want to go with us?"

"No. I'm fine."

"You'll be all right on your own?"

"Sure."

"Don't want to be seen with the old ladies?"

"It's not that," I say, forcing a smile.

My mom is short, and kind of pudgy, with blonde hair held back with one of those hair band things Hillary Clinton used to wear. When I was little I loved the softness of my mom. I could practically bury myself in her if I was hurt, or tired. Then, when I got to be about thirteen, I wished she were thin and tall and stylish, like Kit's mom. But now that I'm seventeen, I'm over that. She's a good mom, even if she's what the magazines call full-figured.

Mom gives me one of her "this isn't the whole story" looks.

"You're not getting sick are you? You look a little peaked."

"Mom! I'm fine!"

"Well, I'll have to take your word for it," she says.

I pick up a copy of *People* and pretend to be reading it. Finally, Mom gives up and leaves the room. I go into the kitchen and turn off the ringer on the phone. It would be just my luck to have Kit call and Mom answer and then they'd both know I'd been lying.

When Mom leaves, I turn the ringer back on the phone. I get a Clucker's Old Fashioned Chicken Pot Pie from the freezer and microwave it. Clucker's is this place down on Fifth Street that makes chicken pot pies from Mr. Clucker's grandmother's recipe. I swear that's their name — Clucker. If they'd been named Woofer, would we have had Woofer's Old Fashioned Doggie Pot Pies? Never mind.

I take my pot pie and a glass of milk into the living room and put it on the coffee table. I turn on the TV, then go through the house turning off lights and closing the blinds. I leave a dim light on in the living room, because that's what we always do when we're gone, and Kit knows it. I sit in front of the TV, the sound way low.

There's a reason people come all the way from as far north as Bakersfield and as far south as San Diego for Clucker's. The filling is thick and yummy, with a melt-in-your-mouth crust. I always eat the filling first, then savor the crust. Mom says I've been eating Clucker's that way since she first started me on solid food.

Why am I thinking so much about Clucker's? Because I don't want to think about how I've treated Kit. That's why. When I get to the crust, it has the cardboard texture of cheap pizza. I should have cooked it in the oven instead of the microwave. I don't care. Liars deserve cardboard crusts.

About ten, the time I might be home from Aunt Grace's, if that's where I'd been, the phone starts ringing. It rings every ten or fifteen minutes, until about eleven-thirty. Then it stops. Before I go to bed I listen to the messages on the machine in the kitchen. Four from Kit, each one sounding sadder than the one before.

"Don't shut me out," is what the last message says. I erase them all and go to bed.

I lie there for a long time, waiting for sleep to come. Wilma, my little black and white border collie/cocker spaniel mutt is curled up next to me on my bed, her head resting on the edge of my pillow, her paws twitching as she runs through fields of doggie dreams. *I'm* wide awake, trying not to think about the major Kit drama, trying not to think about lying to her. Have you ever really tried not to think about something? Try not to think about an octopus. Just try it. See what I mean? So here's what I'm not thinking about, which is the same thing as saying I'm thinking about it all the time. Lesbian. My best friend is a lesbian. I've been sleeping with her for six years. A lesbian. What does it all mean?

I toss and turn, stretch out on my stomach, my back, curl up in a fetal position. Nothing works. Wilma stirs with each turn, but doesn't wake up.

I turn on the light and take the novel we're reading for English from my bedside table. When we were first assigned this book, *The Color Purple*, I didn't think I'd like it. It's a bunch of letters to God, and they're not even written in good English. Sometimes I have to read the same thing over and over just to figure out what it means. That part is getting easier now, though.

In the book, the main character, Celie, the one who writes the letters, is three years younger than I am. She's already had two babies, and her own *father* is the father of her babies. And things get worse and worse. But something about Celie makes me want to keep reading — maybe it's the way she keeps on trying even though her life is already trashed.

I take up on page thirty-six. Here's a coincidence. Celie is having trouble sleeping, too. And get this, after a lot of sleepless nights she writes:

What it is? I ast myself.
A little voice say, Something you done wrong. Somebody spirit you sin against. Maybe.
Way late one night it come to me. Sofia. I sin against Sofia spirit.

I close the book and think about why *I* can't sleep. Like Celie, I ask myself "What it is?" And it doesn't take long to figure it out. If I thought about sin, like Celie does, I'd have to say that I sinned against Kit's spirit when I lied to her. Even if I don't think in terms of sin, I know I was wrong to be dishonest with Kit. I want to call her right now — somehow wash away the lie and put things right between us. I'll call first thing in the morning. But what will I say?

Finally, when the sun is up, I wander into the kitchen. Mom is still sleeping. I force myself to wait until nine, a reasonable time to call people on a Saturday morning. I pick up the phone and dial Kit's number. I still don't know exactly what I'll say. In PC we learned it's best to use "I" statements in tense situations. That way the other person doesn't need to get defensive. I've never, ever had to think twice about anything I said to Kit — I always just said it. But things are different now.

Kit's line is busy. This happens a lot. We call each other at the exact same time. It's because we're both on the same wave length according to Mom. I used to think that was true, but how can I be on the same wave length as someone who's, well . . . a homosexual.

I press redial. Kit picks up before the first ring is finished.

"Did you just try to call me?" I ask.

"Yep."

We both laugh. Then there is a long pause.

"You first," Kit says. "You're the one who got the call through."

A lot of things run through my mind. Stay with "I" messages I remind myself.

"I feel weird about what you told me the other day."

"*You* feel weird. How do you think I feel?" Kit asks.

"I don't know. That's one of the weird things. I always thought I knew how you felt, and now I don't."

There's a long silence.

"Look," Kit says. "It's still me."

We talk in a slow, awkward way until finally Kit says, "This is frustrating. Come spend the night and we'll have plenty of time to talk. We'll rent a movie. Like always."

I don't respond.

"Come on Lynn, stop being so uptight! I'll sleep on the couch if you want, and you can have my bed to yourself."

"It's not that," I say.

"Is, too!"

"I'll check with Mom and call you back," I say.

"Yeah, well I'm not buying any more lies! I can't believe you didn't just come straight out with it yesterday and say you didn't want to spend the night with a homo!"

"I'm confused! Okay?"

"Okay, that makes two of us. But listen, you're not my type. You're my spirit sister. I want that always, but don't flatter yourself that I find you physically attractive."

When we hang up my head is spinning! I go into my room and stand looking at the picture collage on the wall above my desk. There's a picture of my mom and dad, before they divorced. And a picture of Wilma jumping for a frisbee. It's an action shot, like you see in magazines, and Wilma would look exactly like those border collie frisbee champs, except for her cocker spaniel ears flopping in the breeze.

There's a picture of me and Gramma and Grampa, dressed up for Christmas. They look healthy and happy in that picture, and it's strange to think that only a year later, both of them were dead. My gramma died first, of cancer. Then my grampa a month later, of a heart attack. Mom thinks he died of the shock of losing Gramma. Who knows? All I know is they're dead and I miss them. They both thought I was the greatest kid on earth. My mom loves me, but she's more realistic about me than Gramma and Grampa were. I miss being the greatest wonderful kid in the world to somebody.

Besides those few pictures, there are a bunch of me and Kit — at the beach, in the mountains, clowning around in the sprinklers. Also, there are snaps that include Holly and Nicole, too, playing volleyball, and soccer. But check out the one of us dressed like Beauty and the Beast one Halloween. Kit was the beast. Did it mean anything that I was the girl and she was the boy? We were only twelve. Did she *want* to be a boy? Just because she likes girls, I mean *really* likes girls, does that mean she wants to be a boy?

My mom once complained because I had more pictures of Kit up there than I did of my own family.

"But Kit *is* my family," I'd said. "She's my sister."

"Don't talk silly," Mom said, half-angry.

"I'm not — she's my spirit sister."

That's how I felt then, and I still do. Kit has a right to be who she is. I've got to remember that. I go to the phone and call her.

"I'll be over around six," I tell her.

"Cool. Pete's Pizza, garbageburgers, or Clucker's?

"Pizza," I say.

I don't have to tell her I want mushrooms and black olives. She knows. That's the kind of friend I never want to lose.

Things feel strange, but we go through the motions of our regular Friday night routine. We do the pizza pig out and watch "My Dog Skip." On Monday, before the big drama, we decided that "Dog" would be the word for our senior year. I'll explain.

Each September, just before school starts, we decide which word has to be in the title of our Friday night video rentals. Last year it was "moon." So we saw "Racing with the Moon," "Moon Struck," "Paper Moon." We even saw "Moon Raiders," which wasn't all that great, but by the time school was almost out, we were desperate to find another "moon" movie. Most people think that's a weak way to choose a movie, but we like it. We get some offbeat stuff that way. Sometimes we like offbeat.

We cry over "My Dog Skip," and I think about Wilma, and how sad I'll be when she dies.

"You'll probably be thirty by that time," Kit says. "You may not even like dogs then."

"I'll always like dogs. And I'll always *love* Wilma."

"You can't be sure how you'll feel when you're thirty," Kit says.

So we have this long, stupid conversation about dogs, and the role they'll have in our lives when we're thirty, and will Wilma lose her pep when she gets old, and on, and on, and on. I think we do that to avoid talking about what's most on our minds.

It's after eleven when Kit's mom and dad come in from a meeting. Kit's dad, David, goes to an AA meeting almost every day. Sometimes her mom goes with him. They look like a couple you could see in the movies. On the screen, I mean, not just in the audience.

Kit's mom, Jessie, is tall and slim. She's wearing a white linen dress that sets off her dark skin and eyes. She probably could have been a model if she'd wanted. Kit's dad is dressed in khaki pants and a plaid cotton shirt. He's a sheriff, and tough looking — muscular, not paunchy like some of those guys. He's not Mr. Macho, though. Every night before he goes to bed, Kit's dad prays for whoever he's arrested that day, and for other people he's seen who are in trouble. Kit says he's been doing that ever since he started with the AA thing.

"How was the movie?" he asks, sitting on the edge of the sofa, resting his arm on Kit's shoulder.

We tell him about "My Dog Skip," how funny and how sad.

Jessie picks up a piece of cold pizza crust and starts munching away.

"I'll watch that movie some time, when I'm ready for a good cry," she says.

"We've got a fresh quart jar of jelly and a tub of peanut butter for in the morning," David says.

We all laugh, remembering how all through the seventh grade Kit and I only ate peanut butter mixed with jelly. No toast. Just a bowl of the mixture which we'd eat with spoons. Kit's mom said it was hormonal, but I don't even want to think about hormones right now. Did Kit's hormones go crazy some time back then, turning her into a . . . girl lover?

Kit's dad leans over and kisses her on the top of her head.

"Goodnight, sweet Katherine," he says.

Even back when Kit's dad was drinking, his eyes would go all soft when he looked at her. I envy that. My dad's eyes always look the same, whether he's looking at me or some football game on TV.

Jessie gives the usual parental warning about not staying up too late. They really don't care though, as long as we're not loud. I watch as they leave the room. They seem happy together.

When they first moved to our neighborhood, Kit's dad, David, was a major alcoholic. He and Kit's mom were always fighting about how much he drank. Jessie actually filed for divorce — told him she'd get sole custody of Kit and he'd pay hell to see her. No court would give visiting rights to a stumbling down drunk. I guess that scared him. He stopped cold. He told Kit he did it for her — he knew she deserved more in a father than one who could only think about the next drink.

Now they're like some TV family. Right after he quit drinking, David dragged his guitar out of storage and started playing again. Mostly country stuff, but not bad. Kit often sings with him and they sound pretty good together. She's got a strong soprano voice, and his is low and rough, so it's a good contrast. Anyway, things are different than when I first met them.

4

Finally, when we've run out of stupid, shallow stuff to talk about, and it's so late the traffic noises from Main Street have dwindled, and no one else is stirring around in Kit's house, we start talking, for real. Kit tells me more about how for a long time she'd suspected she had feelings for women and not for men. I tell her about my hopes that Conan will pay more attention to me.

"If he does, like if the two of you got together, would it be a big deal that he's black?"

"To me it wouldn't. We're all just people is the way I see it."

"What about your mom?"

"I don't think so. She's not prejudiced."

"Your dad?"

"He'd be *all* twisted. But I hardly ever see him and when I do he hasn't a clue about what's going on with me . . . What about *your* mom and dad? What if you brought home a girl that you . . . "

I can't finish the sentence.

"It worries me to think of telling Mom and Dad. They're so . . . straight. They've been through so much . . . I don't want to hurt them."

Kit goes to get us each a Coke and fix another batch of microwave popcorn. I stay on the couch, thinking.

Kit returns with popcorn and drinks and puts them on the coffee table in front of where I'm sitting. Then she sits cross-legged on the floor, directly opposite me.

"Lynn?"

I look up from dipping my own individual bowl into the giant popcorn bowl.

"What?"

"I had to tell *you*. I couldn't stand it any longer, keeping the real me a secret — letting you go on thinking I'm someone I'm not. As for telling anyone else — I'm not brave enough yet."

"Maybe you could meet a perfect guy and that would change things."

"Believe me. Okay??" she says, annoyed. "I'm as sure of where I stand on the sexuality scale as I am that I have black hair."

"But remember what you said earlier, about not being able to know how you'll feel about things when you're thirty?"

"Dogs. We were talking about dogs. It's not the same. Things won't change for me. I've had a long string of secret crushes on girls — women. I never want anyone of the male persuasion touching me, kissing me. I'm a lesbian and nothing will change that."

This is the first time either of us has said the L word out loud.

"Lesbian sounds so . . . so definite."

"That's what I'm telling you! It's definite! I am definitely a LESBIAN!"

I go out to the kitchen. Kit doesn't follow. I lean against the kitchen counter, my thoughts in a whirl. It's too much to take in, too sudden. I always thought Kit and I would each find *the* boy in our senior year. We'd do that double date thing to the prom, and to grad night, and to all that senior stuff that's supposed to be part of the best years of our lives.

I get another bag of microwave popcorn and zap it. Then I melt butter in a small Pyrex pitcher. I'm stalling for time. It's all too intense. I'm not wild about intense. I zip back into the family room and grab the popcorn bowl. Kit's reading the notes on the "My Dog Skip" video case.

"Be right back," I say.

I empty the bag of popcorn into the bowl, pour butter over it, salt it, and take my time mixing it up.

Not that I want more to eat. I needed a break.

Kit and I both pick at the hot, buttery popcorn. Then, without looking at me, she tells me how important I am to her, and how much she wants me to understand the way things are for her.

"I want to understand. I'm trying," I say.

Kit concentrates on eating popcorn. I go to the bathroom. When I come back she says, "Being at Aunt Bernie's last summer gave me a chance to figure some things out. Like maybe I'm not a freaky pervert after all. Maybe it's okay to be a lesbian."

Then she starts talking about her Aunt Bernie.

"She's totally different from my mom — more relaxed or something. You know how Mom always worries about what other people think."

"That's just being a mom," I say.

"I guess. But Bernie isn't into all that stuff about how people should act, and look, and think. She says she's a free spirit. My dad says she's a nutcase whacko. Hhe smiles when he says it, but he's only half kidding."

"Why did he let you spend the summer with her, if he thinks she's a whacko?"

"He only half thinks she's a whacko. She wanted me to work in her bookstore. One thing my dad really wants me to know is the value of hard work. You know him, 'By the time I was sixteen I was working a forty-hour week.'" She stands, imitating her father, thumbs hooked through her belt loops, rocking back on her heels. "'I helped support my family, kept up with my schoolwork, rode my bicycle twenty miles a day between home and school and work. Not one of those fancy high tech bikes, either. Mine had one gear — muscle gear. Kids today don't realize how easy they have it . . .'"

Kit's imitation is perfect.

"Your dad's pretty nice, though."

"Yeah. He's cool. I get tired of the old hardship story is all."

"My dad does the hardship thing, too, but he doesn't have all the redeeming qualities your dad does."

"Twenty miles a day on his bicycle? Work, supporting the family . . ."

"No, but he tells me 'you don't know how lucky you are to have this computer. When I was in high school I had to do all my work by *hand*. Term papers? I didn't even have a typewriter, much less a computer.'"

We laugh.

"So anyway, Aunt Bernie promised she would work my fingers to the bone, keep my nose to the grindstone, my shoulder to the wheel, every work cliché you can think of. So she convinced Dad I should go. Mom goes along with whatever Dad says. It's like she has no opinions of her own."

"She sure *used* to have opinions," I say, thinking about the time she changed the locks on their doors.

"She had opinions when Dad was drinking. Now that he's quit, they never, ever argue. Aunt Bernie says my mom's whipped."

"Whipped?"

"You know. Not physically, but like she's totally ruled by my dad. I think she's afraid to ever upset him."

After more popcorn munching, and the distraction of Jay Leno, Kit gets back to the subject of her summer away.

"Aunt Bernie's world is *so* not Hamilton Heights."

"In what way?"

"Lots of ways."

"For instance."

"Okay. For instance. The first Sunday I was there, Aunt Bernie took me to church. I was expecting dull. Instead, the place was alive with people of all shapes, sizes and colors, singing and swaying and dancing in the aisle. There was a big celebration of the wisdom of Native Americans, and the sacredness of earth and sky. There were dances and drums and chants, and a lot of stuff I didn't understand, but it was awesome. The Cherokee part of me liked it a lot."

"Did they have any of the regular stuff, like a sermon and choir and that little wafer and grape juice thing?"

"It's hard to compare. Everyone sang. There was bread and wine out in a big patio area, and I guess there was a sermon, sort of."

"What did he talk about?"

"She."

"Okay. She."

"Liberty and justice for all."

"She talked about the Pledge of Allegiance?"

"Just the liberty and justice part of it. She said it was a far off goal, not a reality. Then she went on about all of the people in this country who don't have liberty and don't get justice. So I guess it was a sermon."

"But we have more liberty and justice here than anywhere else."

"Maybe," she says. "But now that I'm thinking about it, I'm not so sure."

I can feel my mind wanting to take a little trip out of here about now. I try to focus.

"What does this have to do with . . . you know . . . liking girls?"

"Nothing. But spending the summer with Bernie, going to her church, working in her bookstore, meeting so many different kinds of people — I started thinking maybe my own differences weren't so bad. Maybe I'm not scum."

"Do you think being in San Francisco turned you into a lesbian?"

"Nothing *turned* me into a lesbian. I just *am* a lesbian!"

"You don't have to get all hostile about it!"

"I'm not *hostile*! I'm trying to tell you this is me! Your lifetime spirit sister! I didn't just *turn* into a lesbian, any more than you just turned straight. You *are* straight. I *am* lesbian. That's how it is! Believe it!"

"Calm down," I say. "You'll wake up your parents."

"It's you I'm trying to wake up! Wake up, Lynn," she says in a sing-songy voice, like she's waking a child. "Look at the pretty rainbow. It takes all kinds to make the world."

I take a deep breath and count to ten. What I *want* to do is grab my backpack and run home, where things are safe and predictable. Where I don't have to be taunted about waking up.

"Sorry," Kit says, probably doing that mind reading thing again.

I run my index finger across the bottom of the emptied popcorn bowl, collecting butter and salt, licking my finger, then repeat the action, making finger designs in broad curves.

"I've felt like such a poser, trying to fit in but knowing in my heart that I was way different. I had a million questions, and I didn't know where to turn for answers. I could hardly raise my hand in class and ask 'What if I'm only turned on by women?' ... And that phony little sex ed class we had in the ninth grade — it was like there was no such thing as homosexuality. Male penis into female vagina — that's it."

I move my greasy finger patterns up the sides of the bowl. Maybe I'm an artist, a popcorn bowl artist. I'll set the completed project with a quick drying clear plastic spray. When I get my designs in thirty bowls of different sizes and shapes, I'll have a gallery showing. Lynn Wright, Popcorn Bowl Artist . . .

"Are you even listening?" Kit asks.

I drag my finger slowly from one side of the bowl to the other, intersecting my first designs.

"Every word," I say. "Male penis into female vagina. That's how we all got here, right? What's wrong with that?"

"Nothing's wrong with that, for you, and the hetero majority. But what about the rest of us?"

Halfway through another swipe across the bowl, Kit grabs it from me and sets it out of reach.

"Lynn. Listen. What about the rest of us?"

I lick the remaining butter and salt from my finger.

"I don't know."

"We're left in the dark, trying to figure it all out, each in our own lonely way. It's so hard."

I look at my friend, her sad eyes, her somber demeanor. Why have I never given much thought to Kit's frequent times of quiet withdrawal? Kit's in one of her moods, I would think, irritated, and wait for the mood to pass, rather than try to understand.

"**R**emember those two women who were camping at Triple Pines when we were up there for volleyball camp?"

I shake my head.

"Sophomores. Volleyball camp," she prompts.

"I remember the camp."

"Those two women. They were on the other side of the lake. They brought some fish over to us. Coach Terry fried it over the campfire. You remember them."

"I remember frying the fish over the campfire. I don't remember the women."

"Both blondes. One was short and heavy and the other one was kind of wiry."

"Uh, uh."

She gives me a look, like I've forgotten the President of the United States stopped by camp.

"I'm supposed to remember two women I saw for five minutes more than two years ago?"

Kit sighs. "Well, *anyway* . . . I watched them row back across the lake. They were side by side on the seat, each with one of the oars. And they moved their oars in perfect unison. They were laughing. Something about them made me think . . ."

"Think what?"

"I'm not sure. I just was . . . I don't know . . . drawn to them. Later, while you had kitchen duty, I took the path around the lake. About halfway around, I saw smoke from a campfire. I walked closer, then stopped at a place where I was partly hidden by trees. I hadn't planned to spy, but . . . They were sitting close in front of the campfire with their arms around each other. One of them said something and the other laughed. They began kissing, lightly at first and then more intensely. The shorter one unbuttoned her shirt, and the other leaned down and . . ."

Pause.

"And what?"

" . . . and kissed her breast. I turned away, desperately wanting to watch but at the same time, afraid. My whole body was warm and trembly. My breasts felt full and there was a sort of feverish feeling . . . you know . . ."

Pause.

"Downstairs?" I ask.

We laugh. Really, we cackle.

"Yeah!" Kit says, gasping for air. "Downstairs!"

We *howl*, wiping tears from our eyes. I laugh so hard I have to make a mad dash for the bathroom, my laughter-strained bladder about to betray me.

When I come back out, Kit is sitting quietly, that look of sad contemplation again showing through her dark, Cherokee eyes.

"I took my time walking back to camp that night, breathing the cool air, willing my body to calm down. But with each step I took, I thought, I want that someday. I want what those two women have. That's what I want for me."

Kit tells me how glad she was to finally know what she wanted, but it scared her, too. She started spending a lot of time at the public library, for information about homosexuality and lesbianism.

"I was *hungry* for information. At the market checkout stands there's all this boy-girl teen magazine stuff. How to act, what to wear, what to say, pictures of all kinds of couples, except boy-boy, or girl-girl. How could I find out about freaks like me?"

"Don't say freak," I tell her. "It's worse than weird."

"That's how it felt, though, inside. Like I was a stranger than fiction freak... Like something out of your mom's pile of old *World Weekly News.* Or worse.

"It didn't help that I was always hearing 'Oh, he's such a fag,' or 'She's a lesbo,' like that was the worst thing anyone could say about another person."

"When did you hear that?"

"All the time. You can't walk down the halls, or sit in a classroom, without hearing stuff like that. Or, 'That's so gay.'"

"Really? I don't hear that."

"You're not listening. It doesn't affect you, so it's like it's not even happening."

"You hear it all the time?" I say.

"All the time," Kit says. "But anyway, I hung out in libraries, hoping to read something about people like me. I couldn't find anything in our school library. Besides, with you working there after school, I didn't want you to see me looking for *homo* stuff."

"You could have said you were working on a report."

"Right. And lie. I was sick of living a lie — get it?"

I reach for the popcorn bowl, wanting to add a few finishing touches to my work of art. Kit gives me a look, but keeps talking.

"There wasn't much in the Hamilton Heights Public Library, either, and there was one librarian who seemed always to be watching as I browsed through the sex section. I decided to try a bigger library, in a place where no one would know me. Remember how I was always taking the bus to the Pasadena Library?"

"I thought you had a lot of homework is all."

Kit laughs. "I had homework, all right — the most important assignment of my life, trying to learn about others like me, trying to figure out if life as a lesbian was even worth it."

I look at her hard, trying to read her expression. What if she'd read something that made her think life as a lesbian was *not* worth it? She turns her head away, avoiding my eyes.

"I stumbled onto a few things, a couple of novels with lesbian main characters, and a book titled *Our Bodies, Ourselves*, which included stuff about lesbians like it was a normal thing."

"Normal?"

"Well, you know, like an everyday thing anyway. Besides, who decides what's normal? I think that's why I've always been so interested in psychology. I was afraid I was some kind of *freak*, and I wanted to understand about all that normal/abnormal stuff."

A close look at the popcorn bowl reveals it's not such a work of art after all. I take it to the kitchen and rinse it out. Kit follows, still talking.

It's as if now that she's started talking about knowing she's a lesbian, and now that I've started listening, she can't stop. The flood gates have opened, and the previously hidden part of her life comes pouring out.

"This summer, in my aunt's bookstore, I found lots and lots of books of the kind I'd been wanting to read. She has a whole section devoted to lesbian literature, and another whole non-fiction section devoted to homosexuality. When I started reading them, I wasn't quite so lonely anymore. There are lots of us in the world, living good, loving lives, doing important work. And the other thing about the bookstore — I had the chance to see people who came in and bought books from *my* sections."

"Does your aunt know that you're . . . "

"We didn't really talk about it, but she kept handing me certain books as they came in — 'you might like this,' she'd say, and it almost always had something to do with lesbianism."

"What about her? She's not married. Is *she* a lesbian?" I ask, secretly wondering if it might run in families.

"No. There's always a man in her life, but she's never wanted to be tied down to marriage."

"But the books?"

"She has books on everything. That's the kind of store she runs."

Finally, after two in the morning, it seems like Kit has said as much as she possibly can, and I've *heard* as much as I possibly can.

"Bedtime," Kit says.

We go into her room. I get my sleeping shirt and tooth brush and take them into the bathroom. Always before, we'd get into our sleeping stuff while we stood in Kit's room, talking. But tonight I don't want to undress in front of her. I know she said I wasn't attractive to her in "that way," but I'm uncomfortable anyway.

In bed, I stay way over on my side, practically hanging off the mattress.

We're quiet for a long time, then Kit whispers, "I really need you to stay my spirit sister."

"For life," I say.

Finally, all of the hours of wakefulness catch up with me and I fall into a deep, heavy sleep. When I wake up, the sun is shining full into the bedroom window. It's after ten, and Kit is already up. Here's what I notice though. As deeply as I slept, I'm still all scrunched up on my side of the bed. Will I ever again feel completely comfortable with Kit?

5

It's October now. The annual heat wave has lifted, and although afternoons are still smoggy, we've not had a Stage Three Alert for at least ten days. A Stage Three Alert, for those of you who don't live in the Los Angeles Basin, advises that children not be allowed to play outdoors. The elderly, those with asthma or heart disease, pregnant women, all should stay inside. But the infamous basin is more conducive to life, now that it's fall.

And about that conversation Kit and I had a while back? She's right about always hearing anti-gay stuff at school. Once I started paying attention, I heard faggot, dyke, lesbo, queer, and lots worse stuff, too. All the time. Just like she said.

Conan waits for me outside of English now, so we can walk together to PC. After school, if his football practice and our volleyball practice get out near the same time, he takes me and Kit home. He drives an old, beat up Hyundai and sometimes it seems like it won't make it up the hill to my house. I don't care if we have to pedal, I just like being in the same car with Conan.

Lately Conan's been dropping Kit off in front of her house, and then driving around the block to my place. When he doesn't have to rush off to baby-sit for his four-year-old sister, Sabina, we sit in my driveway and talk. Sometimes we talk about religion. Or books. Conan reads a lot. He read *The Color Purple* years ago, and it wasn't even an assignment. Sometimes we talk about more personal stuff.

Conan's dad gives him a hard time, wanting him to be super macho. He tells Conan that football comes first. There's big money in football, for someone with Conan's size and talent. Conan wants academics to come first, then football.

His grampa thinks Conan should go into politics, do something important for his people. His mom wants him to go into business administration. Like the dad, she wants him to get rich, but she doesn't want him to get beat up doing it. It sounds as if they all argue about what Conan should do, and no one pays attention to what Conan thinks.

"What about Sabina?" I asked him once, during one of our driveway conversations. "Does she have an opinion on how you should live your life?"

Conan laughed. "Sabina just wants me to be her big brother."

On my side, I've told Conan how I sometimes feel lonely, with just me and my mom. And how it used to bother me, that my dad only managed to see me about twice a year. I told him about how awful it was, seeing my gramma waste away with cancer, and how guilty I feel that I didn't spend more time with her when she was sick. That whole thing is something I hardly ever talk about. As much as I've talked with Conan about private things, I've *not* told him that Kit is a lesbian. I promised not to tell, and I won't. Besides, what would he think?

I suppose you've figured out that I'd like to be more than friends with Conan. I think he feels the same way, but I'm not sure.

Yesterday he'd asked, "What are you doing Saturday night?"

"No plans," I'd said, all hopeful.

"Me, either," he'd said.

Then he started talking about his car, or something totally unrelated. What was that about, I wanted to ask him, but I didn't have the nerve.

On Monday morning, after the Saturday that neither of us had plans, Conan is waiting for me in the driveway when I walk out my back door.

"Want a ride?" he asks.

"Sure. But Kit's coming over to walk with me."

"No problem. There's room for three."

We sit on my back porch steps, petting Wilma and waiting for Kit.

"I almost called you Saturday night," he says.

"Why didn't you?"

"I wasn't sure you'd want me to."

He's looking down at Wilma, scratching her head as if he's not said a word.

"I wish you *had* called," I say.

He turns to me with a broad, open smile.

"Really?"

"Really."

"What were you doing?"

"Not much. Kit came over for a while. I did some laundry. Wilma and I practiced frisbee."

"This mutt's not going to make it in any frisbee competitions. Her ears slow her down," he says, laughing.

"She's good!" I say.

He just laughs all the harder.

"She's a *mutt*," he says. "But she's lovable."

Then he turns serious.

"You're lovable too," he says, so softly I can hardly be sure I've heard him right.

"I am?"

"Uh, huh . . . Am I?"

"Yes," I say, glad he asked the question.

He takes my hand and holds it until we hear the slam of the back gate. We stand and wave to Kit.

"Want a ride?" Conan calls to her.

"Do I! My legs are *still* stiff from the workout Terry put us through on Friday."

I climb into the back seat, to leave room for Kit. She and Conan are talking about sports conditioning, comparing the workouts the football team does to the workouts our volleyball team does. Usually I'd be interested, but right now, I'm floating somewhere above it all, hearing lovable, lovable, lovable, hardly able to believe Conan said that about me. On the way to first period, Conan takes my hand again. Holding hands doesn't sound like much, but sometimes it is.

The lunch table where Kit and I always sit is near where the jocks sit. Usually Holly and Nicole sit with us, but on Mondays they have a meeting with the school newspaper staff. Conan sits with the jocks. Tammy and a bunch of other cheerleader types hang around that table, too. It starts the first week of school — areas are chosen, and then nothing changes. The skaters sit at one place, and the rockers at another. Also, there are the Goths, the skinheads, the gangbangers, even a few rednecks. We never divided up like that back in elementary school.

Did I say nothing changes? Here comes Conan, moving from the jock table to sit next to me. And Robert follows him. Robert Pomeroy — the guy who hangs around Kit. He's on the football team, too.

In PC, Woodsy has written the week's schedule on the board. Monday is group work for our projects. Tuesday is individual reading from a stack of books and magazines that she's collected. Wednesday we have speakers from Project Ten. Thursday is class discussion and Friday is more group work. Although this class may not be as important to me for college as Advanced Placement English, or econ, it's probably the best class I have as far as holding my attention. Today though, my hand still warm from Conan's touch, the word lovable replaying in my brain, my sense of Conan's presence in the chair behind me, all conspire to keep me from concentrating on what Woodsy is saying. It's just my luck that she calls on me.

"What might that mean, Lynn?"

"What?"

She pauses. Just a beat. Long enough to let me know that she knows I've not been paying attention.

"Project Ten," she says, pointing to the board, to the announcement for Wednesday's speaker.

"Ten people?" I say, making a wild guess and feeling the familiar blushing response creeping up the back of my neck and across my face.

"Ten percent," she says. "A certain ten percent of the population will be the topic of our discussion on Wednesday. What segment of the population might constitute ten percent?"

"Poor people?" Kendra says.

"No, but that's a good guess. I'm afraid poor people constitute more than ten percent of our population, though I'm not certain of the figures. Who's working on the 'poverty in America' topic?"

Yvonne, Carmen and Joey raise their hands.

"When you get to your group work in a few minutes, will you please see if you can find a percentage figure that relates to poverty?"

Carmen nods, while the other two look puzzled.

"What other groups might constitute ten percent of the population?"

There are a lot of guesses. Teenagers, alcoholics, people who make over $100,000 a year, people who are deaf, blind, paralyzed. People with cancer. Doctors, lawyers, teachers, on and on until Brian says it's fags.

Ms. Woods points to the big "NO PUT-DOWNS" poster on the bulletin board.

"That's not a put-down, it's a description," Eric says, and he and Brian laugh like maniacs.

"That's a derogatory term, Eric, and it *is* a put-down. It's as bad as nigger, or chink, or any of the other demeaning words I sometimes hear on this campus."

"There shouldn't *be* any fags and then we wouldn't have to have names for them," Brian says, prompting more laughter from Eric and a few others.

Woodsy stands looking at them, as if she's trying to decide how to respond.

"What other terms might you use, that wouldn't be derogatory, to identify the ten percent group which you referred to?"

Neither of them answers.

I sense Conan stirring behind me and turn to see his hand raised.

"I know what Project Ten is," he says. "There was a group at the school I went to before I came here."

"Tell us, Conan," Woodsy says, apparently relieved to turn her attention away from the Brian/Eric comedy team.

Eric whispers something to Brian, who nods and smirks. They are both totally immature. What did I ever like about Eric? Was it only that other girls thought he was a big somebody? And Holly kept telling me what a cute couple we made? Was that all there was to it? If so, then who am I to be talking about immaturity? Uh-oh. There goes my wandering mind. I don't care. I think focus is overrated. I like my wandering mind. Except now I'm not sure what's going on in class. Conan's not talking anymore and Woodsy's looking irritated about I don't know what. So I focus.

"Fags," Eric says.

"And dykes," Brian adds.

Laughter.

Woodsy turns on them.

"Use either of those terms in this class again and you can sit out the rest of the period in the office."

Woodsy reaches into her desk, pulls out two referral slips and hands one to Eric and one to Brian.

"Write your names and the dates on these, just in case we need to use them," she says, then turns her attention to the rest of the class.

"Conan is right. Project Ten is a group for gay and lesbian students, and also for straight students who want to offer their support."

"I don't think it's ten percent," Sean says. "That would mean three people in this classroom are homosexual."

People look around, giggling and pointing fingers. Woodsy says she hopes we will have matured by Wednesday when the Project Ten group comes.

The rest of the period we spend working on our projects. Conan, Sean and I have chosen the topic of drug decriminalization. My first choice topic was teen pregnancy, but when I learned that Conan was choosing drug decriminalization, *that* became my first choice.

Conan has a late football practice today, and Kit and I get out early from volleyball practice, so we walk home together. There is a slight breeze — enough to have blown the smog away. Overhead we have a clean blue sky with cottony clouds, and it feels good to breathe deeply without worrying about pollution particles.

"Are you getting that Project Ten thing in your PC class, too?" I ask Kit.

"Yeah. Cool, huh?" she says, smiling a big smile.

"I guess."

"Ten percent of us out there? Can you believe it?"

"I don't know."

"*I* believe it. And I feel better knowing I'm not a one in a million freak. I'm a one in ten freak," she says with a laugh. She's all jazzed on the subject.

"Look at it this way. There are twenty-five hundred students at Hamilton High. So do the math. There must be two hundred and fifty who are gay or lesbian. Right?"

"Yeah, I guess so. But I only know one," I say.

"No. How about Frankie Sanchez, in choir? I bet he's a ten percenter."

"Why? Because he choreographs the music numbers?"

"Partly. And I don't think he's ever had a girlfriend."

"So?"

"And he's kind of . . . you know . . . delicate."

"Stereotyping, Dr. Dandridge?"

"Maybe. But I'm going to talk to him about Project Ten."

"He probably doesn't even know about it. You didn't, until

today."

"If he doesn't know about it, maybe he should."

Kit stops at my house before she goes home. I get the frisbee from its place inside the garage and we play keep away from Wilma. We laugh hysterically as she makes huge, spinning leaps. Half the time she catches it, no matter how hard we try to keep it from her. Each time she drops it at my feet and looks up at me, I swear she's smiling.

When we tire, we sit on the front lawn, Wilma between us, nudging the frisbee first to me, then Kit, then back to me — her way of begging us to get back to the game.

Kit's black hair shines in the sun. Her smile is infectious as she gives in to Wilma and tosses the frisbee. I can't help thinking how pretty she is, and how she could have practically any guy she wanted. I don't say that, though. I'm sure she wouldn't like to hear it. I'm learning.

CHAPTER

6

Each of the Project Ten speakers tells his or her own story. "His or her" takes on a whole new meaning with one of the participants because she used to be a man, Leonard, but now she's a woman, Leona. She says she's a transsexual. She also says there are a lot of transsexuals in the world, which is news to me.

Just looking at her, you wouldn't know she used to be a man. Maybe her skin is a bit coarse, but no more so than my great aunt Doreen's. Leonard/Leona is tall for a woman, but not *unbelievably* tall. The clothes she's wearing are what I guess you'd call business attire. A nice suit, skirt above the knee, two inch heels (pumps, I think my mom would call them), pantyhose, make-up, the whole thing.

At first I'm totally freaked by her. Why would anyone go through all of those surgeries and hormone treatments, all that physical pain? And this is weirder still. She has a thirteen-year-old son who used to call her Dad and now he calls her Auntie Leona. How creepy would that be?

My mind drifts from Leona to my own dad. He's not great the way he is, but what if he came for a visit and he'd turned into a she?

I don't think I could handle it. I feel sorry for Leona's son.

"Why didn't you just stay the way God made you?" Eric asks.

Leona gives Eric a long look, like she's trying to decide how to answer him.

"I *have* stayed the way God made me. God, or the creator of the universe, or the life force, whatever, made me want to be a woman. For as long as I can remember, I've known I was female. My deepest longing was to have my body reflect the real me. God gave me the longing. My doctors gave me the body."

She doesn't go into detail about her operation, but even so, the mere mention of surgery is enough to draw groans from the boys. Their body language says even more than the groans. Every single boy in my line of vision has his legs crossed and his hands folded low on his lap, as if protecting that particular region of his anatomy. I turn back to look at Conan. He, too, has taken the protective position.

Even though the idea of such a surgery repulses me, I begin to understand Leona's choice. She's doing the best she can to live the life that seems right to her. I can respect that.

There are three more people on the panel besides Leona. There's a gay man who's probably in his thirties, and a younger lesbian, and an older woman who is straight, but is part of a support group.

Raymond, the gay guy, talks about how difficult life as a teenager was for him — how isolated he was. Then he talks about how good life is now. He has a good job, his family has finally accepted him as he is, and he's in a loving, committed relationship. He takes some pictures, 8 x 10s, from a folder and holds them up for us to see. There's one with his partner and their golden retriever, and another with them decked out in running gear, numbers on the front, ready to run the L.A. Marathon.

"We have a life together," he says.

Then he shows a picture taken at their wedding. They are both in tuxedos, standing at the altar of a big, fancy church. They are facing the congregation, beaming. There are flowers and candles, and it looks like any other wedding picture, with the one major exception of there being two grooms and no bride.

"That's sick," Brian says.

"I think it's sweet," Tiffany says, batting her eyelashes at Raymond in her cheerleader style.

"It's *disgusting*," Eric says, flashing Tiffany a look that is less than affectionate.

Woodsy walks over to where Brian and Eric are sitting, as if to reprimand them.

"It's okay," Raymond says to Woodsy. "I choose to be open about my life, which means I occasionally get labeled 'sick,' or 'disgusting,' or worse."

Raymond puts the pictures back in his folder, then looks at each of us in the classroom, one by one.

"Ten percent," he says. "Chances are, two or three of you in this classroom, today, know you are gay, or bi, or have some heavy questions about your sexual orientation. And you're wondering if what your fellow students say about you is true. Are you sick? Are you disgusting?"

We are all quiet, sort of sneaking looks around the room, wondering who the two or three might be.

"If my being here lets you know life can be as good for you as it can for the other ninety percent, it's worth it to me to hear the labels. If it lets you know you're not alone, that's what I care about. You have every right to be who you want to be."

"Yeah, well don't get close to *me* any of you ten percenters or you'll wish you hadn't!" Brian says, fist closed, macho football biceps flexed.

Eric laughs, as do a few others — mostly boys.

Raymond asks, "Do you ever wonder why homosexuality brings out such anger in certain people?"

No one answers.

"The worst gay bashers are usually people who are uncertain about their own sexual orientation. So if they fight noisily and fiercely to stamp out homosexuality, that must prove they're the straightest of the straight. Right?"

He looks directly at Brian, then Eric.

"More likely, it proves the gay bashers are on shaky ground with their own sexual orientation."

Raymond sits down, and one of the women starts talking. I'm watching Brian and Eric, who are both looking at Raymond as if he were raw sewage. I wonder about Raymond's theory. Brian's had practically every H.H.S. girl who's haveable, so he *must* like girls. But then, I wonder. Maybe it's more like he uses girls to prove a point. Maybe that's why he's still angry with Kit, because he couldn't prove anything with her.

I've lost track of what's going on. The younger woman panelist is talking about her parents. Leona is listening intently, her neatly manicured hands folded sedately on the table in front of her. I go back to the daydream about what if my dad showed up one day as a woman, so I miss most of the rest of the talks. One thing grabs my attention, though. They say that even though only ten percent of the population is gay/lesbian, thirty percent of teen suicides are from that group. It doesn't take a math genius to figure out that gay/ lesbian teens are at much greater risk than the rest of us are. I remember the remark Kit made about trying to figure out if life as a lesbian was even worth it.

The straight woman, Julie, talks about how important it is for us to be supportive of our gay/lesbian/bi/trans friends.

"What do you mean, bi?" Nicole asks.

"Bisexual. . . "

"Someone who swings both ways," Steven says.

"Right," Julie says. "Someone who may have sexual feelings for both men and women."

She's a member of a group called PFLAG — Parents and Friends of Lesbians and Gays. Her son is gay, and she talks about how hard it was for her to accept that, and how important PFLAG has been to her. She hands out information about various groups and resources for gay/lesbian youth. I'm amazed at the length of the list. She talks about high school groups, like Project Ten, and GSA — Gay Straight Alliances, and free counseling services. There are also numbers for a suicide hotline, and child protection services. I guess some kids get beaten up when their parents discover that they're gay.

On the way out of class I hear Eric say to Tiffany, "Homosexuality is as much of a sin as murder."

Conan asks him, "How do you figure?"

"It's all in the Bible."

"Lots of stuff's in the Bible," Conan says.

"Yeah. And it's all the word of God. And people like those fags and dykes and that other pervert had better start facing up."

Something must have happened to Eric over the summer. I don't think he was like that before. I watch as he and Tiffany walk down the hall together, holding hands. Eric is talking a mile a minute and Tiffany is nodding her head in what I guess is agreement. Better her than me.

After school, I meet Kit on the volleyball court. We're the first ones there so we decide to practice serves. Kit's across the court from me, volleyball in hand. I wait for the serve while she talks on and on about the speakers in PC, like she's on some kind of natural high or something.

"Were the same people in period two?" she asks.

"I don't know. Did you see Leonard who turned into Leona?"

"Yeah, and Raymond, the gay guy, and Heather, the lesbian, and the other older woman, Julie?"

"Ummm. I think so. I don't remember anyone's name, except Leona and Raymond."

"It's so cool that they came to talk to us! You know, what Heather said, about how hard it was to tell her parents but now they're her best support . . . "

"I got distracted wondering what it would be like to have a dad turn into a mom."

"You mean, you weren't even interested enough in a lesbian's experience to listen?"

"It's not that. I was just distracted."

Kit bounces the ball once, tosses it high in the air and slams it across the net in her strongest power serve. I catch it and serve it back, trying, and failing, to match her power. She lets the ball bounce past her and stands looking at me.

"It doesn't seem right, that Heather is up there pouring her heart out and you're too distracted to listen."

"Don't take it all personal," I say.

"It's just . . . it's so important . . . "

She looks like she might cry.

"Sometimes I feel so alone . . . and Heather . . . talking about . . . you know . . ."

"I'm *sorry*," I say. "Tell me everything Heather said. I'll listen. I won't daydream . . ."

"ALL RIGHT GIRLS!" Coach Terry's voice booms across the court. Some of the others who've gathered by the benches sprint out to the court and I know that's the end of any conversation for at least an hour.

Terry lines us up for a pep talk about the coming game with San Martino.

"They're tough, but we're tougher. This is going to be our best season yet."

She leads us through a series of stretches, then says, "Kit, opposite side hitter, Carmen, setter, Lynn, middle blocker . . . " until she's designated all positions for an hour's worth of practice games. After the games, we go to the weight room and do a circuit that Coach Terry has set up especially for her volleyball players. Then sprints and, finally, more stretches.

By the time Coach Terry is through with us, we are worn out and sweaty. We shower and change, then decide we need to replenish our energy and spirits with a stop at Barb 'n Edie's. Over garbage-burgers and Cokes, we talk about PC.

"It's good to hear about other people's problems," I say.

"Does that mean you think being a lesbian is a problem?"

"Hey — it would be for me. But if it's not for you, or for Heather, then cool."

Kit takes a big bite of her juicy garbageburger and munches thoughtfully.

"I felt so good today in PC, hearing those people talk about finding the strength to be themselves — how everyone has that right."

"It seemed strange to me," I say.

"Right," she says, getting that look on her face that tells me I've said the wrong thing.

"So now, when I'm sitting here with you, I don't feel so good anymore. Like you think *I'm* strange."

"You're so sensitive these days! Whatever I say, you take it the wrong way!"

"Listen to what you're saying, though! First you can't be bothered to pay attention to someone who's talking about an issue of huge importance to me, and now you're saying that the gay/lesbian thing was *strange*?"

I am surprised at the strength of Kit's emotion. We've never had one of those roller coaster friendships where we're mad and yell at each other, and then don't speak, and then make up. We've never been like that. I don't want it to be like that.

"Are we fighting?" I say. "Because if we are, I don't want to."

We look straight at each other for about a minute, trying to decide.

"I guess if we have to ask if we're fighting, we must not be fighting," Kit says.

"Guess not," I say.

That gives us both a much needed laugh.

Later that night, just before bedtime, I check my e-mail. There's something from Dad, saying he'll pick me up on Saturday and take me to his company's family picnic. I guess I'll have to go. I've outgrown my dad, but he doesn't know it yet.

There's another thing about how to make $$$ over the Internet. Delete! Then — a note from Kit:

There's a big Gay Pride celebration over at Griffith Park this Saturday. Will you go with me? You don't have to be gay to go. All kinds of people will be there. — Kit

I e-mail her back that I've got to go to that stupid annual company picnic for my dad's work. She knows that's not a lie,

because I complain about it every year. This year I'm relieved to be
going, though. As out of place as I feel at my dad's company picnic
— Daddy's little girl and all that phoniness — I'd feel like I was
from another planet at a Gay Pride gathering.

I want to be Kit's spirit sister, but I don't want to get all involved
with Gay Pride stuff. I can't believe *she* does either. She even says
she doesn't want anyone besides me to know right now. If she *does*
go to the park on Saturday, I hope she'll stay away from the TV
cameras.

Kit shows up at my house Sunday morning. My mom and I are
doing our traditional Sunday thing, eating pancakes and bacon and
watching the Sunday morning show.

"Hey, Always," Kit says to my mom, flopping down on the
couch beside her.

Here's something else I need to tell you. About five years ago,
Kit nicknamed Mom "Always," because we could never beat her in
Trivial Pursuit. Always Wright. Get it? Mom refuses to play Trivial
Pursuit with us anymore, since the time she almost lost. She says she
doesn't want Kit to start calling her "Sometimes." "Always" is bad
enough. Her real name is Claire, but Kit likes Always better. Mom's
a good sport about it.

"Join us for breakfast?" Mom asks.

"Sure," Kit says.

"Well . . . get up off your cute little duff and go fix it," Mom
laughs, giving Kit a playful poke. Really, sometimes I think Mom
likes Kit better than me.

"Pancake mix is in the bowl on the sink and the bacon's in the
bottom drawer of the fridge," Mom says.

Kit goes bounding into the kitchen and I follow. She grabs the
package of bacon, pulls off four pieces, tosses them into the frying
pan, turns up the gas on the two front burners and stirs the pancake
mix.

"You should have been at Griffith Park yesterday," Kit says,
talking low so Mom can't hear. "It was soooo cool!"

Kit reaches into her jeans and empties a pocket full of telephone numbers and e-mail addresses on cards, or tiny slips of paper. One number is on the back of a matchbook cover. I thought people only did *that* in movies from the fifties.

"Look! All of these people want to talk to me! Yesterday, at Gay Pride, I was an insider."

I flip the pancakes Kit seems to have forgotten in her enthusiasm for being in the middle of things. She turns the bacon. I notice she's smiling. She looks happy. I always think of Kit as a happy person. That's how she was when we started being friends and that's how she's always seemed to me. But seeing her happy now, I realize that she's been on the quiet side for — how long? Last year, after a choir party had mostly ended with couples, I asked her if anything was wrong. Was she worried about anything? She brushed it off, and I didn't pursue it. I guess maybe I didn't want to know — I wanted to keep thinking she was happy, that everything was fine.

"Fry up a few more slices of bacon for me, would you?" Mom calls from the family room.

"You got it, Always," Kit says.

She adds bacon to the skillet and stands over it, cooking first one side, then the other. When it is exactly the way Mom likes it, Kit picks up the scraps of paper from the counter and shoves them back into her pocket. Smiling, she gives me a thumbs up sign and carries her plate of pancakes and bacon, plus extras for Mom, back to the other room. There is a lightness to her walk that I've not seen for a long time. I hadn't even noticed it was missing. For a spirit sister, there's a lot I haven't noticed.

7

Mom is off to San Jose on some kind of business trip, so I get to drive her car today. It's a Lexus, not new, but way more comfortable than Conan's Hyundai. I'm in the driver's seat, waiting for Kit. The first thing I notice about Kit when she walks through our back gate is that she is not smiling.

"Hi," I say, as she reaches the car.

"Hi."

She tosses her backpack in and climbs into the back seat. It's funny, that unspoken recognition of who belongs where. When Conan first started hanging out with me and Kit, whoever got to the passenger seat first took it. Now, if Conan is driving, the seat next to him is saved for me, and vice versa.

"Hard times?" I ask Kit as I ease out the driveway.

She sighs. "My dad is being such a shit! He's complaining that I spend too much time on my computer. This guy they arrested yesterday had gone nuts, got all violent in a coffee shop, thinking he was some character in a computer game."

"What's that got to do with you?"

"Nothing! I don't even play computer games! But now he's

checking on me every ten minutes or so, to see what's on my screen. Puhlease! Hasn't he heard of the right to privacy? All I need is for him to come in and see an e-mail message about gay pride!"

We swing by for Conan. Sabina watches from the doorway as Conan gets into the passenger seat Kit has left vacant for him.

I put the car in reverse and wave to Sabina. She doesn't even notice me, she's so busy blowing kisses to Conan. Conan laughs and blows about a million kisses back to her.

"She's cute, isn't she?" he asks, his eyes all dancing. "*She* loves me, too," he says to me.

From the back seat, Kit groans. "The sugar content in this car is giving me diabetes," she laughs, punching Conan on the shoulder.

Myself, I like the sugar content.

Today is a minimum day — teacher workshops or something. We're out by noon and decide to go to the beach.

"Is it okay with Always?"

"She didn't tell me *not* to take the car to the beach."

"She didn't tell you *not* to jump off a bridge, but you've got sense enough not to do it, don't you?" Kit says, mimicking every mom in the world.

That gets us laughing.

Then Kit says "In your heart you know Always won't like it."

So then we have to explain to Conan why Kit calls my mom Always, which gets us laughing again.

I'm pretty sure my mom won't care if I drive to the beach. Besides, it's a perfect day. We stop at our houses for the necessities — bathing suits, towels, sunscreen, and then we're off. We take the 10 to the 605, then south to the 405, and down to Huntington Beach. It's got to be one of California's all-time ugliest drives. My great-aunt Doreen says this used to be beautiful, all orange groves and avocado orchards, strawberry farms, and, best of all, blue skies. Hard to believe. Now it's look-alike houses and strip malls, warehouses and factories. The skies are so thick with pollutants that just breathing leaves a nasty taste in your mouth and a heaviness in your lungs.

Hardly anyone is on the beach today. Not like the middle of summer, when you can hardly find room to spread out a towel. Here, because of ocean breezes, the sky is blue, the air clean. It is totally worth the drive through heavy grayness to reach this place.

"C'mon!" Kit challenges, rushing into the surf. Conan and I follow her lead, racing to the white foamed waves, diving beneath them, breathless with the first shock of cold water. We swim out past the breakers, where Kit lies floating on her back, as still as a piece of driftwood, bobbing on the surface of gentle swells.

The green flag is up, meaning the surf is gentle today. No riptides or undertow, no huge waves to turn you upside down and slam you head first into the sand. At the other end of the beach, a few surfers wait lazily on their boards, hoping for a wave big enough to be worthy of their energy. Surfers don't much like the green flag days.

Conan swims closer in, catching a breaking wave and stiffening his body for the ride to shore. I tread water, watching as he rises to his feet and turns to wave at me. I wave back, then look toward the horizon. Two small sailboats bob slowly along, somewhere between here and Catalina Island. I think how this ocean reaches to Japan and beyond, up to the Arctic and down to Antarctica. I wonder where the water that now holds me up has been.

I'm lost in thought, totally peaceful, when Kit swims in front of me, splashes me full in the face, then swims away at top speed. I swim after her, gaining, until I'm even with her shoulders. I heave myself over, shoving her under. She comes up sputtering and laughing, masses of hair hanging down in her face.

"Even?"

"Even," I agree.

She leans her head back in the water, then comes up with her hair hanging neatly down her back.

Conan swims out to us, his big body graceful in the water. The three of us form a sort of circle, treading water, not talking, feeling the rise and fall of the powerful sea. Later, when my fingers are as wrinkled as prunes, I swim to shore and flop down on my beach towel. The sun is warm on my back, the salt air refreshing to my smog weary lungs.

I am hovering somewhere between sleep and wakefulness when I sense Conan's presence.

"You need sunscreen," he says.

I turn to see him smiling, holding a tube of SPF 15 lotion. He kneels beside me and begins rubbing lotion onto my shoulders and upper back, then across my lower back, inch by inch, massaging the lotion deeply into my sun warmed skin.

"Legs, too," he says, and squeezes lotion along my left leg, thigh to calf. His hands are warm and gentle and I get a tingling sensation in places Conan has not yet touched. I want to turn to him, hold him close, kiss him with all my might. Instead, I lie still, basking in his touch.

When Conan has smeared every inch of my back and legs with sunscreen, he lies down beside me.

"Thanks," I say.

He grins. "Turn over and I'll get the rest of you."

"No, your turn," I tell him, taking the half used tube of sunscreen and starting on his back.

He laughs his deep, rolling laugh. "Like I'm going to get sunburned?"

"Like it feels good," I say, rubbing lotion into his broad, walnut-brown back.

"Ummmm. You're right."

"Besides, you *can* get sunburned, no matter how dark you are."

"Whatever you say, nurse."

Conan closes his eyes as I continue protecting his skin, whether he thinks he needs it or not. He is absolutely still and I wonder if he is drifting off to sleep, or if he too is getting tingly in places covered by his trunks. I wonder if he wants to turn to me, and hold me, as I wanted when our situations were reversed.

The mood is broken when Kit runs up from the shore, dripping wet, laughing, shaking herself as if she were a dog, spraying us with water. When she goes to the restroom, Conan says, "Robert wants me to set him up with Kit."

"He's already asked her out, and she says no."

"He thinks she likes him anyway. You know, they're always laughing about stuff at lunch. He wants her to give him a chance."

"Conan . . . I don't think so."

"Wouldn't it be good, though, for Kit to have someone too? Like today. She wouldn't be like . . . a third wheel."

"A third *wheel*?"

"I don't mean that in a rude way . . . just, don't you think she'd like someone special, too?"

"Maybe. But it won't be Robert."

"Well, I told him I'd see what I could do. So will you at least talk to her?"

"Tell him not to get his hopes up."

Late in the afternoon, when Conan and I are out in the water, I notice Kit talking with a girl over by the vending machine. I don't want to stereotype anyone, but this girl looks like . . . well . . . a lesbian. I watch for a moment, long enough to see them exchanging slips of paper which I assume are their telephone numbers, then I feel guilty about spying and turn my attention to the next wave, letting it carry me in.

Back on shore, Conan and I sit leaning into one another, waves occasionally washing sand from our feet and legs. I dig into the sand where I see little air bubbles erupting. Two tiny sand crabs scramble in the palm of my hand, tickling as they try to dig in. I put them back in the damp sand and watch them scurry down-ward, to their buried safety. Conan stands and offers me a hand.

"Another swim?"

I dig for another handful of crabs and shake my head. Conan gives me a quick, sweet kiss on the top of my head, then rushes into the ocean, pulling with strong, powerful strokes to reach the calmness of unbreaking waves. I'm still digging for crabs and releasing them when Kit sits down beside me.

"That girl I was talking to?" Kit says, waiting for a response.

I nod.

"She goes to Sojourner High — says they've got one of those GSA groups on their campus."

"Sojourner? The alternative school where all the druggies and delinquents go?"

"Star says it's a cool school, just with a bad rep."

"Who would name their kid Star?"

"Can I get to the point here?" Kit asks. "People from Hamilton come to their meetings, and it's not all gays, or lesbians, or bis, or trans, or whatever. It's their straight friends, too."

I keep digging for crabs.

"I thought you didn't want anyone else to know?"

"You don't have to be lesbian or gay to go there."

"But that girl . . . Star . . . She knows, or else why would she be talking to you about it? Did you give her a secret sign or something? I've heard there are secret signs."

"She just started talking to me, said she'd noticed me around and didn't I go to Hamilton High. That's all."

Kit digs up a handful of wet sand and lets it sift slowly through her fingers, beginning a drip castle like the kind we used to make back when we were eleven and came to the beach with our moms.

"You know how I'm not wanting to live a lie anymore?"

"You're not lying to anyone."

"Not with words. But Robert keeps asking me out and I keep turning him down. I know it hurts his feelings. He says he's sure I like him, so why won't I go out with him."

"He asked Conan to set you up with him."

"I wish he'd give it up."

"Couldn't you go out with him, just as a friend?"

Kit snaps her head up from the castle and gives me an angry, piercing look.

"Don't you get it? That would only make things worse — to be going out with a guy who likes me, 'like that,' when I will never like a guy like that!"

"Okay. Okay. Turn down the volume!"

"It's like a lie when I keep letting people assume I'm straight, when Nicole asks me if I don't think some guy is so fine, and I just smile. It feels phony."

"I don't get what's phony about it," I tell her.

"Okay. It's like . . . remember when I told you about Miss Hughes? When we were freshmen, and everybody was all ga-ga over Freddie Prinze Jr.?

"I was totally obsessed with Miss Hughes, but all the time I let people think I was nuts over Freddie."

Pause.

"I felt like a liar then, and I feel like a liar now, whenever I let someone assume I could like some guy. Get it?"

Another pause.

"I guess there's another lie you've been living, too," I say.

Kit looks at me, all puzzled.

"You let me believe we told each other everything. I spilled my guts to you, and I thought you told me your innermost feelings. Spirit sisters and all that. But you never said anything about Miss Hughes, or any of the rest of it."

Kit sighs.

"I was afraid to tell you. I knew it was weird, and I didn't want you to think I was weird."

We go back to building our sand castle, adding more steeples around the edges. Kit's strong, dark hands drip sand on the tops. Her face is set. It must have been lonely for her to keep a whole heart-load of thoughts secret. If I'd been her — honestly? I probably would have kept secrets, too.

"I don't think you're weird," I tell her.

Her face softens. She looks up and smiles.

"Thanks," she says. "I don't think you're weird, either."

Long after our castle has been washed away, Conan joins us. Three in a row, we watch as the giant orange sun slowly descends below the horizon. Light fades, leaving a rich pink glow over the distant inky blue sea. I listen to the eternal coming and going of waves breaking against the shore. I wish I could express what I feel right now, that the earth is ongoing. That in spite of pollution, the forces of nature will prevail. That life is good, and friends are precious, and that it all has to do with love, one way or another — loving our planet, and each other, and ourselves.

The tide slowly washes in, pushing us gradually back. We settle at a safe distance, sensing the movement of the darkening sea. Catalina is hidden from view. The moon casts a reflection on now black waters.

Kit starts singing a song we learned for a choir skit last year.

"Blue moon, you saw me standing alone . . ."

I join in with the alto part. Conan, although he's not in choir, knows the song from somewhere.

" . . . without a dream in my heart, without a love of my own . . ."

The song is lonely at first, then ends with lovers finding one another, and the moon turns from blue to gold. Very weak, I've always thought. Tonight though, the song, along with the accompanying sound of the steady, ongoing ebb and flow of the sea, fills me with a sense of harmony. Kit and Conan must feel it, too.

We are silent after the song, until Conan says, "I want every day to be like this one."

Kit and I nod in agreement, then, reluctantly, pack stuff up for the long ride home.

CHAPTER

8

It's like there's this "everything's in harmony" beach glow that carries us through the week. Kit's dad read an article about how computer use in high school raises IQ levels, so he's quit checking her computer screen.

Mom says she's glad we had a good time at the beach, no problem that I drove there without first clearing it with her.

Conan and Sean and I give our PC report on drug decriminalization, and it goes really well.

Friday night it's Kit's turn to stay at my house. We rent "Dog Day Afternoon," just because it has the required word in the title. It turns out to be a really great movie, with a bunch of Academy Awards. It's a weird story, though, about this bisexual guy who robs a bank to get money for another guy's sex change. Okay. So I'm not explaining it very well, but it really is a great movie. After it's over, Kit and I talk for hours, about how tortured people can be when the world thinks of them as one way, say, as a man, and they think of themselves in an opposite way, as a woman.

"Like Leonard/Leona," I say.

"Except I think she's only Leona now. I don't think she wants to be identified as Leonard anymore."

"Well . . . it's hard for me not to think she's still both."

"Work on it," Kit says.

I'm already in bed when I hear the hum of my computer and see that Kit is bringing up her e-mail. She's got messages from churlygirl and sadchck and a bunch of other people I've never heard of.

"Come look at this," she says.

"Do I have to?" I whine.

She laughs. "Don't be such a slug."

I get up and stand behind her, looking down at the screen. She points to a message from strgrl.

"This is Star, the girl I met at the beach."

It's an invitation to a GSA leadership training class, tomorrow, at Sojourner High School, for gay, lesbian, bi, trans, questioning, straight youth, who want to start or strengthen GSA groups on their campuses.

"What's this bi and trans stuff?"

"You know — like they talked about in PC. Transgender, like Leona, and bi — can go either way."

Kit sounds like she's talking about something as simple as different hairstyles. I don't exactly see it that way.

She opens a message from churlygirl. "Hope to see you at Sojourner on Saturday. It'll be cool!"

"Go with me," Kit says.

"I told Conan I'd meet him at the mall."

"What time?"

"Around four."

"So??? This thing is over at one."

"Well . . . I told Mom I'd help do stuff around the house, too."

"Why don't you just say you don't want to go?" Kit asks, turning back to the computer screen. I go back to bed.

The truth is, I'm not sure if I want to go or not. I want to be supportive and all, but mostly I want to do it without being involved. As soon as I think that — be supportive without being involved — I know what a stupid idea it is. I mean, how can you *not* be involved, if you're going to be supportive.

"I'll go," I say.

"Forget it. I don't need any favors," Kit says angrily.

I get up and go to the bathroom, brushing and flossing one more time. What's *with* her anyway? When I go back to my room, she's answering the e-mail. Neither of us says anything until after she turns off the computer and gets into bed. We lie in the dark, with plenty of distance between us.

"I don't want to have to beg for your support," Kit says.

"And I don't want to have to go places where I'm uncomfortable, just to please you."

After about a thousand inhale/exhales in the quiet night, I tell Kit, "I'm going tomorrow. Because I want to."

"If it's awful we'll leave," she promises.

The meeting's not exactly awful, but it sure is an experience unlike anything I've ever had before. As soon as we walk into the Sojourner media center, it feels like I'm in a foreign country. I want to turn around and walk right back out the door. Kit's already talking with Star. She wouldn't notice me leaving. I turn to go, but this person, Leaf, hands me a sign-in sheet and starts talking to me.

"Is this your first meeting here?" Leaf asks, arching a pierced eyebrow complete with a small silver hoop.

I nod. Leaf is wearing cargo shorts and a bright red and yellow Hawaiian shirt. I can't tell if this person is a girl or a boy. Very full lips, and a rather dainty demeanor, with a slightly husky but melodic voice. Maybe it shouldn't make any difference, whether I can identify Leaf by his/her sex or not. But I keep trying to figure it out. I realize I'm staring. I walk away from the door, to the other side of the room, where I practically bump into Frankie Sanchez.

"Hey," he says, giving me a surprised look. "There's a bunch of sodas over there in the cooler. Can I get one for you?"

"Thanks," I say. "Maybe a Sprite, or 7-Up?"

"Come with me, and see what you want."

Frankie and I walk back across the room to get sodas. Just as I bend down to check out the choices, Leaf comes over. Now that I'm eye level with Leaf's way hairy legs, I know he's a guy. If it weren't for those legs, though, I'd never have figured it out.

Kit leads Star over to us.

"This is Lynn, my best friend," she says. "Lynn, this is Star."

"Hi," I say, smiling.

She nods, then turns her attention back to Kit.

"Come on," she says, pulling Kit away. "I want you to see this cool display."

Kit lets herself be drawn to the other side of the room, and here I am with Frankie and Leaf, not knowing what to say. I'm eyeing the door again when I hear a familiar voice asking that everyone take a seat on one of the chairs in the circle. It's Mrs. Saunders, Emmy, the librarian I told you about a while back.

"Lynn! Nice to see you here."

"Where's Rosie this morning?" I say, walking over closer to where Emmy's standing.

"She's home with my husband . . . It's so sweet. She loves having a dad who pays attention to her."

I guess I look puzzled because Emmy adds, "Rosie's biological father doesn't come around very often."

"I know how that goes," I say.

Frankie waves at Emmy. "We should probably start soon."

"You're right," Emmy says, again asking that everyone take a seat. Slowly, people find places in the circle of chairs. There are about twenty people I guess. Nora Thomsen and Caitlin Ratchford are here, also from choir. I don't know them very well. They're juniors and they hardly talk to anyone except each other, and sometimes Frankie.

Really, it's weird, but I've never even heard Caitlin's voice, except for when she's singing. Whenever I say hi, Caitlin smiles, and Nora says hi back.

Kit comes over and sits next to me, with Star practically glued to her other side.

Frankie introduces himself as the president of the Sojourner GSA, then introduces Emmy as the advisor from Hamilton High, and Guy Reyes as the advisor from Sojourner. He asks that we review the dos and don'ts of participation in the group. Frankie mentions confidentiality, and someone else talks about no put-downs.

Really, the rules for this group are the same as in peer communications, except they include not introducing ourselves by sexual orientation. *That* was the first thing I planned to say in my introduction. I'm here as a friend, not a . . . What *would* I have said? Not as a homo? Not as a lesbian? I'm here as a normal person? Lucky for me, there's a plan for what we say when we introduce ourselves. It's called an "ice-breaker." All I can think is that an ice-breaker would have been good equipment for the Titanic. Maybe this ice-breaker will help me get rid of the sinking feeling that lives inside me right now.

Okay. This is the ice-breaker. We say our names and what we had to eat for dinner last night. Some of the dinners sound so funny that before we're halfway around the circle, everyone's laughing uproariously. It starts with Leaf's catsup and butter sandwich on whole wheat bread, and gains with a girl's Rice Krispies Treats with peanut butter and jelly. Then there's a string of vegetarians with gardenburgers and sprouts. The girls from choir, Nora and Caitlin, were part of the gardenburger set. That's according to Nora, who spoke for them both.

Next, people describe big batches of greasy fries, onion rings, fried zucchini, Cokes and chips. Killer foods, if you believe the American Heart Association.

By the time it gets to us, pizza and soda sounds like a health food meal. Here's the thing though. Because we all laughed together, we're no longer strangers. Even Leaf, who I think it's safe to say nearly everyone thinks is weird when they first meet him, seems like one of the group, not like a weirdo.

Frankie and Star lead the next exercise. Frankie introduces it as "Change Seats" but Star calls it "Move Your Ass." I'm surprised Emmy doesn't correct Star's language. I guess it's different than during actual school. In the library if anybody uses "ass" in front of Emmy, they'd better be talking about a donkey.

The game is kind of like musical chairs, without the music. Chairs are removed from the circle until there are exactly enough chairs for everyone, minus one. It starts out simple — move your ass if you have a driver's license. About half the room, including me and Kit, get out of our chairs and race to find another. Frankie's left standing. Which means he has to come up with the next statement.

"Move your ass if you use e-mail."

Nearly everyone races for a seat.

A girl with bright red hair and about ten bead bracelets on each wrist holds her arms out for all to see and says, "Move your ass if you have a Pride bracelet."

I'm one of the few who doesn't move.

Now it's Star who is left standing.

"Move your ass if your parents ever kicked you out of their house."

A lot of people move, including Leaf and Frankie and Nora.

"Move your ass if you have a friend who's committed suicide."

I'm shocked this time, when seven people, including the adviser from Sojourner High, move. Toward the end of the game, as the topics get more serious — ever had an eating disorder, ever been mistaken for a gender other than your own, ever been beaten up because of your gender identity — I find myself not changing chairs, and surprised at how many people do.

After that we gather in groups of four or five and talk about how we can strengthen or start GSA groups on our campuses. I drift away then. I don't much care whether Hamilton High has a

GSA group or not. It sounds like a lot of trouble to me, and anyway, whoever wants to go to a GSA group can go to the one here at Sojourner.

On the way home, Kit talks about how cool everything was — the people, the games, the plans for GSA.

"You ended up sitting through the last part of that 'Move Your Ass' game."

"I didn't have any reason to move. Besides, I didn't even know what they were talking about with that gender stuff. I dropped Latin because I couldn't get genders, and I still don't."

"It's not about grammar, you airhead."

"Well, what then?"

"Gender, gender, you know, it's your, like your . . ." Kit stops talking.

"You know," she says.

"No, I don't get it, and I don't think you do, either!"

"I *do* get it . . . I just can't explain it."

When we get to my house we take sodas out on the steps, as we've done for years, after school, or waiting for my mom to come home from work, or playing with Wilma.

Kit brings up the gender word again.

"Okay. I can explain it. It's like with that Leona person. Everybody said she was a boy, because she had a boy's body. That was her *biological* sex. But by *gender* she identified more with girls."

"So what am I?"

"Female."

"Sex or gender?"

"Both."

"What about you?"

"Female."

"What about Leaf?"

"I guess he's physically male, but his gender is female. Do you think?" Kit says.

"It's confusing. I like things better when people are just male or female, and they act that way."

"Thank you, Dr. Laura," Kit says.

"What do you mean by that?"

"Just think about it," Kit says. "I don't want to argue anymore."

"Fine with me." I say.

"So, let's talk about happy stuff."

"Okay. I think I'm in love. I mean, Conan, isn't he just the best?"

Kit smiles at me. "He is an amazingly nice guy."

"Handsome, too."

"Yeah, I guess. In a Conan kind of way."

"No, really, his smile, his eyes. It's like a person's soul could sink way deep into his eyes and be safe there."

Kit laughs. "I'm happy for you, but I wonder what Always is going to say when she meets him."

"It'll be okay. I'm pretty sure. I think he's more worried about having me meet his folks than I am about him meeting Mom."

"How about your dad?"

"He can go years without meeting Dad."

Wilma comes up to us with the frisbee in her mouth. She drops it at my feet. I throw it up as high as I can and watch her jump and twist to get it.

"Beautiful," I tell her. "Isn't she beautiful?"

Kit doesn't respond, and when I turn to look at her, she has a look in her eyes that I've not seen before. I don't know how to describe it — soft like, and far away.

After I've thrown the frisbee about twenty times, and Wilma's caught it nineteen, I turn my attention to Kit.

"What's on your mind?" I ask. She just smiles.

"Something's on your mind. C'mon, out with it."

"Promise not to tell?"

"Promise. Like I ever tell anything you say anyway."

"This is special . . ."

"Okay! Just tell me!"

"I've got a date with Star."

I throw the frisbee to Wilma another ten times.

"Say something," Kit begs.

I take a deep breath.

"What's wrong?"

"I thought you weren't coming out until after high school, that's all."

"I'm not exactly coming out! I'm just going to a coffee place with Star. No drama."

"It is *drama*. I can tell it's a *ton* of drama, the way you were all moony eyed with her. And she couldn't leave your side all day!"

"So? You're going out with Conan! You're all moony eyed with him! Are you saying it's okay for you to be in love, but not for me?"

"No, but . . ."

"But what??? You'd be all happy if I went out with Robert, but you're unhappy that I'm going out with Star? Get over it! Are you with me, the real me, or do you want me to be some pretend Barbie doll, like my mother does?"

Kit goes into this prissy thing, "Oh, could I borrow your high heels for tonight, please??? And your wonder bra??? I want to be so pretty and sexy for Robert . . . Is that who you want for a friend? Because if it is, it ain't me, Babe."

We burst out laughing with the "it ain't me, Babe" remark. That's the song my mom played constantly for a whole year while she was deciding to divorce my dad, and then for about a decade after. It's like her signature song, or something. We barely ever listened, but it was played so much, over and over, that we both knew the whole song by heart by the time Mom's favorites returned to Otis Redding and the Beatles.

We laugh so hard I think I can't stop, and I hope it's real laughter, not that phony stuff people do when there's tension.

When we stop laughing we sit a while longer, mellowed out.

CHAPTER

9

It is crowded at the mall, but I see Conan right away, over by the carousel — not that he's hard to find in a crowd. We check out the toy shops, for a birthday gift for Sabina. He decides on a puzzle, because his sister's so smart. Then he buys a sparkly bracelet, because she's so cute. Finally he buys a cuddly stuffed dog, because she's so lovable.

"I've got enough money left for two smoothies. Want one?"

At Jivin' Juice, Conan orders a blackberry smoothie, and I get a banana pineapple combination.

"I worked all morning helping my dad in the yard. Anything to be lifted, I'm the man, according to him."

I take a swallow of my drink, savoring the taste, happy with my choice, happy to be here with Conan.

"We trimmed a tree way back, and then we sanded and put a coat of paint on the picnic table, so it'll be ready for Sabina's party. What about you? What've you been doing this morning?"

"Well . . ."

I don't want to keep any secrets from Conan. But if I tell him about the GSA meeting, will that be like breaking a promise to Kit?

"And . . . " he says, looking at me expectantly.

"Well . . ."

"Is there someone else?" he asks, almost in a whisper.

"No, no, it's not that at all!"

"Well, then, what is it that you can't tell me?"

"I went somewhere with Kit. I don't think she wants anyone to know. That's all."

Conan laughs.

"You mean that GSA thing? Were you there with Kit?"

"How did you know?"

"You know Susan?"

"No, unless she's the one that eats Rice Krispies Treats with peanut butter and jelly for dinner."

"Sounds like Susan," Conan says. "She lives next door to me. She told me Kit was there, but she didn't say anything about you."

"So much for confidentiality," I say, miffed.

"Hey, it's no biggy."

"It could be, to some people," I say.

Conan seems distracted. I follow his gaze. Two men are sitting across from us, staring. They're probably around my dad's age. You know the phrase, if looks could kill? That's what comes to my mind. If looks could kill, Conan and I would be dead by now.

"What's with *them*?" I whisper to Conan.

"Just a couple of racists, I guess," Conan says. "Come on. Let's move down to the waterfall."

"Why should we? It's a free country," I say, blazing a look back at the men.

Conan picks up our drinks and starts walking. I catch up to him.

"Some people get *all* worked up when they see a black guy with a white girl. That's been the cause of plenty of lynchings," he says.

"But this is the twenty-first century. Right?"

"Right. We're just moving away from bad energy. That's all."

We sit on a bench near the waterfall, catching a light spray from the misty water. Conan takes my hand in his and rests his cheek against it.

"See. Good energy is always better."

Every time I'm with Conan and things are quiet, like at the beach, or here, I feel like I belong with him. I hope I can tell him that some day.

Another Monday morning. Another glow from another perfect weekend with Conan.

There's a knock at the back door. I know it's Kit, wanting a ride to school. Mom always lets me take the car on Mondays, when she rides to work with a friend.

Even though I'm expecting Kit, I don't recognize her when I first open the door. I blink, then look again.

"Well . . .?" Kit says. "Like my new do?"

All that's left of her beautiful, thick, shiny black hair is about an eighth of an inch of fuzz on top of her head. The rest is gone. She's in jeans and a white tee shirt, not the usual preppy stuff her mother always insists that she wear. She's wearing a heavy plaid flannel shirt. Around her neck is a woven choker thing with the colors of the rainbow repeated every quarter inch or so. On both wrists she has those Pride bracelets with brightly colored beads — purple, blue, green, yellow, orange and red. She is beaming.

I try to smile.

"What'd your parents say?"

"Dad's on the early shift this week, and Mom's visiting Gramma and Grampa for a few days."

"She'll have a FIT when she sees you."

"I know," Kit says. "But it *is* my hair."

"Was," I say.

Kit laughs, but it doesn't seem so funny to me. I back the car out of the garage and Kit climbs into the back seat.

"Star helped me with my hair," Kit says. "First she pulled it all together at the bottom, with rubber bands, then she took the scissors and cut it as close to my head as she could."

I'm watching the road, but what I'm seeing is Kit, on a stool somewhere, with Star cutting away at her hair.

"It's cool," Kit says. "We wrapped it securely, from one end to the other, and then we took it to a place that makes wigs from human hair. They loved my hair!"

"Who doesn't? Didn't?" I ask.

"But listen to this. The wigs are loaned out to cancer patients. And they look really natural, because they're real hair. The woman at the shop said they would probably get four or five very nice wigs from what we brought in."

I glance at Kit in the rearview mirror. It's all I can do to keep from crying, thinking about her beautiful hair, and how she hardly even resembles her old self.

"She said I'd made an important contribution."

"But that's not why you did it," I say.

Pause.

"I did it because I'm sick of having people assume I'm like ninety percent of the population."

I wonder how others will react when they see her and I'm getting all nervous. Kit, though, is glowing. Like I was earlier this morning, when the weekend with Conan was all that was on my mind.

When Conan gets in the car he does one of those classic double takes you see in old cartoons.

"Wow! Look at you!" he says with a big smile.

I wonder what he means. My mom always says if you see a really ugly baby you can always say, "Look at this baby!" with a lot of enthusiasm. That way, you're not lying, and you don't hurt the proud parents' feelings.

Conan reaches back and rubs Kit's fuzzy head.

"Nice," he says. Then, turning to me, "Don't get any ideas, though."

Am I the only one who sees a problem here? It's not like people aren't going to notice anything or say anything at school. I don't even want to turn into the parking lot when we get there. We could just keep going. I'm sure we could find one of those old hippie communes somewhere in Oregon — the kind that takes people in and doesn't judge them by their appearance. Then we wouldn't have to watch Kit being humiliated for her strange new look. Or maybe I'm overreacting. If nobody else thinks it's a problem am I getting all whacked over nothing?

So okay. I'm not hijacking my friends to Oregon. I follow the line of cars into the parking lot and grab the nearest space. As we walk toward the main building, I notice people noticing Kit. She walks along with us, talking and laughing as always. Conan takes my hand, which usually is enough to light up my morning, but today, in spite of Conan, and sunshine, my mood is dark.

At first it's like silence surrounds us when we walk together in the halls. The paused conversations, the turning of heads, the widening of eyes, are noiseless. In choir, there's kind of a low buzz, which I'm pretty sure centers on Kit's hair, or lack thereof, not to mention her clothes and accessories.

It's not until volleyball practice that anyone actually says anything to Kit about her hair.

As we walk onto the court, Coach Terry says to Kit, "Nice cut."

I can't tell if she's being sarcastic or sincere.

"Thanks," Kit says, flashing a big smile.

When Kit practices her serve, all eyes are on her, appraising. I don't think it's the serve they're watching. As great as it is, they've seen her serve thousands of times.

Kit tosses the ball upward, flawlessly placing it exactly where she wants it. As she tips her head back to watch the rising ball, right before she connects for the serve, I get an image of Kit's long volleyball-braid, thick and black, hanging past her well-muscled shoulders. I blink and it's gone. Get over it, I tell myself.

It's only hair. I stare, trying to get used to the new look. There before me is the back of Kit's head, buzzed on top, shaved up the neck and sides. Her rainbow choker stands out like a collar on some weirdly groomed poodle. God! GOSH! As soon as I think the poodle thought I'm filled with guilt. My spirit sister. My very best friend through thick and thin, and I'm comparing her to a *dog*. What is my *problem*?

Usually, after showers, the whole team bunches up in the same area, drying off, getting dressed, talking and joking around. Today there are two bunches. Me and Kit near the center, where we all usually gather, and the rest of the team at the other end, away from us. Talking and joking is *so* not happening.

Conan's still at football practice, so it's only me and Kit on the way home. I pull Mom's car into the garage, and dump my backpack on the porch steps. Wilma drags her frisbee out.

Kit and I walk through the gate, with Wilma happily following behind. We sit under the tree, taking turns throwing the frisbee for Wilma.

After a while, Kit says "Aren't you going to ask me about my date with Star?"

"I already know she butchered your hair. Is there more?"

Pause.

I breathe in the freshness of tree-filtered air. I scoop up a handful of dirt and let it slowly sift through my fingers. I remember the candles, the *World Weekly News*, the little fan, the pitcher of water, our vows. I ease up on my attitude.

"Tell me about your date with Star."

Pause.

"Please. I'm sorry about the butchered remark."

Kit nods. "It was cool."

"What'd you do? Besides the obvious, I mean?"

"Well, after we took my hair to the wig shop, we went to this coffee place up in Pasadena."

"And . . ."

"And it was unbelievable! As soon as I walked in, it was like I was at home. There was a band, and people were dancing. It was mostly women dancing together, but there were some gay guys, and also a few men and women dancing. It was an out and proud crowd. It was *awesome*."

"Did you dance?" I ask, trying to picture this place in my head.

"We danced until my feet fell off!"

Wilma gives a short, sharp bark, looking up at me expectantly, then lifting her frisbee and dropping it.

"I thought you didn't like to dance," I say to Kit.

"I didn't like dancing with *Brian*. I don't like dancing with *guys*, touching their sweaty hands, having them put their hands on my butt and press me close to them, so I feel their nasty thing pushing against my pubic bone."

"You make it sound so repulsive!"

"It *is* repulsive. To me anyway."

Wilma barks again. I pick up her frisbee, concentrating on throwing it just the right height and distance so she can show off one of those high, twisty catches. It's not easy, though. The frisbee is so chewed up now, it's totally out of balance. It acts like some kind of cross between a frisbee and a boomerang.

"Dancing with Star was like nothing I've ever experienced before," Kit says. "It's like we each knew how the other would move, no awkward stepping on feet, or one going one way and the other going opposite. We were in unison, without thinking, or planning, we just were."

"That's how it is with Conan," I say.

"Yeah? Well then you know how nice it can be."

After about twenty more frisbee throws, Wilma deposits the frisbee at the back gate instead of bringing it back to me. It's her way of letting me know she's finally had enough. She comes back to the tree and wedges her way between me and Kit. As Kit reaches down to pet Wilma, I stare at her bracelet.

"All of the colors," she says, "Each as beautiful as the other. Like all of the different kinds of people in the world."

"Right. Like you see a bunch of purple people running around," I say, knowing how stupid I sound.

"Get a clue! It's symbolic! It stands for all kinds of diversity — race, color, gender, culture — you know."

"But doesn't it sort of . . . stereotype you?"

Kit gives me a disgusted look.

"Really, half the kids at that GSA meeting were wearing those rainbow things."

"I don't care about that. I'm sick of looking like Barbie in my little skirt and sweater. I'm sick of the little gold charm bracelet my mother always wants me to wear. I'm sick of looking like some girly-girl. That's SO who I'm NOT. I'm finding my own way. That's all."

We hear a car come into the driveway.

"That would be Mom," Kit says. "Time for the great unveiling."

"Are you worried?"

"Well . . . Look."

Kit lays her hands flat on her jeans — each upper thigh. When she moves them away, they leave two distinct, damp, sweaty imprints.

"Shall I go in with you?" I ask.

She shakes her head. "I think I'm on my own with this one."

I get up, relieved, and brush my hands clean.

"Call me later," I say.

"I'll e-mail. It's more private . . . See you in the morning?" she asks, reaching for her backpack.

"Sure. Conan'll pick us up."

I walk to the gate. Wilma follows.

"Good luck," I call back to Kit.

"Thanks," she yells back.

I go into the house and start my homework, but it's hard to concentrate. My head is full of worry for Kit, and love for Conan, and will I get into a good nursing program, and what will we have for dinner, and why all of a sudden am I getting these zits on my face when it's not even near my period and I've not eaten any chocolate in weeks.

It is after midnight by the time I've finished my homework and get around to checking e-mail. That's sort of a deal I've made with myself. I don't open e-mail until my homework is done — like a reward from me to me. I've got a message from Haley. She was one of the ten-year-olds in my cabin at summer camp. I taught her to swim, so now we're friends forever. I'm e-mailing her back when the flag comes up that I have a new message. It's from Kit.

When my mom saw my hair she went into total meltdown. She kept screaming, my beautiful baby, my beautiful baby! What's to become of you? My dad said nothing. I mean NOTHING! He just sat there, looking at me. It's like he wasn't even hearing my mom. She kept asking me where she'd gone wrong, why would I want to hurt her like that. I told her, It's not about you Mom. I got my hair cut is all. That's not all, my dad said. You think I'm on the donut and coffee patrol? I'm out there, on the streets. I know what's up. The rainbow necklace, the Pride bracelet, the haircut, is not all. All the time he was saying this, he was calm, and sort of distant, but then it looked like he might cry. DAMN! I haven't seen my dad cry since the last time I saw him drunk.

There's more to tell you, but I'm tired of writing. The worst thing is that my dad left without saying where he was going. Like in the old days. Mom's all worried, crying about how if Dad starts drinking again it's all my fault.

I immediately e-mail back to Kit, telling her to come over so we can talk — I'll leave my bedroom window open for her. I stay awake for a long time, and even when I sleep I'm only half-sleeping. The other half is listening for Kit. She doesn't show up.

CHAPTER

10

When I pour my morning glass of orange juice, I find a note from Mom on the kitchen table. Her friend from work made a batch of lasagna for us, way too much for two. Why not invite my new boyfriend over to help us with it?

Mom's been hinting around that it's time for her to meet Conan. At first I told her Conan and I were just friends. Which was true, at first, sort of.

The other night she told me, "I don't care if you are just friends. You talk to him every night on the phone, he takes you to school, you spend a lot of time together on weekends, and I want to meet him."

Mom has this thing about knowing all of my friends. It was okay when I was ten, but I don't think it's necessary now. In six months I'll be legally classified as an adult.

Kit looks haggard when she shows up in the morning. We sit on the steps, waiting for Conan.

"How're things at your house this morning?"

"Quiet," Kit says.

"Your dad?"

"He was there this morning, when I got up."

"And?"

"Not drunk. But his sponsor was sitting at the table with him, drinking coffee. Judging from the way they looked, they'd been up all night."

"His sponsor?"

"You know. The twelve-step thing. Everyone has a sponsor to help them stay on program. I guess he'd been tempted to drink, so he called this poor guy in the middle of the night."

"How about your mom?"

Kit starts laughing a kind of sad, hysterical laugh.

"What?"

"You know how I told you Dad was talking about the rainbow stuff last night?" she gasps out.

I nod. Kit struggles to catch her breath.

"Well, for a minute it was like Mom got her hopes up. She stopped screaming and sobbing and she said, 'Rainbow? Rainbow?' And she got this sort of hopeful smile on her face."

Kit is again consumed by laughter. But it's more of a harsh laughter than a fun laughter.

"I don't get it."

"She thought it had something to do with Rainbow Girls. Remember how she tried to get us to join that group, where they have secret handshakes or something and they're always running around in formals? Remember?"

"When we were in the eighth grade?"

"Yeah. She had this plan for us, to help us become ladies. Rainbow Girls!" She points to her bracelet. "Rainbow Girls!" She laughs.

I laugh, too, but at the same time I feel sort of sorry for Kit's mom.

"She doesn't still think you're wanting to be a Rainbow Girl does she?"

Kit gets serious.

"No. Dad told her she was way off base. She was so far off base she wasn't even on the field."

"Then what?"

"I don't know. Then I came in and e-mailed you and Star and went to bed."

"I left my window open for you all night," I tell her.

"Thanks."

"Do you want to stay at our house tonight?"

"No. We've moved into the not speaking phase now. When I passed them in the kitchen this morning it was like I was invisible. That's okay. It's easier."

From the look on Kit's face, I'm not convinced things are easier.

Conan pulls into the driveway, all smiles. He gives me a big kiss as soon as I get in the car, then looks back to greet Kit, who looks all tense and worried.

"Hey. Who died?" he says with a laugh.

When she doesn't respond he says, "That's a joke. At least, I hope it is!"

"Sorry," Kit says. "I guess I'm not in a joking mood."

"What's up?"

Kit sighs. "Nothing. I don't want to talk about it."

Conan is quiet for a while, as if all he's thinking about is driving. Then he glances in the rear view mirror. "I thought we were friends. I thought I was more than just a ride to school."

While we're waiting at a signal, Conan turns around and looks at Kit. She looks out the window.

"Just a family fight," she says. "That's all."

In PC, during journal writing time, Conan whispers, "What's with Kit?"

"A big argument."

"Yeah? . . . And?"

"I guess her mom went over the edge about Kit's new look —
wants to know where she went wrong. And her dad's not
speaking. That stuff."

Conan nods his head as if he understands. "I hate when my
family gets all on my case about stuff that's really none of their
business."

"Like what?"

"Like . . . just stuff," he says, and turns back to his journal
writing. Conan doesn't talk much about family things, except for
his sister. I wonder if his dad is doing more of that barbarian
stuff, or if something else is going on.

Between second and third period I catch up to Kit on the way
upstairs.

"Are you worried about the fight with your parents?" I ask.

"We never fight. Everything's been good for the past four
years. And now . . . seeing my parents all down . . ."

Kit is on the verge of tears. By this time we're near the library.
I lead her inside, to a table in a far corner. We sit next to one
another and I wait to hear what Kit will say next. The warning bell
rings, signifying five minutes to class time, but we don't move.
Kit takes a series of slow, deep breaths, trying, I think, to avoid
a real cry fest.

"All I'm trying to do is be who I am, and my parents are going
nuts — just because I got a haircut!"

"And the rainbow stuff," I remind her.

"Is it wrong for me to be who I am? Should I keep pretending
to be someone else?" she asks in a strained whisper.

One of the hardest things I've ever had to deal with has been
Kit's "I like girls" revelation. I've wished she would just keep
going along with things, the old way, like she's one of the crowd.
But now, if I'm honest with myself, I know I was wrong.

"Don't pretend," I tell her. "Be you — awesome volleyball
player, budding psychologist, true friend, spirit sister, Star's
love, lesbian — be your own true self."

Tears are streaming down Kit's face, full force now. I'm all teary, too.

"Thank you," she whispers.

Emmy walks past our table, barely pausing, and sets a box of tissue down between us. We wipe our faces dry and for the first time today I see Kit smile. Then the smile fades.

"I don't want people to be hurt, or angry. I don't want my mom to be all sad about me, and worried about Dad falling into his old ways. What if he really does start drinking again? Because of me?"

"One day at a time. Isn't that what your parents always say?"

Now Kit does smile, full out.

"I wish I'd thought to remind them of that last night when mom was carrying on about what was to become of me and Dad was acting like there'd been a death in the family!"

Emmy stops by the table again. She glances at Kit, hair, bracelet, clothes, looks at me, then back to Kit.

"Can I help?"

Kit shakes her head.

Emmy sits down across from us.

"That old cliché about these being the best years of your life — what a joke, huh?"

"So far," Kit says.

Emmy glances around the library, as if to be certain everything is going smoothly. She pulls a pencil out of her pocket and erases a mark on the table. She takes one of those deep, yoga breaths.

"Rosie was born the summer before my junior year," she says.

I don't know why that should shock me. It's not like the days of the Scarlet Letter or anything. But Emmy seems so . . . together.

"You were a teen mom?" I ask, like she didn't just tell us that.

"Neither of us is pregnant if that's what you're thinking," Kit says.

"What I'm thinking is that you're upset. And that life in high school is not always easy."

"Well, duh," Kit says.

I don't know why Kit has to be so rude. Just because she's in the middle of a big drama, doesn't mean she has to take it out on Emmy. I try to smooth things over.

"Was it hard being a mom when you were still in high school?" I ask.

"It was the hardest thing I've ever had to do — so far anyway. I was always tired, trying to take care of a baby, and keep up with school. I never had any money. I didn't even graduate on stage, with my class. It was a big disappointment at the time, but . . . it doesn't seem like such a big deal now."

"Why didn't you graduate on stage?" Kit asks, her tone more civil now.

"I took the proficiency test and transferred to community college after my junior year. I needed to get on with things."

Emmy goes to check out a book for a student, then returns.

"All I'm trying to say is, things can be hard, and they can get better. I love my life now — Rosie, and Carl, and my job."

She looks intently at Kit.

"Whatever the problem is, don't give up hope."

Kit nods.

"It was hard being one of *those* girls. Some of my teachers said I'd ruined my life, I'd never make it to college . . ."

"That sucks," Kit says.

"But there were others, too, like Woodsy, and Mr. Michaels, who encouraged me . . . I want to be more like them than like the others. That's why, when Frankie asked, I agreed to be an advisor for GSA . . ."

"Mrs. Saunders?" a frail looking freshman boy asks. "Can you help me find a book?"

Emmy gets up to help him.

"I didn't mean to get carried away with my life story," she says, smiling as she gets up from her chair.

I smile back. Even Kit smiles back. In a few minutes Emmy stops by our table with passes back to class.

"We can take a hint," I say, laughing.

Kit and I gather our things.

"You okay?" I ask.

Kit nods. We exchange a quick hug and go on to our third period classes.

It's silent reading time in English. I open *The Color Purple* and look at the page. I'm not actually reading. I'm thinking about Kit, and what a terrible denial of a person it is to expect them to pretend to be something they're not. It's like saying "I can't accept you the way you are. You're not worthy."

Kit's never asked me to be anything other than myself. I'm glad I didn't ask that of her either. What do I care if she's a lesbian? She's Kit.

Miss Banks gives me a look, like she knows I'm not reading. I don't get how she can tell from such a distance whether or not my eyes are moving across the page, but she can. Maybe that's something teachers learn in college — or at least back when *she* was in college.

Another look from her. A major frown. I turn my attention to *The Color Purple.*

I'm at a part where Celie and Shug, the woman Celie's husband *really* loves, are having a heart to heart. Celie tells Shug about a terrible time, when she was fourteen, and her father raped her. Shug holds Celie and comforts her and then — they get all sexy with one another. I'm so surprised! Is Celie a lesbian? Is Shug? How is it I never notice something's up before I'm hit over the head with it?

I reread a couple of pages. I'm happy for Celie, that she finally has a chance to feel love, and show it. That's the important thing, love. Not the rules of love, but love itself. I'm going to remember that whenever I'm uncomfortable seeing Star and Kit being affectionate with one another.

Conan meets me after school, just before he has to go off to football practice. He tells me he loves lasagna, so I guess I'll set the table for three tonight. I shouldn't be nervous. I know my mom's not racist. My stomach feels kind of fluttery, though. I don't think Conan will be exactly what she's expecting.

As soon as I get home from school, I call Mom.

"I've got to tell you something about Conan before you meet him tonight."

"It sounds like he's got two heads or something."

"He's black."

"And?"

"And I didn't want you to be surprised."

"Thanks, but remember, I teethed on the civil rights movement." She laughs. "Whenever there was a demonstration against segregation, Gramma and Grampa were right there, marching, pushing me along in my stroller. By the time I was three I knew every single verse to 'We Shall Overcome.'"

By the time dinner's over, it's as if Mom and Conan are best friends. As far as I'm concerned she asks way too many questions. Conan doesn't seem to mind, though. He just smiles and keeps answering. That is, between bites of lasagna. It's pretty amazing to see how much food he can eat in one sitting.

Conan asks Mom about her work, which she loves to talk about. He even turns the tables on her and asks her about *her* goals in life.

"Well, for the past several years my boss has been trying to get me to move up to a job that requires a fair amount of travel. I've not felt like I should be running off and leaving Lynn on her own. But now . . . I'm thinking about taking it next fall."

"You never told me that!" I say.

"You never asked."

"What would you be doing?"

"Workshops. Training people how to use our software. My territory would be the west coast and Hawaii."

"Mom! That would be so cool!"

She laughs. "It's not certain yet. Don't start packing your bags to join me on a business trip."

After dinner Conan and I clear the table and load the dishwasher. Then we go outside and sit on the steps. It's cold out, and Conan pulls me close enough that I can feel the warmth of his body.

"You're never cold, are you?" I ask.

"Never around you," he says, giving me a long, slow kiss.

"Now I'm not cold, either," I tell him.

We kiss again and he puts his hand under my sweater and lightly caresses my back. The feel of his warm hand on my skin is pure pleasure. He knows that.

"More?" he whispers.

"Yes," I say, even though I don't know what he means by more.

"Let's find a better place," he says, standing and holding his hand out to pull me up.

I tell Mom I'll be back in an hour or so, that we're going to get ice cream. When I get in the car, I notice the dog Conan gave Sabina for her birthday.

"Does she like her birthday present?" I ask, pointing to the huge stuffed animal.

"Oh, no," Conan groans. "She forgot Fluffy!"

He looks at his watch.

"She's probably giving Mom a terrible time about going to bed without it . . . Fluffy. I want my Fluffy," Conan cries in what I take to be an imitation of Sabina.

"It *is* pretty cute," I say, rubbing the soft white fur on Fluffy's head.

"Sabina wants me to get a dog license for Fluffy, so if she gets lost we can call the pound and they'll help us find her," Conan laughs.

"I've got one of Wilma's old licenses."

"That'd work. I'll get it when we come back."

11

We drive to a tree-lined street in the rich section of town and park at the end of the cul-de-sac. We push the front seats back as far as they'll go and try to stretch out, keeping our bodies close. Conan is practically trapped by the steering wheel. We trade places but the Hyundai is still very confining. Somehow though, we manage to get close. Conan pulls me against him and reaches under my sweater to unfasten my bra. He pulls my sweater up and kisses my breast gently, then my mouth.

"I love you," he whispers. "I love how you make me feel."

He guides my hand downward. I can feel his warmth and hardness even through his jeans. We kiss again, strong and forceful. Then — the beam of a flashlight through the window. Some guy walking his dog, but I guess he thinks he's Mr. Neighborhood Watch or something. He looks for a moment, then walks on. Conan gets back in the driver's side, starts the car, and drives out of the cul-de-sac. The guy with the flashlight watches.

I lay my head on Conan's shoulder, thinking how comfortable I am with him. I've never done that much before. Guys have tried to touch my breasts, or put their hands between my legs, or get me to touch them, but I've never let it happen. It didn't appeal to me. Even with Eric, who I really liked for a while, we didn't go beyond heavy kissing. I didn't want to. But with Conan, I keep wanting more.

"Are you mad at me?" he asks.

"Oh my gosh! Mad? Why?"

"You know, because I got . . . all . . . worked up?"

"Oh, Conan," I say, scooting as close to him as I can possibly get, "the only one I'm mad at is the guy with the flashlight."

Conan laughs and gives me a quick kiss on the top of my head.

"We'll find a better place next time," he promises.

We've just turned onto my street when red lights flash behind us and there's a quick, short burst of a siren.

"Shit!" Conan says, slowing to the curb and stopping.

The blast of a bullhorn — "GET OUT OF THE CAR WITH YOUR HANDS UP!"

"We weren't speeding," I say.

"Do what they say. Show both of your hands, open, when you get out."

Conan opens the door, then puts his hands up and gets out of the car. I do the same.

"UP AGAINST THE CAR, SPREAD EAGLE!"

There are two sheriffs and they both have their guns out. One is pointing at Conan and the other at me. My heart is pounding in my ears. I'm shaking so hard I can hardly stand. Across the roof of the car Conan whispers, "Stay calm, Lynnie. Don't move unless they say to."

One sheriff, the skinny one, stands back, where he can see us both, gun trained on Conan, but watching me, too. The fat one holsters his gun, walks up to Conan and starts patting him down.

"WHY???" I scream, frantic.

"Chill," Conan says.

"He's right," the fat sheriff says. "Chill."

In the eerie lights, flashing red, I see Conan's face across from me. It resembles Conan, but it's a face I've not seen before, frozen hard, without expression.

Through my sobs I hear the rumbling of a trash container and then the voice of my mother, screaming, "What's going on here?" Then the pounding of her feet, getting closer to me.

"STOP RIGHT THERE!" comes the voice from the bullhorn.

I turn my head to see the skinny sheriff with his gun aimed at my mother.

"MOM!"

She stops. "THIS IS MY DAUGHTER!"

"Don't come any closer," the sheriff says.

"I live right there," Mom says, pointing to our house. "I'm Claire Wright. This is my daughter, Lynn, and I want to know what this is all about, Officer . . ." Mom squints her eyes, struggling to read the sheriff's name tag, ". . . Officer Barcley."

Officer Barcley lowers his gun.

"We got a call regarding a car of this description and license number. Suspicious activity."

By this time, the fat sheriff has Conan sitting on the curb with his hands behind his back, in handcuffs. Officer Barcley is watching Conan while my mom tries to talk to him. The other guy is searching through Conan's car.

"What *kind* of suspicious activity?" Mom demands to know.

Officer Barcley doesn't bother answering, but stands watching Conan.

"Officer Barcley!" It's the voice Mom uses when she means business. He doesn't even turn to look at her.

"Nothing here," the fat guy calls out, standing and closing the car door.

"You can put your hands down now, and step away from the car," Barcley says to me.

I stand back from the car and wipe my face. Conan turns sideways to see what is going on.

"Hey! Did anyone tell you to move?"

Conan turns back, facing the street, never changing his statue like look.

Mom runs to me, hugs me tight. My knees are weak with relief. I sink toward the street. She guides me to the curb and gently eases me down. She sits beside me, holding me, while I collapse in body-wracking sobs.

"Officer Barcley!" she calls, more insistent than ever.

I'm dimly aware of the sheriff sauntering over to where we're sitting.

"We got a complaint. These two were somewhere they had no business being," he says.

"Where?"

"Where they didn't belong."

"We were just . . . in the Heights . . . where they de . . . de . . . decorate all those giant pine trees at Christmas," I gasp, between sobs.

"On a public street?" Mom asks.

"There've been some robberies up there recently . . ."

"On a *public* street?" Mom repeats.

"On a public street, parked, with no business being there. You should watch the company your daughter keeps, Mrs. Wright."

I feel my mom stiffen, take a breath, as if to speak, then exhale slowly, remaining silent. I can't stop shaking. She tightens her arms around me.

The other sheriff, the fat one, wanders over. Conan still sits on the curb, handcuffed, as if they've forgotten he even exists.

"You can take your daughter home now," the fat one says.

Mom stands. I still feel weak and shaky.

"Thank you, Officer . . . Lee, we'll wait here until you're through with Conan," Mom says.

"You may as well go on home. This might take a while."

"Oh?"

"We're running a computer check on the car and the suspect."

"Suspect?"

"The car may be stolen. There may be a warrant out for Mr. Parker here. At the very least he's in violation of the curfew laws.

We'll have to hold him in custody until a parent can come get him."

Mom looks at her watch.

"It's only eleven-ten, Officer Lee. He would have been home before eleven if he hadn't been stopped."

"Maybe. Maybe not. We're just doing our jobs, trying to keep the community safe for honest, law abiding citizens."

Another squad car pulls up and stops behind the first one. Kit's father and his partner get out.

"Hey, Claire, Lynn," he says, flashing a questioning smile. He glances at Conan, then turns to the sheriff named Barcley. "What's up?"

They talk quietly, out of earshot. Officer Lee goes back to the squad car and checks the radio. "Nothing on the Parker guy," he calls out.

Both seem disappointed.

Kit's dad comes over to where we are standing.

"Do you know this guy?" he asks Mom, nodding in the direction of Conan, still sitting on the curb with his hands behind his back. Why don't they let him up?

"He's a friend of Lynn's. Actually, I think he's a friend of Kit's also. I know they all ride to school together most of the time."

"What's his story?"

"Story? I don't know any *story*, David," Mom says.

"Hey, I'm not the enemy, you know?" he says, giving Mom the same look I've seen him give Kit when he's trying to get through to her.

Mom nods.

"Right. I'm just a *little* upset. I come out of my house to find my daughter and her friend being held at gun point . . ."

Mom almost loses it, then pulls herself together.

"All I know about Conan," she says, gesturing in his direction, "is that he's a student at Hamilton High, big man on the football team, a friend of our kids. He seems to be a very nice young man.

It certainly doesn't appear he's done anything wrong tonight. As far as I know we are all still at liberty to park on public streets unless there's a no-parking designation!"

"You're right. But we have to take him in since it's past the curfew."

"It wouldn't *be* past curfew if he hadn't been stopped."

"But we can't have him driving around without adult supervision after curfew. That's against the law."

I stand looking at Conan's back, the bulk of him, frozen in position. His arms must be tired. I want to go to him, but it's as if he's in a zone that can't be crossed.

"Release him to me," Mom says. "I'll see that he gets home legally."

Kit's dad weighs the suggestion. He goes back to talk with the other three, again quietly enough that we can't hear them. The toughest acting guy, Barcley, shrugs and walks away. Lee follows. Mr. Dandridge walks over to where Conan is sitting and unlocks the handcuffs. Conan sits rubbing his wrists.

"You're released to Mrs. Wright," David says.

Conan rises slowly, now rubbing his arms and moving them around, probably trying to get the circulation going again. I go to him, put my arms around him, hold him tight. He is stiff and unyielding, his face still set. He says nothing. We walk together toward my mother.

"Come on," Mom says. "Call your parents so they won't be worried. We'll have a cup of hot chocolate and then I'll get you home."

Conan nods silently, not making eye contact. I go to the car to get my purse. Stuff is strewn all over. Everything's out of my wallet — driver's license, student I.D., social security card, pictures. Only the five-dollar bill is still where I left it. Tissue, lip gloss, breath mints, pen, markers, everything's been emptied out. I search around and under the seats until I think I've found everything. I look in the back seat, just to be sure I'm not leaving anything behind. There is Sabina's stuffed dog, its back ripped open, its head pulled off, stuffing strewn all over.

"Conan!" I call, the trembling starting again.

He and Mom walk to the car.

"What's all that?" Mom asks, as I gesture to the mess in the back seat.

"It's Fluffy," I say, choking back tears. "Conan's little sister's favorite stuffed animal."

Conan picks up the emptied head and drops it back down. His face is still ice. "Figures," is all he says.

After the phone call to his parents and the hot chocolate, Mom rides with Conan in his car, and I follow behind in her car, so I can take her back home. The lights are all on in Conan's house when we pull up. I want to say goodnight to him, but by the time I'm out of the car he's already at the front door, where his father and grandfather stand waiting. Conan turns and waves to us and disappears into his house. I wonder if Sabina is still awake, waiting for Fluffy.

When I see Kit in the morning, I tell her about how Conan and I were pulled over, and the way we were treated.

"I don't know how things would have turned out if your dad hadn't come along."

"Right. And if it had been you and me parked, talking, up in that ritzy section, would anyone have alerted the cops? And if they did, would we have been pulled over? And if we were, would either of us have been handcuffed, or would anything in our car have been destroyed?"

"I know. It sucks."

"Liberty and justice for all — not *even* close to a reality," Kit says.

CHAPTER

12

Kit asks me to go to the next GSA meeting with her. I don't have a good excuse not to, so I go. We meet Emmy in the faculty lot, and she drives us over to Sojourner in her van. Frankie, Caitlin and Nora go, too. When we get to the meeting room, Star is waiting. She takes a new Pride bracelet from her pocket and gives it to Kit. Kit gets that melty look again. They hug. Then Star slips the bracelet on Kit's wrist, just above the one she's already wearing.

The Sojourner High teacher, Guy, is there. There are two boys and two girls, including Star, who go to Sojourner. They're way more "out there" than the Hamilton High group. Just the hair alone. One of the boys, Jerry, has a mohawk that stands about four inches high, straight up. It's bright green. His eyebrow is pierced, his nose is pierced twice, with two little diamond studs at the edge of each nostril. He's weighed down with metal stuff hanging from his belt, and big spiky bracelets and a neck cuff. Another boy has hair that's been bleached white and divided into beaded strands, each about an inch long. The girl has her head shaved. She's got dark motorcycle style glasses, so dark you can't see her eyes. She's wearing a Hell's Angels T-shirt, greasy, torn jeans, and big heavy boots. There's a tattoo of a Harley-Davidson on her upper arm. Kit should bring Motorcycle Girl home to meet her parents. Maybe the contrast would make them think Kit's new style is not so bad.

The meeting starts with the usual review of rules. Then we go around the circle saying our names. Emmy hands out 3 x 5 cards. She explains the routine, for the benefit of new people. I think Kit and I are the only new people. The rest seem to know each other already. Anyway, the way this works is that everyone writes something about their past week on a card. Usually it's related to gay/lesbian issues, but it doesn't have to be.

"We try to get the best and the worst of the week. Then we talk about the issues that have been presented," Emmy says. "For people who are shy, or scared, keeping experiences anonymous feels safer."

Guy passes around a plate of chocolate chip cookies while we're writing on the cards.

"Oh, good, it's Guy's turn to bring cookies. None of those store bought Mother's Cookies things that Emmy always brings," Jerry says.

Both Guy and Emmy laugh, so I guess she's not insulted.

"I got up early this morning to bake these," Guy says.

I don't know what to write on my card. The best part of my week, maybe of my life, was those few minutes with Conan when we were parked on the tree-lined street. That's the farthest thing in the world from a gay/lesbian issue, though. The worst part was being stopped by the sheriffs, but I don't want to talk about that. I write that the worst part of my week was seeing how hard things are for my friend — how negative her family is. Then, I can't think of anything else, so I just say the best part was getting closer to my boyfriend.

The best part for one person was that his mom had joined PFLAG, an organization for parents and friends of gays and lesbians. The worst was that his dad went into a rage, forbidding his mom to go to the meeting.

"That's my card," Jerry, the guy with the Mohawk says. "I just walked my mom to the car and stood between her and my dad until she backed out the driveway."

"You said your dad was in a rage?" Emmy asks.

"Yeah. Yelling and screaming and stomping. That's my dad."

"Does he ever hit?"

Jerry looks down at his boots, not making eye contact. "Naw. Not anymore," he says.

It's obvious who the next card is from. The best part of her week is Star, Star, Star. The worst is the situation with her parents.

There's talk about how to get more people involved in GSA, and why it's important to have such a group.

"We might get more people out if we moved the meetings to Hamilton," Emmy says.

Jerry moans. "That leaves me out, man. I'm not supposed to set foot on that campus ever again."

"We might be able to work something out, just for the meetings — if you're always with me," Guy says.

"That place gives me the creeps," Motorcycle Girl says. "People staring, looking down their noses."

"It's not all like that, Dawn," Frankie says.

"All *I've* seen," Dawn, earlier referred to as Motorcycle Girl, says.

What's with these people anyway — Star, Dawn, Leaf. Did their parents give them names that made them become ten percenters, or did they change their names to fit some ten percenter stereotype? And who am I to talk anyway, when I'm named after an actress? So now I'm following unruly name thoughts, and I'm thinking about how when I was thirteen I wanted my mom to change her name from Claire to Grumpy because I thought Grumpy suited her personality. To say she didn't like the idea is a giant understatement — if there even *is* such a thing as a *giant* understatement. Can something be understated and giant at the same . . .

Oops. Back to the meeting.

I regain my focus just as the decision is being made to move the GSA meetings to Hamilton High. We can meet in the back room of the library. Emmy says it's not very busy at lunchtime, and the library tech and aides can handle the desk. Guy's sure he can work things out with Mr. Cordova, the dean, to get an okay to bring Sojourner kids on campus. I gather that most of them were kicked out of Hamilton High and security is not happy to have them back as visitors.

When we leave, Jerry says to me, "See you next week."

I nod, but I think maybe not. The truth is, I'd rather eat lunch with Conan.

We're a few minutes late getting back to class. Emmy writes a note to Mr. Michaels, our choir teacher. It's embarrassing that we're all in the same class and have to walk in together.

Someone from the tenor section mutters, "Must be homo group today."

Mr. Michaels looks up from his roll book, but I can tell he didn't hear exactly what was said.

Even though it's only October, we're already working on Christmas music. Because Kit's a soprano and I'm an alto, we don't sit together. She's in the very front, and I'm on the other side, a few rows back. I can see some of the boys looking at her, smirking, like someone's said something rude. I bet it was Douglas West. He's in the tenor section.

I've known Douglas since seventh grade and he always wants to be the clown. The trouble is, he hasn't figured out yet that his smart mouth isn't really funny. A lot of guys outgrow that stuff, but I bet he'll still have a junior high school mentality when he's getting those sixty-year-old senior discounts at the movies. I give him a dirty look. Not that he cares. Here's what gets me, though.

He sings like some kind of angel. He has a solo part in "Shenandoah." When he sings, "Oh, Shenandoah, I'm goin' to leave you/ Away, you rollin' river," it is so perfect and pure that I'm convinced of his absolute goodness. That only lasts while he's singing, though.

On Monday there's a notice in the bulletin about the new Hamilton High GSA group meeting. When Woodsy reads the notice in PC, Eric starts with his sin against God and nature thing again.

Woodsy reminds him for about the zillionth time that he's entitled to his own beliefs and opinions, but he is not to express anything that puts another person down. I don't think he gets it.

Our lunch group is changing. It used to be me, Kit, Holly, Nicole, Conan, and Robert — the six of us. We shared food and laughed and we were all together. Then, Frankie joined us and now Nora and Caitlin sit with us, too. Even though we all still sit together now, our conversation is fragmented. Conan and I usually just talk to each other.

"I found another Fluffy for Sabina," he says, looking down at his double helping of pizza.

"Great. I'll give you Wilma's old license for the new Fluffy."

"That'd be good. I told Sabina Fluffy must have got loose, and without a license, we couldn't find her."

"Why didn't you tell her the truth?"

Conan looks at me like I've just said something in a foreign language.

"Well?"

"She ain't needin' to hear that mess o' shit yet."

Speak of a foreign language. I never hear Conan talk like that. I look at him, surprised. His face has that frozen look again, like it did the other night, when we were stopped by the sheriffs.

"Conan?"

"I hate those honky cops!"

"My mom wants to file a complaint against them."

"Oh, man. How to make things worse! Then they'll be stopping me every time I leave my house!!"

"She says it's a case of racial profiling."

"No shit." Conan laughs, but it's not a happy sound.

I don't know what to say — he seems so far away from me right now, with his cynical laughter and his frozen face.

I slip my hand into his. He doesn't pull away, but he doesn't let me make eye contact, either. He lets out a deep sigh.

"Tell your mom to let it rest. I know she's coming from a good place, but . . ."

"It's not fair, though."

Conan sits gazing at a tree over by the administration building.

At the other end of the table, Robert is talking to Holly. He finally gave up on Kit when she showed up with her close buzz and rainbow stuff. In the middle, Kit, Frankie, and Nora talk about e-mails and chat rooms, gay websites and GSA stuff. They also spend a lot of time talking about where the best gay coffee places are. Caitlin always sits next to Nora, listening. But I still haven't heard her talk.

Kit is finding the "fit" she's not found before in high school. Not that she hasn't always been one of the core players on the volleyball team, or an important singer in choir, but I mean socially. When I think about how things have been in the past, I realize that Kit's main social life has been with me. That's sort of been true for me, too, I guess. Except that I've had boyfriends, and done some extra stuff. Last year I was in the school play. I may try out again this year.

Anyway, Kit is in the middle of things with these new friends. But I miss the all-together feeling I had when just the six of us ate lunch together.

Conan's got that far away look. I squeeze his hand, hoping to bring him back from wherever he's gone in his mind — that place he's not invited me to be.

He concentrates on stuffing his garbage into a paper bag, then throws it, about fifty feet, into the trash can. Eric and Justin, both over at the jock table, give him thumbs up signs and Conan smiles. Then, finally, he looks at me. I lean into him and rest my head against his shoulder.

"What did your folks tell you about cops when you were a little kid?" he says.

"You know. If I was lost or in trouble, I should go to a policeman. Policemen were my friends. The usual."

"See that wasn't the usual in my family. They told me if I was lost, find an older black woman and she'd help me. Stay away from policemen. Stay away from whitey. If for any reason a policeman approached me, be polite, give my name and address, but no more."

Like in the old war movies, I think, where prisoners gave only name, rank and serial number.

"When I got my driver's license, my grampa made me go through this whole routine. First he showed me tapes of that guy, Rodney King, being beaten practically to death by L.A. cops. 'That's what happens to niggas who never learned what I'm about to teach you,' he told me. Then he made me practice what I'd do in all kinds of circumstances."

"What kind of circumstances?"

"You know. Circumstances like when we were stopped the other night . . . My grampa made me sit in the car, at the end of our driveway. He drove up behind me and flashed his lights. 'I'm a honky cop,' he yelled. 'What're you gonna do?' I opened the door to get out and he yelled 'you're dead! Assaulting an officer with intent to do bodily harm!'"

"That's sick," I say.

"He wanted to keep me safe. He made me practice sitting still in the car, with my hands resting open fingered on the steering wheel — not moving until he gave me instructions, and then I was to follow those instructions to the absolute letter."

"It sounds like that training stuff they did during Vietnam — what to do when captured by the enemy."

"Absolutely. We practiced for two weeks, every day, before I was allowed to drive on the streets."

"Don't you think that's a little extreme?"

"Maybe. But I'm still alive. Not like my friend," he says, once again turning his attention toward the tree.

The warning bell rings. I want to stay right at this table, next to Conan, and hear the rest of his story. I want to know about his friend who's no longer alive. But he's already standing and has his backpack slipped over a shoulder.

"Gotta go."

"Don't forget to drop by later for the dog license," I tell him.

"Okay," he says, but I wonder if he'll remember. He seems so far away from me right now.

As he walks past the jock table, Justin gets up to join him. I watch them walk away toward the gym. Justin jabs Conan in the arm and nods in the direction of our table. Conan keeps walking. The rest of the guys still sitting there are looking toward our table. Brian is looking directly at Kit. The others are laughing in that mean way people laugh when they've been putting someone else down.

"Let's get to class," I say to Kit. We walk off together, with Frankie, Caitlin and Nora following right behind. I hear more harsh laughter and something about fairy tales . . . or is it tails? No one acknowledges they've heard anything, but there is no more conversation. My face grows hot, and I look down at the ground in front of me. Why is it *I'm* blushing, when the jocks are the ones who are being buttholes?

13

When Conan stops by in the late afternoon, he has Sabina with him. They stand on the porch, Sabina clutching the new Fluffy to her chest and standing as close to Conan as she can get.

"This is my friend, Lynn," Conan says, lifting Sabina up so she and I are eye level.

"Hi, Sabina."

She hides her face in Conan's jacket.

"Shy," Conan says with a bright, gentle smile. I'm so relieved to see Conan relaxed and smiling, I give him a big kiss on the cheek. Sabina shoots me such a look!

"Shy, and jealous, too, I guess."

She wraps her little four-year-old arms around his tree-stump thick neck.

"*My* Conan," she says.

"We have to share," I tell her. Then I run back into the house to get Wilma's old dog license. Wilma follows me back outside. As soon as Sabina sees Wilma, she wants to get down and play. I show her how to throw the frisbee and she and Wilma are instant friends. Conan puts the license on Fluffy's collar and pretends

Fluffy is jumping for the frisbee. This causes Wilma to race around the yard in wide circles, barking at the toy dog from a safe distance. We laugh until we are out of breath — Sabina, too. She leaves Conan's side and comes to sit next to me on the lawn. She runs her hand lightly across the back of my own hand.

"My mommy has fingernails, too," she says. "And my Aunt Brenda, too."

"My mommy has fingernails, too," I say, wondering if we're playing that Sesame Street game about what's the same and what's different.

Conan and I watch Sabina and Wilma play while we talk about the football game coming up. Until now they've been playing practice games, but this one counts. There's also talk of some college recruiters being there to watch two of Hamilton's major players. Conan is one of them. Brian Marsters is the other.

"I guess it would be good if I could get a scholarship," Conan says. "But I don't want college to be only about football for me. I don't know if I can play serious football and keep up with classes at the same time."

"What if you don't get a football scholarship? Or what if you don't *take* a football scholarship?"

"Other than that my dad would disown me? I'm not sure. I might go to community college."

Selfishly, I hope he *does* end up at community college, because that's probably where I'll be studying nursing. I don't even want to *think* about Conan leaving town.

It is nearly dark when Conan and Sabina leave. He gives me a quick kiss, and a smile, and I don't feel so insecure with him anymore. Sabina also gives me a kiss.

"My mommie has a soft cheek, too," she says.

"Mine, too," I tell her.

She waves to me until they turn the corner, and I go back to my room for a long session of homework.

Late at night, just as I'm getting ready for bed, Kit knocks at my window. I open it and let her in.

"I can't go home until I straighten up — which is exactly what she means — *straighten!*"

"Does this mean you've started talking again?"

"Screaming's more like it — at least with my mom. Get rid of the rainbow necklace and bracelets. Let my hair grow. Dress right. Get rid of these . . ."

Kit turns to face me and I see that she now has a row of five silver studs embedded in the curve of her left ear.

"Quit staring," she says.

"Sorry. It's just . . . doesn't it hurt?"

"Not as much as pretending to be straight."

I can tell she's upset by the way she breathes. It's her trick to keep from crying, or losing her temper — very deep, regular breaths.

A long time ago, back when her dad was still drinking, she told me that when he and her mom would get into screaming fits, she concentrated on breathing. It didn't change things, but it made them less noticeable.

She stands there, still by the window, holding her backpack and a little suitcase.

"So can I stay or not? I can go to Star's if you don't want me to stay."

"No. I mean, yes, stay. Don't go to Star's."

"Sure?"

"Sure."

"How about Always?"

"She won't care," I say, though I'm not certain how she'll feel once she gets a look at the new Kit. She hasn't even seen the haircut yet.

Kit flops down on the bed, pulling a pillow over her head. I sit down next to her. She moves the pillow and looks up at me, her eyes glistening with tears.

"Mom says I'm ruining their lives."

"What does your dad say?"

"Nothing. At least not to me. As far as I can tell, he's staying away from home."

Kit pulls the pillow back up over her head. By the time I've brushed, flossed, and put on my pajamas, Kit is sound asleep. I lie in the dark for a while, thinking how quickly families can change. Only a few weeks ago I was thinking how perfect things were at Kit's house.

As soon as I hear Mom's alarm go off, I get up and go into her room. She's still in bed. I want to prepare her for the new Kit, before they meet in the kitchen and Mom goes into cardiac arrest.

"Mom?"

She half opens her eyes.

"Can I talk to you for a minute?"

She nods, patting the edge of her bed and motioning for me to sit down.

"Kit spent the night last night."

"That's fine," she says, sounding groggy.

"Her mom kicked her out."

She leans up on her elbow, her eyes fully open.

"Why?"

"She's mad at her."

"I could have guessed that, if she kicked her out. *Why* is Jessie so angry? It doesn't sound like something she'd do."

I wish I'd planned what I was going to say. It seems too complicated now that I've started the conversation.

"Lynn? Why is Jessie mad at Kit? Is Kit in some kind of trouble?"

"Not exactly."

"Is she pregnant?"

"No way."

"Well, then?"

Mom nudges me over and gets out of bed. She's wearing a giant T-shirt that she's had forever. It says, "A woman without a man is like a fish without a bicycle." I don't exactly get it, but

I think it has something to do with my mom deciding single was better than married.

"I've got to get going, Lynn. Can you come to the point?"

Mom gets her underwear and pantyhose from the dresser, then turns back to me.

"Why did Kit get kicked out?"

"Well . . . I guess her parents don't like the way she looks."

"Oh, come on! They've been looking at her all her life, and suddenly they don't like the way she looks? Could I get a little more of the story here?"

Mom reaches into her closet for one of her many "business" suits and hangs it on the door. I know she's in a hurry, but it's hard for me to figure out what to tell her. I mean, I'm not just going to blurt out that Kit's a lesbian.

"Kit got her hair cut real short, and . . . some other stuff."

"What other stuff?"

"Just don't be shocked when you see her. That's all. And can she stay here again tonight?"

"Yes. But she's got to let David and Jessie know where she is."

"Why? They don't care or they wouldn't have kicked her out."

"I don't know exactly what's going on here, but I'm pretty sure they care." Mom glances at the clock. "We'll talk more this evening. Right now I've got to hurry or I'll be late."

Kit and I are in the kitchen, drinking orange juice, when Mom comes in for a quick cup of coffee. In spite of my earlier warning, when Mom sees Kit she lets out a piercing scream.

"Your hair! Your beautiful hair!"

Then she takes in the rest, the piercings, the rainbow necklace.

"Oh, Kit," she says.

Mom pours a cup of coffee and stands sipping it, looking from Kit to me and back again. Then she rinses her cup, puts it in the dishwasher, and grabs her keys from the holder near the door.

"Well . . . I'll see you both this evening. I'll bring home chicken pot pies. Okay?"

In PC Conan hands me a big fat note, all folded up, and asks me to read it later. My heart sinks to the bottom of my stomach. Okay, so I'm going to be a nurse and I know that doesn't really happen, but I swear I feel my heart sink. He's going to break up with me. I know it. I haven't even told him how much I love him yet, and he's breaking up with me.

"Can't I just read it now, and get it over with?" I ask, barely able to hold back tears.

"No. Read it when I'm not around."

I face forward. The note sits folded on my desk, "Lynnie" printed across the top fold. Woodsy is saying something to the class, but all I hear is a buzzing in my head — breaking up, breaking up, breaking up. Then Conan taps me on the shoulder. I can't look.

He leans forward and whispers, "What do you mean, 'get it over with'?"

I shake my head. What's to talk about?

"Lynnie — you said you wanted to read it and get it over with. Get *what* over with?"

I turn to look at him and I guess my face shows a lot.

"Oh, Lynnie. It's not that!"

It's like a dam bursts and rivers of tears rush down my cheeks. I grab the note and run out into the hall, so relieved, embarrassed, overcome with tears, that I can't possibly sit in a classroom. I'm leaning against the wall, trying to get control, when Conan comes out of the room. He puts his arms around me and holds me tight.

"It's just that, what's in the note . . . I don't like to talk about it . . . sometimes I cry, and you know, it's okay for you to cry," he says, wiping my tears with the back of his hand, "but for a guy? I don't want you to see me cry. That's all," he says.

"Let's take a break," Conan says.

We go around to the double doors closest to the gym, where Larry, one of the campus supervisors, stands guard. He's leaning against a table when we come through the doors.

"Conan, my man," he says, all smiles, shaking Conan's hand

and clapping him on the shoulder at the same time.

"We gonna beat Wilson Friday night?"

"Count on it," Conan says.

They do a high five and laugh.

"We gonna take CIF this year?"

"Count on it," Conan repeats.

"My man! I'm bankin' on you to deliver!"

"Count on it!"

They high five again, laughing.

"Hey, Larry. Me 'n Lynn gotta get something from my house. It'll only take a few minutes."

Larry's smile fades.

"Oh, Conan, you know the rules, man."

"Yeah, but this is important. I'm not leavin' to make trouble. You know that."

Larry nods. He looks around, then, seeing no one else, waves us on.

"Be quick," he says.

I can't believe how Conan managed to get us through the gates of our tightly closed campus. I guess football players have a lot more power than volleyball players.

We go to Starbucks and sit at a back table.

"Read it," Conan says, nodding at the note I still have clutched in my hand.

I unfold the note and start reading, while Conan goes to get lattes for us.

Dear Lynnie, I'm writing this because it's so hard for me to talk about what happened, but I want you to know. I don't want us ever to hide anything from each other. Getting stopped by the cops the other night, and having them rip apart the stuffed dog my sister loved so much, made me think about some things I've been trying to forget. Things I've not had to think about too much since we moved to Hamilton Heights. Where I lived before was in what's considered a bad part of L.A. Drive-by shootings, drugs, gang stuff, poverty, you know. I pretty much stayed out of trouble — it helps to be big. I went to a magnet school in another part of town, played football, avoided that gang shit. My best friend Mark, from when I was five, did the same. My grampa met us at the bus every day, walked us home, made sure we did our homework. Mark's mom worked until late, so he usually had dinner with us. When I went to a magnet school, Mark did too. When he signed up for football, I did too. That's how it was. No drugs, no alcohol, no gangs, just clean-cut American boys, living a clean-cut American life.

Conan brings my drink to me. I watch as he gets a newspaper from the basket by the door, then takes it and his cup to another table, where he starts reading. I, too, go back to my reading.

*Mark's dad was almost never around, but now and then he'd show up and try to make up for lost time, be the big man — he'd bring video games, or take Mark to a Lakers game or a Rams game. They usually invited me to go, too, but my grampa always said no. When I appealed to my mom and dad, they said no, too. When I asked why it was "because I said so, that's why." So one day Mark's dad showed up in this black Lincoln Continental, straight off the showroom it looked like. And he tossed Mark the keys. Told him to be back by midnight. Mark came straight to my house. It was one of those rare times when no one was home to tell me no. I climbed into the passenger side and we took off. We drove to the beach, and up in the Hollywood Hills, then around the observatory. It was like riding on air. Mark wasn't a reckless driver. We didn't speed, we just took it easy and drove all over, feeling good. We were on our way back to my place about eleven or so, allowing plenty of time for Mark to get the car back. Cops pulled us over on a side street off Vermont — a dark, industrial area. As soon as the red lights hit, I put my hands on the dashboard, fingers spread apart. We didn't do nothin'! What kinda shit **is** this? Mark said. I told him to calm down, put his hands on the steering wheel, but he opened the door and got out.*

*This is my dad's car! he yelled. I've got a license! I saw him reach
into his jacket pocket, to show I.D. Don't! I hollered — but my
voice was lost in gunfire. I saw him fall and I knew he'd never be
up again. I sat there, frozen, my hands still on the dash, my
fingers still wide open, like my grampa taught me. They handcuffed me. Made me sit on the curb, like the other night. Only that
night I watched the cops take their time calling an ambulance. I
watched them step over Mark's body like it was nothing more
than a dog turd in the street. I watched the ambulance attendants
look for a pulse, then pull a blanket over him. It took hours for the
coroner to arrive, before Mark could be moved. It turned out the
car'd been stolen. They said the cop thought Mark was reaching
for a gun when he reached into his jacket. All I know is Mark's
dead, and he didn't deserve it. That's what I couldn't tell you. No
one else here knows, and I don't want them to. But it's different
with you.*

I fold the note back up and sit looking across the room at
Conan's broad back. I am so sad, for him, and for Mark, and even
for the policeman who made the mistake. I wonder why life has
to be so hard. Conan turns and looks at me. I walk over to him.
He gets up and takes my hand and we walk back to his car.

"I'm sorry," I say.

We get in the Hyundai. Conan sinks heavily into the driver's
seat.

"The last thing Mark ever said to me was 'what's this shit?' I
keep wondering the same thing."

Tears well in his dark eyes. He looks away.

"You can cry with me," I tell him.

"I don't want to" he says, and then he's sobbing. We hold one
another, in the Hyundai, in the Starbucks parking lot, both of us
crying — Conan for his friend, and me for Conan and the whole
sadness of the world.

When our tears subside, I tell Conan I can't go back to school.
My eyes are so puffy they look like slits. I'm all shaky. We go to

my house, where we finish off the leftover Chinese food. Conan is still hungry, so I introduce him to Clucker's Chicken Pot Pies. That's a hit.

When he's finally licked the tin clean, we stretch out on the floor next to the stereo and listen to whatever disks my mom left in the player. It starts with Otis Redding, "Sittin' on the Dock o' the Bay."

Conan starts laughing. "My folks always have this on, too. They're *big* Otis Redding fans."

"You know what you told me? About your grampa?"

"You mean how he made me practice what I'd do before I could drive?"

"Yeah. And what he said about whitey and all that?"

"Ummmm," Conan says, scooting a little closer to me.

"Does he hate white people?"

Conan doesn't answer immediately. Which makes me think his grampa probably *does* hate white people.

"I wouldn't say that, exactly," he says. "It's just . . . my grampa's got a history. He was in the Black Panthers back in the sixties, so he was kind of a radical."

"Maybe he won't like me," I say.

"But maybe he will. I like you," he says, nuzzling his head up against my neck. "I love you."

"I love you, too, Conan. I've been wanting to tell you."

We kiss, long and deep, and one thing leads to another. We do a lot to get close, skin to skin, kisses, caresses. We don't have sex, like the whole intercourse thing, partly because we don't have any protection, and partly because I'm not sure I'm ready for that. Conan says he can wait. Besides, he knows lots of other ways to help us feel good.

After we've both . . . you know . . . been satisfied . . . we lie next to one another, our clothes all unbuttoned and half off, breathing together as if we share some deep, internal rhythm. Right now, I feel closer to Conan than I ever have anyone else in the world. Right now, life doesn't seem quite so sad.

In the evening, while Kit and I are cleaning up the dishes, her dad knocks on our back door.

"David," Mom says, sounding surprised. "Come in."

Kit stops drying the pitcher and stands listening intently.

"Is Katherine here?"

"She and Lynn are in the kitchen, cleaning up."

Kit sets the dishtowel and the half-dried pitcher on the counter and stands facing the doorway. David walks in, then stops. His worry lines have deepened.

I return to my dishwashing task. The only sound is of muffled news from the TV. David takes a step toward Kit.

"Katherine," he says, in a soft, strained voice.

For a moment she's frozen. Then she steps forward into her dad's waiting arms. Mom gestures me toward the family room.

"Leave them alone, so they can talk," she says.

I go to my room and start my homework. Halfway through English, Kit comes in and starts packing her stuff up.

"He wants me to come home," she says.

"What about your mom?"

"He says we have to all work it out together."

"But . . . does he know?"

"He knows certain styles."

"But . . ."

"He asked if I thought I was a lesbian. I told him I didn't think, I knew."

"And he's cool?"

"He's sad. He says life will be harder for me. But he said . . ."

She struggled, trying not to lose control — that steady breathing thing again.

" . . . he said he loved me to the depths of his soul . . . and nothing, no matter what, would ever change that."

She cried then. I did too. We cried from relief that she could be herself with her father, and that they would work things out as a family. But I was also crying for what I've never known — a father who loved me to the depths of his soul.

CHAPTER

14

Okay. I'm back. We left off weeks ago, the end of October, and now it's almost Thanksgiving. First quarter is over. I got an **A** in physiology, PE, peer communications and **B**s in the rest. Miss Banks gave me an **A** for originality of thought on my *Color Purple* paper, but only a **C** on organization — "RAMBLING AND DISJOINTED," she'd scrawled across the top in her bright green, fine-tipped marker. So, there went my **A** in English.

When I reread the paper, I could see what Banks meant, though. I don't care. I'm glad I followed my "originality of thought" ideas, rather than choosing an easier theme.

I could easily have written about racism, or sexism. But I decided to write about how when love followed the rules of the day, with men being dictators in marriages and families, everything turned sour. But when it went beyond the rules, like with Celie and Shug, and others, love blossomed. Okay, so I'm still rambling. But I've been wondering lately about all the rules that are attached to love — wondering if we need them. Anyway, I still have a chance for an **A** in English on my semester grade. We'll see.

I'm kind of sorry to be finished with *The Color Purple*. Those two characters, Celie and Shug, made a big impression on me. I'll miss them.

I've added a medical careers course to my schedule. It meets on Saturdays, which isn't all that great, but if I do well in it, along with physiology, I'm almost certain of getting into the RN program at the HHCC.

Things with Conan? Cool! I can't believe how I jumped to the conclusion that he wanted to break up with me. That's *so* not Conan.

Speaking of Conan, though, we've won our last two football games against teams that decimated us last year. Everyone says Conan and Brian make the team. The *Hamilton Heights Daily News* is playing up the barbarian thing — **THE BUCK STOPS AT THE BARBARIAN! BARBARIAN BATTERS BRUINS!** Conan claims he hates that stuff, that it's a team thing and no one person is any good without the others. I think he likes the attention, though. And his dad is *all* happy because it looks as if Conan will be getting at least three or four offers for football scholarships.

Anyway, Conan's a hero. Every one at the whole school knows him. Of course, he's hard to miss because he is literally the biggest man on campus. As much of a hero as he is at school, he's the biggest hero of all to Sabina. Finally, after lots of visits to our house, and frisbee throws with Wilma, she *tolerates* seeing me kiss her brother. She and I have become great friends, but she'd still prefer to be the only love in Conan's life.

At school, some of Conan's fame slops over to me. The "in" kids go out of their way to say hello to me now. I was invisible to them before Conan. Not that I cared. That group always seemed kind of phony to me. The first time I heard Tammy Spears, the Barbie-style cheerleader that half the guys on this campus are ga-ga over, yell "Hi, Lynn," in her sweet, chipper voice, I looked all around to see where the other Lynn was. I'm used to it now, though. I smile and wave and say hi back, knowing I would become invisible again if Conan and I were no longer a couple. Never happen.

What else is new? Remember how I thought Eric must have had a big change over the summer? I was right. He had some kind of religious experience. We don't talk much anymore, but one day he asked me if I knew Christ.

"I know *of* him," I'd said.

"But does he live in your heart?"

"Not that I know of," I told him.

He launched into a mini-sermon about finding the way, and being saved, and I don't know what else. He's president of the Christ First club now. Tiffany's in it, too. They wear necklaces with little gold crosses. Everyone in Christ First wears them.

Enough about that. Where was I? Oh, yeah — our winning football team. That's not Hamilton High's only winning team. Our volleyball team's won every league game so far. Even so, the *Daily News* doesn't bother to report girls' volleyball events. The *Hamilton High Times* does, but that's because Nicole's the editor. I don't care. I'm in it for the game, not the glory. Good thing!

Kit seems pretty happy. We've been through some changes these past months, but we're both pretty happy. Kit spends a lot of time with Star, and I spend a lot of time with Conan. Our Friday nights aren't the same. I go to the football games, so I can cheer wildly for Conan. Then there's always a party somewhere, after a game.

Kit and Star go to a gay coffee bar in Pasadena. It's become kind of a Friday night thing for them, and also for others in the GSA group.

At first I didn't like Star. But I'm over that now. She includes me in her "stupid jokes" weekly e-mail messages, like "what did the fish say when it swam into the wall? Dam!" And "What do you get from a pampered cow? Spoiled milk."

Besides the laughs, I respect how Star hasn't let life get her down. When her mother found out Star was a ten percenter, she threw all of Star's clothes out on the front lawn. Star was only fifteen, but her mother told her to think of herself as an orphan from that time forward. Guy Reyes helped her find a place to stay at a church sponsored shelter. Then a PFLAG woman took her in. Star works full-time at an electronics store, installing car stereos. She's nineteen and she's just this June going to graduate, but she's done it all on her own.

Star told me about the PFLAG woman — her adopted mother, is how she refers to her. The rest I learned from Kit. We still usually sit out under her tree when we get home from school. And we still call each other at the same time. And I still go to GSA meetings with Kit, because we're spirit sisters. For life.

Last Saturday night Kit stayed over at my house, like old times. We ate pizza and watched "My Life as a Dog." It was one of those movies we'd never have rented, except it had "dog" in the title. It turned out to be a perfect choice — really funny and really sad in the way good movies can be. It also had some "gender identity" stuff in it. (See how I can throw that term around now?)

One of the main characters was a girl who pretended to be a boy. She was a real roughneck on the soccer field, and at boxing — probably Dawn was like that when she was younger. Anyway, get this, when the girl in the movie started getting boobs, she bound her chest with tight ace bandages so no one would know, and she kept playing soccer on the boys' team.

It seems like everywhere I look now, movies, TV, life, I see examples of people who are not exactly of the straight and narrow 100 percent heterosexual persuasion. I wonder why I never noticed before?

After the movie we crawled into bed, each on our own side, with plenty of space between us. We turned off the lights. It's easier to talk in the dark.

Kit told me what a hard time her mom is having with her "new look." Kit hasn't even used the "L" word with her mom. Neither of her parents know about Star.

"It's strange," Kit said. "Star's one of the best things that's ever happened to me. Sometimes, it's like I'm exploding with happiness. The sad thing is, I can't *begin* to share that with my parents."

"Not even your dad?"

"My dad accepts the idea of me *being* a lesbian, but I think it'd send him over the edge if he thought I was *acting* like a lesbian."

The conversation drifted to S-E-X.

"I can't explain how I feel with Conan. I don't even know the words . . ."

Psychologist Kit went to work.

"Try excite," Kit said.

"Ummm. Yeah."

"Try arouse."

"Ummm."

"Try you love your hands and your mouth all over him. Try you love his hands and his mouth all over you."

"KIT!"

"Try, WATCH OUT, THERE'S A FIRE DOWN BELOW!"

"STOP!" I said, laughing.

"BLAST OFF!"

"STOP NOW!" I begged, laughing even harder, Kit joining in.

We caught our breath.

"You better be using protection."

"We're not doing it the make babies way," I told her.

"Oh, so you're doing it *our* way?" she asked.

"What do you mean?" I said, not sure I wanted my sex life with Conan to be compared to lesbian sex. Whatever that is.

"Star and I aren't doing it the make babies way, either."

"Well, duh!"

"No. Think about it. Excite. Arouse. Hands. Mouth. Fire

down below . . . What're you doing that we're not?"

"Nothing, I guess, when you put it that way. Except one of us has really different equipment."

That got us laughing again.

Then Kit said, "You're missing a lot, being with a guy."

"What do you mean? I think *you're* the one who's missing something."

"No, look. It's natural for women to know what women want, what feels good. Men only know what they want. I bet Conan doesn't make you feel as good as Star makes me feel."

"And I bet the opposite, but I'm not going to try to prove it."

It was another one of those crazy conversations that only spirit sisters can have.

Here's how I look at things now. Kit and I are both crazy in love. We're happy. That's what matters. It's what I hoped for, for our senior year. I just didn't expect Kit's love to be a girl. I'm pretty used to that idea now, though.

While we're caught up on things, I should tell you about GSA. One day when I was studying in the library, waiting for Conan to be finished with football practice, Emmy came and sat beside me and took a poster out of a tube.

"Frankie designed this," she said, laying the poster out flat.

"Wow! Beautiful!"

It looked professional, with bright rainbow colors, and purple block print — like a movie poster you might see on the wall at Blockbusters.

"He did it on his computer — some graphics program he has," she said.

Besides the color, the art-deco design, the poster announced that the Gay Straight Alliance Club was now meeting at Hamilton High, and it gave information about meetings.

"We'll put it in the glass case in the main building. More people will see it there than if we post it in the library. What do you think?"

"Sure," I said, not caring much one way or the other.

It was nearly closing time in the library and hardly anyone else was there. Rosie came out of Emmy's office and sidled up to me, hiding something behind her back.

"Finished with your homework?" Emmy asked.

Rosie nodded, still with her hands behind her back, her eyes sparkling.

"I think she wants to show you something," Emmy said. Then, to Rosie, "Go ahead, Sweetie. Don't be shy with your old friend Lynn."

Grinning, she brought her right hand around, waving a sheet of paper in front of me.

"What?" I said, making a grab for it.

She jerked it out of my hand, giggling.

"What? What?? Please? Pretty please?"

She handed her report card to me and watched as I read it.

"Hey! Outstanding in math facts!"

I give her a high five. The rest of the report card was also good, except for an S (satisfactory) minus in art.

"I don't like the smell of the paints," she explained, as she walked over to the drinking fountain.

I stacked my books and put them into my backpack.

"Conan's probably finished by now," I said.

"Yeah, it's quitting time for me, too," Emmy said, carefully rolling the poster and putting it back in the tube. "I'll see you Thursday."

I zipped my backpack.

"You are coming to the meeting, aren't you?"

"I'm not sure yet," I confessed.

She gave me one of those looks like I sometimes get from my mom. Like she was looking into my head, and not sure she liked what she saw.

"Lynn . . . we need you."

"Why?"

"Don't you see, the better the mix of gay/straight students, the more credibility our group has? If you and Conan come to meetings . . . you both have a lot of respect here, and that lends respect to GSA."

"I don't know . . ."

"We need support. Your presence will make things easier from the very start."

Easier for *who*, I wonder. Not for me.

"Think about it. Okay?"

"Okay," I said, but not very enthusiastically.

When I talked to Conan, I told him I'd go to the meeting if he would.

"You know, I'm all for tolerance. And I think it's a good idea to have the club meet on this campus."

"But?"

"But I've been taught to lay low, except in athletics. That whole thing about my grampa teaching me to stay alive . . . "

"But this isn't like dealing with cops."

"No, but it opens things up for ridicule, which makes me mad, and then one thing leads to another."

"I'm not going either, then," I told him.

But the next day, out of the blue, Frankie told me how much he appreciated my support.

"It's hard, you know, feeling like a freak, and like no one in the world will ever like you."

He looked as if he might cry. He walked away before I could say anything. I watched him move his swishy little butt down the hall, students moving away from him, no one speaking, the only recognition a few rude comments. For a moment I forgot my own trivial hang-ups, and my heart hurt for Frankie.

On the day of the first meeting, Kit brought a pastrami sandwich for us to share so we wouldn't miss out on lunch. Between Kit and Frankie, I had to go.

Now our lunch table has become an extension of GSA, which

is cool with me, except some people can be such jerks. They walk past us and make stupid remarks, stuff about faggots and dykes. Frankie Fudge-packer, some guy said yesterday, and poked Frankie on the shoulder. Not hard. Just the insult, and the poke. We pretend not to notice. It's so juvenile — it doesn't deserve a response.

Besides Frankie's poster in the glass display case, we post notices on a few classroom doors, and on the doors to the library. Last week some of our posters were torn down. Jocks, probably. Emmy says not to jump to conclusions, or to stereotype jocks. She reminds me that Conan's a jock, but he's not a jerk. Which is true.

Just yesterday, Conan told me he talked with Brian and Justin and some of the others at football practice — suggested it made the team look bad to have players being rude, like they were at lunch-time. All *that* did was cause Conan to get hit doubly hard at practice. Conan thinks Brian's got a grudge against Kit because he couldn't even make it to first base with her. That's probably all Brian thinks about with girls — base hits and home runs, if you know what I mean.

15

I'm totally surprised to find Eric waiting for me outside my first period class this morning.

"Can I talk to you?" he says.

"Sure."

"As a friend?"

I nod.

"You know, we had some good times together and . . ."

What is this, anyway? He knows I'm with Conan. He *can't* be wanting to get back together.

" . . . and, well, as a friend, I want to talk to you about Kit."

"What about her?"

"Well . . . now that she's so . . ."

He stumbles, looking embarrassed. For a guy who can be so mouthy around his friends, he doesn't do very well one on one.

" . . . so . . ."

"Out?" I say.

"Yeah. Out. It's a sign that she's getting aggressive."

"What?"

"And you're together a lot. And . . ."

"And?"

"And . . . well . . . she could influence you to . . . become a lesbian."

I laugh. I can't help it. "I don't know where you get your ideas, but things don't work that way. Kit's my *friend*. That's all."

"Well, I'm your friend, too, and I'm trying to help. These people have their ways."

"These people . . .???"

Conan rounds the corner.

"Hey, Lynnie," he says, smiling his special for me only smile.

"Hi, Eric."

Eric gives Conan a friendly nod, and the three of us walk on to Peer Counseling together. At the door, Eric reminds me to think about what he's said, and then walks to his desk on the other side of the room.

"Should I be worried?" Conan says, glancing in Eric's direction.

"I don't even know what he was talking about," I say.

"That I love you more than he ever, ever, possibly could," Conan says, smiling.

The jock table is louder than usual today, with guys looking our way, pointing at Kit, laughing. We all pretend they're not there and try to continue our conversation. Their laughter and gestures become more outrageous. Conan walks over to their table and says something, but they laugh all the harder.

"Admit it! You know what she needs!" Brian says, which gets them going even more.

After lunch, when Kit and I go to get books for afternoon classes, we see some kids standing near our lockers. At first we're not sure what they're looking at. Most of the jocks are off to the side and down the hall a bit, watching the watchers. When they see us, there's this air of weird anticipation.

Kit and I both see the object of interest at the same time. It's fastened by duct tape and hanging from a string, resting right in the middle of her locker door. It's a big, plastic penis, and written in heavy red marker across the gray metal locker are the words "You want it!" and "For Kitty's pussy." Dribbles of white glue string down the locker door accompanied by the words "Here, Kitty, cum for Kitty."

There is a moment of absolute silence, everyone watching while we take it all in. Then, from the jocks down the hall, the hooting begins. Someone starts up with "Here, Kitty, Kitty, Kitty!" and others join in. Brian puts his hand on his crotch and performs exaggerated pelvic thrusts.

"Something for Kitty's pussy!" he yells, and the words and laughter swirl around us, echoing off walls of metal lockers.

"Let's go," I say, taking Kit by the arm. She doesn't move. "Kit?"

Woodsy appears, and the hall suddenly empties.

"Oh! What is this?"

She yanks the plastic penis down, walks us to her classroom office, and closes the door.

"What all was going on out there?" she says.

"Just this," Kit says, pointing to the plastic thing, which is now sitting on Woodsy's desk.

"And the writing," I say.

Kit nods. "And the yelling. And the laughing."

"And Brian . . ." I start to tell about what he did, but I don't know how to describe it.

"He made a motion, like a sex thing, and yelled that it was something for me," Kit says.

Her voice is steady. She's not crying. She seems totally calm. But I can tell by the way she's forcing deep, regular breaths, that she's struggling. Me, I haven't learned the breathing trick. My face is hot, my hands are shaking, and I could cry buckets any second.

"I hate those pricks!" Kit says, in a voice so low it's almost a growl.

"Who all was involved?"

"Pricks!"

"Names would help," Woodsy says.

"Brian Marsters. And Justin. Mostly football players," I say. "I don't know all their names."

"Brian's the biggest prick of all!"

Woodsy motions for us to sit down.

"Listen, Kit. I know you're very angry, and you have every right to be. But what we need to do now is try to put together as thorough and factual a report as possible. That will help us treat this incident with the seriousness it deserves."

She gets last year's yearbook from her desk and turns to the picture of the football team.

"See if you can come up with names," she says, putting the book on the table in front of us.

She picks up the phone and calls the school secretary, Miss Ramirez.

"Jackie? I need someone to cover my class this period, so I can deal with a problem . . . No, it's not necessary to call security, but I need to get with Mr. Cordova."

She listens for a moment, then asks, "Is he gone for the day?"

She looks less than pleased.

"Well . . . Mr. Maxwell it is, then. It needs administrative attention. I'll be down in about fifteen minutes. I'm bringing Lynn Wright and Kit Dandridge with me."

Woodsy hangs up the phone. Then she hands each of us a tablet on a clipboard and a ballpoint pen.

"Write a thorough statement. Remember the who, what, when, where, why and how, business. List all of the names you can come up with of students who were in the hall."

That's not easy. For sure Brian was there, the loudest of them all. And Justin. But it seems like there were a lot more, and now I can't get a clear picture in my head. Robert, sort of standing in the background? And I think Douglas from choir was there, too. I'm not sure, though.

I look carefully at the football team picture. Anthony Black, that's the name of the guy who was standing next to Brian. I add his name to my report.

The only two I'm sure of are Tammy Spears and her friend, Tiffany. Then I remember Eric. Was he watching, or was he one of the ones who was yelling?

The phone rings. "Yes, Mr. Maxwell. Yes, it's important . . . Yes, I understand you're busy . . . a matter of school safety . . . no, weapons were not involved . . . fifteen minutes."

Woodsy hangs up.

"I wish Mr. Cordova had been in," she says, more to herself than to us.

All I know about Mr. Maxwell, the principal, is that he has the biggest office in the administration building and he's sometimes referred to as Manly Max. He works out in the weight room right after school's out, every day. From what I hear he likes to show off how much he can lift, and challenge some of the guys to weight lifting contests. He's always at football games, welcoming everyone and praising the football team as if this year's winning streak were his own personal victory. He loves Conan. Well . . . so do I. I guess that's one thing we have in common.

"How're you doing?" Woodsy asks, glancing at my incomplete paper. I can take a hint. I continue writing, "There was a long piece of string taped to the top of Kit's locker, with a big plastic penis dangling from it." Then I think, how do I *know* it's a *big* penis. How big are those things supposed to be, anyway? I mean, it's not like I've gone around measuring. The only penis I've ever so much as touched was Conan's, but I sure didn't look. Besides, he had his sweats on. He'd taken my hand, and guided it down inside his pants and . . .

Woodsy is looking at me again. I'm aware that my face is all hot, probably fire engine red. I get back to the report.

In the unattended classroom beyond Woodsy's office, things are getting louder and louder. Woodsy lets out one of those long-suffering teacher sighs and goes into the classroom to give them a busy-work assignment.

"Write non-stop for fifteen minutes. Don't worry about spelling or punctuation. Let the ideas flow," she says. "Then exchange papers with someone. Read each other's work and talk about areas of agreement and disagreement. Take the last fifteen minutes to rewrite your paper neatly, making changes according to any new insights. Do pay attention to spelling and punctuation on your rewrite."

Just as she's coming back to our table, Mr. Harper steps into the office. "Jackie asked me to cover for you. You sick?"

"No, but there's been an incident that needs to be dealt with," Woodsy says.

"Can I help?"

There's a roar of laughter from the classroom.

"Yes. Calm the beasts," Woodsy says, smiling. "Their assignment is on the board."

"You know I'm giving up my lunch for this," Harper says.

"But you'll be getting all that extra pay for it."

They both laugh.

"It was me or Rini," Harper says, then looks at me and Kit. "Me or *Mr.* Rini."

"Thank goodness you took it. I wasn't even thinking about the possibility of him covering my class when I wrote that assignment on the board."

Harper steps out, reads the board, then sticks his head back in.

"Your use of polysyllabics would protect you."

They both laugh again, then Harper closes the door.

"We should wrap this up," Woodsy says. "Go over your statements to be sure they're as accurate as possible. Then sign your names at the bottom."

"See if you think I got everything in," I say, passing my paper to Kit.

She slides her paper over to me.

She's put in pretty much the same stuff I have, except she's written with such pressure there are places where the pen has gone clear through the paper.

"I didn't see Robert," she tells me.

"He was standing way back."

"Sure?" she asks, picking up her pen to add Robert's name to her statement.

"No, don't change it," Woodsy says. "Witness accounts often differ. We each notice different details, and miss different details. The important thing is that the statement is true for you, to the best of your memory and understanding."

Woodsy makes two copies of each of our statements. She puts the originals in a folder which she labels Ben Maxwell, stashes a set of copies in her file cabinet, and hands me and Kit a copy of our own statements.

"Hold on to these," she says.

On the way out of the classroom I read the assignment Woodsy has written on the board. "Write fully and freely about your opinions, observations, and experiences related to ho-homophobia." Mr. Harper is at the board giving a vocabulary lesson on homophobia. Homo = same. Phobia = fear.

Miss Ramirez buzzes Mr. Maxwell to tell him we're here. Then we wait outside his office for what seems like a long time. Woodsy keeps checking her watch. Finally, the door to the big office opens and Coach Ruggles walks out, followed by Mr. Maxwell. Ruggles is in his Hamilton High Bulldogs coach shirt, khaki pants and beat up athletic shoes. His belly hangs over his belt, hiding the buckle. Supposedly he was a big football hero here about twenty years or so ago. Hard to believe now. I wonder if Conan will be all paunchy twenty years from now. I'll still love him, even if he is.

Mr. Maxwell is wearing what he always wears on Fridays when we're having a game. Well, for *football* games. He doesn't dress out for volleyball. Anyway, he's in a blue suit with a gold shirt and gold tie. Personally, I think it's too GQ for a football game, but Nicole says he likes to maintain a certain image.

Thank *gosh* for a wandering mind. I mean, I'm so angry and nervous about the whole locker thing, and worried about having to talk with Mr. Maxwell about it, but then at the same time, my mind lets me escape to stupid wardrobe stuff. Cool. I look over at Kit, who sits stiff and straight, her fists clenched. I don't think her mind's been wandering.

Coach Ruggles and Mr. Maxwell are enjoying some sort of two person football rally, back-slapping and high-fiving, talking about this being the year for the championship, how we're unbeatable, and on and on.

Woodsy checks her watch again, stands, and takes a few steps so she's directly in Mr. Maxwell's line of vision.

"Later, Coach," Mr. Maxwell says. They do one more high five, and then Mr. Maxwell opens his door and motions for us to enter.

Mr. Maxwell places three chairs in a row along his huge, glass covered mahogany desk. "Sit," he says, using the command I taught Wilma when she was just a pup.

The three of us sit down and Mr. Maxwell goes to the other side of his desk and sits down in one of those save-your-back chairs. On the wall behind him are several framed diplomas, awards from the PTA, Rotary Club, Chamber of Commerce and other organizations I've never heard of. I guess he's important.

On one side of the desk is a picture of a younger Manly Max and two other guys, dressed in bicycle gear, numbers on their shirts, bicycles in the background. He looks all buffed out. I see how he got the "Manly" nickname.

When I lean to my left I can check out the family picture he has sitting at an angle on his desk. I'm on the verge of a Maxwell family fantasy, about the two little boys and the littler girl, and the chunky mom and the manly looking dad, when Mr. Maxwell's voice, stern and sharp, jolts me back to reality.

"Tell me what's going on here."

16

My head is spinning. Somehow Maxwell is shifting everything around so it's like *we're* the ones who were out of line!

"I warned Mr. Cordova and Mrs. Saunders we were asking for trouble if we let this homosexual club meet on campus!"

"In all respect, Mr. Maxwell, it isn't a 'homosexual' club," Woodsy says. "It's a gay, straight student alliance."

"Whatever you call it, if it walks like a duck and quacks like a duck, chances are it's a duck," he says, giving Kit a long look. "I understand Frankie Sanchez is the president of the club?"

Woodsy shrugs her shoulders and turns to Kit, who nods her head.

"Walks like a duck, then," Mr. Maxwell says, smirking.

Woodsy catches her breath. Straightens. She's sitting at least a foot away from me, but I can feel her reaction as if we were side by side, touching.

"The issue here is one of extreme, pornographic harassment of a group of students against another student."

"Ms. Woods, girls, let's be sensible. As I said when I reluctantly, against my better judgment, allowed this new group to meet on our campus, we were opening a can of worms. You can't have students flaunting their total disregard for tried and true mainstream values without getting a reaction from those who uphold our American way of life."

"This harassment is *not* our American way of life, Mr. Maxwell," Woodsy says, picking up the dildo and slamming it down on the desk in front of him. "These acts are against the law! The *American* law!"

"So is spitting in the street, but let's face it, it happens. Now think about it. This little group should go back to meeting at Sojourner High School, and save their outlandish dress for somewhere besides this campus. Then things such as this simply wouldn't happen," he says, indicating the reports and dildo on his desk top.

"Mr. Maxwell, the *issue* is what these boys have done! It's not about how people dress."

"I beg to differ. These students call attention to themselves with their extreme dress, bizarre hair styles, flamboyant manner-isms — these things incite . . . "

"We have to take action to ensure the safety of all of our students, Mr. Maxwell, no matter how they dress or wear their hair."

Woodsy points to a thick book sitting on the shelf behind Maxwell's desk. "If you will hand me your copy of the education code . . ."

"I need no instruction from you in the contents of the ed code! Of course I will take action to ensure the safety of our students. Katherine and Lynn, I'll call your parents to come pick you up. Stay home on Monday. That will give things a chance to settle."

"I have a test on Monday," Kit says.

"I'll arrange for you to make it up," Mr. Maxwell says.

"Are you *suspending* these girls?"

"Nothing official, of course."

"If you're telling them they can't come to school on Monday, it sounds like a suspension," Woodsy says.

"It's an *informal* suspension. None of this will go into their records," he says, as if he's doing us a big favor.

"And Katherine, I'm sure we can make an exception in the no hat rule for you. When you return on Tuesday, if you'll wear a hat . . ."

Kit's fists are clenched so tightly, it wouldn't surprise me if her palms were bleeding. She stands and flashes Maxwell a look of pure disgust, then turns and walks out the door.

Woodsy runs after her. Maxwell is right behind.

"Don't you leave this office without permission, young lady! We're not through here!"

"*I* am!" she yells behind her, then takes off on a run.

"Call security!" Mr. Maxwell yells to his secretary.

"Don't, Jackie," Woodsy whispers.

Miss Ramirez picks up the radio, giving no recognition to Woodsy. She presses the side button and says, "Come in, security. Principal's office. Come in."

From where I'm standing, I can see that she's holding the "off" button at the same time she's pressing talk. She tries three more times. On the fourth, she releases the off button and security answers immediately. Mr. Maxwell takes the radio from her and asks that campus supervisors apprehend Katherine Dandridge and bring her immediately to his office. But I know Kit. She's blocks away by now.

"Would you please call Katherine's emergency contact and transfer the call to me when you reach someone? Also get me in touch with Lynn's contact."

Jackie gets the emergency card file and starts shuffling through it.

"Wait here until someone can come get you," Mr. Maxwell says to me.

"I have physiology now," I tell him.

"Yes, well we don't want any more trouble today do we? I'll see to it your teacher allows you to make work up."

"But . . ."

"No."

I wonder why I don't have the guts to run out of here, like Kit did.

"Ginny," Maxwell says, gesturing for Woodsy to go back into his office.

"I have a class in seven minutes," she says.

"This won't take long."

Woodsy follows him, not bothering to close the door.

"Your young friend Katherine just added defiance of authority to her troubles."

"Maybe she'd had enough humiliation for one day. Really Ben, you want her to wear a hat?"

"It makes sense."

"None of this makes sense. You've suspended an innocent victim of sexual harassment, and her friend, and you're doing nothing about the perpetrators."

"Perpetrators? Rather harsh, and legalistic, don't you think?"

"They've broken the law."

"Well . . . boys will be boys. I'll talk with them."

Woodsy stomps out of Maxwell's office, slamming the door behind her. If she were in a Saturday morning cartoon, she would have steam coming out of her ears and nose and mouth.

Mom walks into the office, looking worried.

"You all right?" she asks.

I nod.

She tells Miss Ramirez she'd like to speak with Mr. Maxwell.

"I have no idea what this is about," she says.

Miss Ramirez picks up the phone and buzzes. "Mrs. Wright is here. She'd like to talk with you . . . Yes, I'll tell her."

Miss Ramirez hangs up the phone and says to Mom, "Mr. Maxwell is on the other line with an important conference call, and then he has a 2:00 appointment. He's asked that I schedule you for first thing Monday morning."

Mom stares at Maxwell's closed door. For a minute I think

she's going to barge right in. Thank *gosh* she doesn't. All I want is to get out of this place.

We stop for a latte and I tell Mom the whole story, repeating myself when Mom would ask "they did *what*? — they said *what*?"

"How awful that must have been for Kit. You too, but Kit, poor Kit. Her father's right you know. Life will be much harder for her because of the lesbian thing."

I tell Mom about how Kit ran out of Mr. Maxwell's office.

"Do you think she's okay?" Mom asks. "Do you know where she went?"

"She's probably at Star's."

"Do you know Star's number?" Mom asks, pulling her cell phone out of her purse.

She hands the phone to me and I dial. I know Mom must be really worried, because she's always ranting and raving about how rude people are who have telephone conversations in public places.

I count ten rings, then click off.

"Try her house," Mom says.

Same thing. Now I'm worried, too.

Mom asks, "Where else would she go?"

"I don't know. Maybe she just doesn't want to answer the phone."

"Well, we can try again in a few minutes," Mom says, tipping her cup up and drinking the last drop of latte.

"I still don't understand why you and Kit got suspended."

"He said it wasn't official."

"If you're forbidden to go to school, that's official. And what about those boys? Are they just getting away with everything?"

"He said he'd talk to them."

"Oh, balls!" Mom yells loudly enough to turn heads.

"Mom!"

She looks around sheepishly, then lowers her voice.

"This thing stinks to high heaven! I'll meet with him Monday morning all right, and you'll be in school, too! And Kit, too!"

When we pull into our driveway, there sits Kit on our back steps, throwing the frisbee for Wilma. Her hair, which had grown out about an inch, is freshly shaved.

Mom sits down beside her, putting her arm around Kit's shoulder. I pick up the frisbee and give it a high toss.

"Hard day?" Mom asks.

Kit nods.

"Been home yet?"

She shakes her head. I don't know how to describe the look on Kit's face. It's . . . dark . . . and heavy . . . and amazingly sad. I think of Kit on the volleyball court, first practice in September, spiking the ball, laughing, joking around. I know she says it's better for her to be who she is, but "better" is not how things seem right now.

"It's cold out here," Mom says. "Let's go inside and warm up with a cup of tea."

Kit and I follow Mom in. I drop my stuff in a pile on my bedroom floor, then go back to the kitchen. Mom's already got the teapot started.

"You should call home," Mom says to Kit.

Kit rubs her hand over her freshly shaved head.

Mom does one of those double take things, like she's just noticed that even the fuzz is gone.

"What? Did you stop at a barber shop somewhere along the way?"

Kit smiles. "I'll buy you a new shaver, Always. I promise."

Through all of our talk about the plastic dildo and the glue "cum" Mom never looked shocked. Angry, maybe. And sympathetic. But now she looks shocked — like Kit crossed over some line with this make yourself at home business.

"Really. I'll go down to the drugstore and get one for you right now!"

"I'll drive her down there, if it's that big a deal!" I say. Like Kit hasn't already been through enough today. Now she's got to worry that Mom can't handle the borrowed shaver?

Mom shakes her head, as if trying to clear away whatever trash is floating around in there.

"No. No. It's fine. I'm more worried about hair in these old pipes . . ."

Kit says, "there wasn't *much* hair. Besides, I did it in the back yard."

Then we all start laughing, like it's the funniest thing in the world, Kit shaving her head in the backyard.

The phone rings. The teakettle whistles. Wilma howls, matching pitches with the teakettle.

I go for the phone while Mom gets the teakettle. Wilma's "singing" gets us laughing harder and I can hardly catch my breath to say hello.

"Is Katherine there?"

I hand Kit the phone.

"Your mom."

"Hi, Mom," Kit says, her laughter abruptly ended.

There is a long silence, then Kit trying to talk.

"But Mom . . . No . . . but I couldn't stay . . . you don't underst . . . But Mom . . ."

Kit hangs up.

"She never listens to me! She totally believes Principal PRICK!" Kit is pacing now, stomping. "If she'd ever once be on my side . . ." Kit slams her hand down hard on the counter top. Wilma darts under the table. Mom reaches for Kit and holds her shoulders.

Softly, Mom says, "Calm down, Kit."

"I don't want to freaking calm down! FUCK CALMING DOWN!" she screams. And then, just as I think she might pick up the teakettle and hurl it across the room, she crumples down on the kitchen floor.

"Sorry," she says, gasping. "Sorry." She starts sobbing. Her whole body is shaking. She's rocking, and crying, holding her face in her hands. I drop down next to her, rubbing her back, not knowing what else to do. Mom, too, kneels on the floor, pulling Kit to her, trying to comfort her the way she once did me when I was little.

"Shhhhh. It's going to be okay. You're okay . . . Get the throw off the couch, Lynn."

I bring it in and wrap it around Kit's shoulders. Sitting as close to her as I can possibly get, I continue rubbing her back. Wilma creeps out from under the table and lays down next to me, with her head resting on Kit's knee. Gradually, Kit's shaking becomes less intense and her sobs diminish. We are there, the four of us, huddled together on the floor, when Kit's mom comes bursting through the back door. She stops suddenly, her look of anger changing to one of puzzlement, then of concern.

"What is it?"

Mom stands up, rubbing her legs.

"Kit's been very upset, Jessie."

Jessie looks down at Kit, whose face is still buried in her hands.

"Katherine?"

Kit shakes her head, not looking up.

"I was just fixing us some tea," Mom says. She reheats the water to just below howling level, gets out another cup for Jessie and pours four cups of tea. Next to me, Kit lets out a big sigh, hands me the throw, and goes into the bathroom. I toss the throw on the couch and follow Kit. She's splashing cold water on her face. I hand her a clean washcloth.

"Thanks," she says, holding the cloth under the cold water, wringing it out and plastering it over her tear-swollen face.

"You okay?"

"Yeah."

She does the washcloth thing again, this time holding it to her face, then sliding it slowly across her freshly shaven head.

"All at once everything piled up on me. When I left school, I went straight to Star's. She always helps me figure stuff out, like when things seem all mucked up. I can tell her anything."

"Like it used to be with me?" I say, sort of hurt.

"You were still being held captive by Mean Max, so I couldn't exactly talk with you. Besides, you know how it is, sometimes, besides talking, you need to have someone kiss you, and put their arms around you and just . . . love you to pieces."

I nod.

"I tried to call you at Star's as soon as I got out of school."

"She wasn't home when I got there. She's *always* home Friday afternoon. I was already way freaked out from the nasty jock attack, and then having to put up with that crap from Maxwell . . . and then, when I couldn't find Star . . ."

A knock on the door. "Katherine? Can we talk?"

"Yeah, Mom. In a minute."

"Your tea's getting cold."

"All right, Mom."

Kit drops her voice to a whisper.

"So anyway, when I couldn't find Star, I started worrying, maybe she didn't love me anymore. Maybe she was all decked out in her leathers, catting around like she used to do, before me."

"I don't think so. If Star's not totally in love with you, she's got to be one of the world's great actresses."

"But you know how when one thing goes wrong, and then another, it seems like nothing's right?"

"Yeah," I say, thinking back to the time when my dad left, and I realized I wasn't very important to him. For a while I couldn't believe I was important to anyone, my mom, even my gramma and grampa.

"So I came here. On the way though, I saw Leaf, who told me Star'd been called in to work, to cover for someone who's sick."

"So you were relieved?"

"Totally. But there's all that stupid school stuff. Like I can afford to be suspended. And how fair is that? And those buttholes! I know Woodsy's absolutely on our side, and so will Emmy be, and all the GSA kids. I was okay out there, playing with Wilma and all. But then when my mom started being Mean Max's echo . . . I folded."

Kit smiles. I rub my hand across her head. We laugh. There's another knock on the door, this time louder. We go out to the kitchen and pour fresh tea. By now, David is here, too. He gets up from the table and walks over to Kit. He envelops her in his arms, holding her close.

"They won't get away with this, Sweetheart. They definitely shouldn't be playing in the game tonight."

"Now, David. We've been through that already. Pulling those boys from the game could only make things worse . . ."

David turns to Jessie, as if to say something to her, then changes his mind.

"Let's take a look at your witness statements," he says.

I get mine from my backpack and Kit takes hers, all folded up, from her jeans pocket. David spreads them out on the table and starts reading out loud. Suddenly, I notice the time.

"Excuse me," I whisper to Mom. "Conan'll be here in about five minutes."

I rush into my room and do a quick change of clothes, a gold fleece top with blue jeans, my answer to the blue and gold dress expectations. Brush my teeth, brush my hair, deodorant, breath freshener. I'm set. When David sees me in school colors he looks incredulous.

"You're going to the game? After today?"

"I go to all the games now. To watch Conan."

"The Barbarian?"

"Not exactly," I say. I guess David's been reading too much of the *Daily News* sports page lately.

I honestly don't want to go to the game, but at least I'll be with Conan after the game. And more than not wanting to go to the game tonight, I don't want to stay home, caught in reliving everything at our kitchen table.

Conan knocks at the back door, on time as usual. Usually he

comes in to say hello to Mom, and to pet Wilma, but tonight I say my good-byes as I open the door and lead Conan back to his car. Maybe David would be nice, but maybe he thinks Conan is like the other jocks. And who knows how Jessie would act? There's too much heavy drama in our kitchen right now.

Just out the driveway and onto the street, Conan reaches his warm hand to the back of my neck. He runs his fingers gently through my hair. I take his hand and kiss it. He pulls my head over against his shoulder.

"I heard," he says.

"I suppose *everyone's* heard by now."

"Yep. How's Kit?"

"She totally freaked out," I say. "But she's better now. Her dad says he's not going to let those guys get away with it."

"Her dad the sheriff?"

"Yeah. David."

"What's he gonna do?"

"I don't know."

"I'm sorry they did that," Conan says. "It makes the whole team look bad."

"Not to mention how it made Kit feel," I say.

"That, too."

We ride the rest of the way to school in silence.

CHAPTER

17

Conan has to be at the gym hours before the game, so I always hang with Nicole and Holly. They get here early too, because they ride with Robert. I'm not sure, but I think Robert and Holly are kind of together now. I guess he's over the heartbreak of Kit.

We usually get corn dogs and sodas and then stand in the parking lot watching Frankie put the band through various drills, practicing for half-time.

Band and choir kids respect Frankie's talent. When choir goes to festivals, we don't just stand and sing. We move. And we look good. And it's Frankie that comes up with the moves, and teaches them to us. Same thing with band. Some of the half-time stuff they do looks as good as college. Too bad they sound so awful. They'd be marching in the Rose Parade this year if they could only play the music.

Anyway, tonight I don't want to be hanging around out there, maybe having to answer a bunch of questions about what went on today. Some people live on that kind of drama, but I don't like it. I've brought my book and a flashlight. Because she knows how much I loved *The Color Purple*, Emmy gave me *The Way Forward Is with a Broken Heart*, which is by the same author.

I read until I hear the band start "The Star Spangled Banner," then go to the bleachers. Mr. Maxwell is standing on the sidelines, hand over his heart, singing out. Nicole and Holly wave to me from the cheering section and I make my way up to them.

I try to tell myself it's my imagination, but it seems like everyone is looking at me. I slide in next to Holly.

"Where were you?" she asks.

"I was reading."

"Reading?"

"Yeah, you know, deciphering those small black marks on pages of paper . . . You should try it sometime."

"Very funny," she says.

Drum rolls call our attention to the kickoff.

Robert receives the ball and carries it for fifteen yards. Long enough for me to be deafened by Holly screaming, "BOBBY! BOBBY! BOBBY!" Even after everyone else sits down, Holly is still standing and screaming.

So I guess I was right. They're a couple.

"Enough," I say, tugging at her jeans pocket.

She looks around, embarrassed, and sits down.

W hile the players are getting their act together on the field, Holly tells me she heard what happened at Kit's locker today. Nicole leans in to hear what I have to say.

"It was gross."

"I heard there was some kind of . . . thing," Nicole whispers. I nod.

"Was it a joke?"

"Would you think it was a joke if you'd found a plastic penis on your locker?"

We turn back to the game in time to see a red and white jersey zipping out in front of everyone, weaving his way to a touchdown. The other side, Rancho Verde, goes nuts.

This time, Brian receives the ball and Conan runs interference, stepping out of flying tackles as if they're nothing, keeping the way open for Brian. He is finally stopped by two tackles hitting him at once, but Brian is already free, into the end zone. Now it's our side's turn to go crazy. The cheerleaders run out, Tammy smack in the middle, and lead the **"BRIAN, BRIAN HE'S OUR MAN!"** chant.

In my mind I see Brian's crude gestures, hear the chant *he* led earlier today, "Something for Kitty's pussy!" I'm angry all over again! Butthole Brian's being treated like a hero, and Kit and I are suspended? The whole thing sucks. Nicole and Holly are on their feet, yelling for Brian. Whose side are they on anyway?

Now comes the "Barbarian" chant. It starts low and slow, then ends in a roar.

"baaarRRRRR **BARIAN!!**"

Even though I'm not wild about the whole barbarian thing, I yell it out anyway, because it's for Conan.

Another play. Another cheer for Brian, who just gained six yards. The team is filled with the enthusiasm of winners. That's how they've been since their second practice game win. But tonight they're over the top. High fives all around. Thumbs ups. Laughter. Back slaps and butt pats. I get a quick image of Kit, collapsed in quaking sobs on our kitchen floor just hours ago. But Brian and Justin and the rest of them, the perpetrators, in Woodsy's words, are so energized you could hook them up to a generator and light all of Hamilton Heights tonight.

Conan's family is sitting off to the side, down close to the front, with the families of some of the other black players.

I haven't met Conan's parents or his grampa, yet. I just know it's them because I've seen a picture in Conan's wallet. Also they're passing Sabina back and forth between them, holding her high so she can see the field. Sabina waves Fluffy over her head whenever Conan's name or number is mentioned.

At half-time I walk down to see Sabina. As soon as she sees me, Sabina jumps from her mother's lap and comes running to me, arms out. I pick her up, happy to see her.

"Fluffy seems to be enjoying the game," I say, rubbing my face against the stuffed dog.

"She cheers for Conan."

"Ummm. You too. I could hear you from way . . ."

"Sabina. Come here, Baby," her mother says, suddenly standing in front of me, reaching for Sabina.

"Oh, hi," I say, smiling. I shift Sabina to my left side and extend my right hand to Mrs. Parker. "I'm Lynn."

"Hello," she says, looking at me blankly, not taking my hand. She moves closer to Sabina and takes her from me.

"I'm Conan's . . ."

Mrs. Parker's look stops me. Conan's what? What was I going to say. Girlfriend? Friend?

"Lynn has fingernails, Mama. And she has a soft cheek," Sabina tells her mother.

"That's nice, Baby," Mrs. Parker says, turning away and walking back to her seat.

"Don't forget Fluffy," I say, following after them. I hand Fluffy to Sabina.

"Hi," I say, as the dad glances toward me. He gives me a silent lift of the chin, then looks away.

"Thank the nice girl for bringing Fluffy to you."

"Thank you," Sabina says.

I turn to go back up to my seat, wondering what's with Conan's family. It's like they don't know I exist! Or worse, they know I exist and they don't like it. I'm mulling it all over, trudging back to Nicole and Holly, when someone calls my name and grabs my arm at the same time.

"Mr. Maxwell wants to see you."

It's Larry, the campus security guy who hero worships Conan.

"Let go!" I say, shaking my arm loose.

He grabs my arm again, then lets go when he recognizes me. "I'm supposed to walk you down to see Mr. Maxwell," he says, his voice friendly now.

"I don't want to see him."

"No, come on. You have to. Don't make things difficult."

On the sidelines, Coach Ruggles and the old coach, Coach Howard, are conferring. Even though Howard's retired now, he still comes to every football game — half the practices, too, from what I hear. Standing next to them, but looking up at me, scowling, is Manly Max. He gestures for me to get down there. Conan's parents and grandfather, who wouldn't look at me when I tried to talk to them, now can't take their eyes off me. How embarrassing. I drag along behind Larry, wanting to be invisible.

As soon as I step off the lowest bleacher, Mr. Maxwell is in my face. "You are *not* to be present at any school functions until Tuesday, Miss Wright."

"Why? I'm not officially suspended," I remind him.

"Suspended, nonetheless."

"But . . ."

"Leave. Now."

"What did *I* do? I didn't do anything wrong!"

"You've *defied* my authority by coming onto school grounds when you're SUSPENDED! GET OFF THIS CAMPUS IMME-DIATELY!"

I run down the sidelines, out the gate, and into the parking lot. I'm vaguely aware of the noise in the bleachers, everyone cheering the teams as they come onto the field for the second half.

Conan's car is parked in the back, close to the gym. By the time I get there I'm way out of breath. I fumble around for Conan's key, then open the passenger side door. As I'm getting into the car, Larry comes running up. He stands, gasping, blocking the door with his body so I can't possibly pull it closed.

When he finally catches his breath he tells me, "Mr. Maxwell wants me to make sure you leave campus."

"I'm not going back in there. Don't worry."

"But you're still on campus. You've got to get off campus." What's with these people? It's like I'm public enemy number one.

"It's my job," Larry says. "I don't even know what this is all about. I've got to see you off campus right now, though." He holds the door open, waiting. I wait. He waits. Finally I get out of the car, slam the door shut, and walk to the back gate.

"Don't even *think* about coming back," he calls after me.

I've already thought about it. I walk out the gate and down the street. What I know about Larry is he's not going to miss any more of the game than he has to. He's probably already back there, talking jock talk with Manly Maxwell. I round the corner and check things out. Larry's nowhere to be seen. I go back to Conan's car. This time I get into the back seat. I open the window, just a crack, and sit slumped down, out of sight. I hold my book low and read by the dim flashlight glow. The muffled sounds from the game — announcer, cheers, drums — rumble through me, like thunder from a distant storm.

I turn off the flashlight and close the book, allowing myself to think the thoughts I keep pushing aside. I relive the day, trying to make sense of all that's happened. What do those guys get from being so cruel? Why are *we* being punished? What's the deal with Conan's family? What did Kit's dad mean when he said this thing isn't over yet?

The crowd is louder now — lots of Barbarian cheers. Lots of Brian cheers. Trumpets blast into the **CHARGE!** yell, and suddenly, I understand. Our suspension has nothing to do with us. It has to do with football. No way was Manly going to suspend the players and risk tonight's game. Justice is definitely not as important as football. I'll bet if the cholos or the skaters had been involved, *they'd* all be suspended and Mr. Maxwell would have been a lot nicer to me and Kit.

A louder than usual cheer erupts, signifying another victory for the Hamilton High team, another step toward the championship. The band starts up on the one piece they do well, the alma mater. I sing along softly, remembering the times we've sung it in choir, at the end of our concerts, when Hamilton High alumni all crowd onto the stage and sing with us. Maybe it sounds phony, but there've been times when we sang the alma mater and my heart filled with pride.

As the song ends, "we'll remember you all our lives, dear Hamilton High," and the roar of triumph again fills the air, I rest my head on the back of the driver's seat. I've loved this school. I really have. But now — it sucks.

The tears I've been holding back all day come in a rush.

18

"**H**ey. Lynnie."

Conan shakes me gently. I open my eyes to see him leaning into the car on the passenger side. He smells of soap. There is a band-aid over his left eyebrow and his eye is swollen, but he's wearing a very happy smile.

"Sorry it took me so long. Were you sleeping?"

"I guess," I say, rubbing my eyes as I get out of the car and slide into the front seat.

Larry comes rushing up to Conan.

"Hey! My man! You kicked butt!"

High five. Ten step handshake. Laughing. Larry glances at me, pauses for a nanosecond, high fives again.

"Really, man. They was watchin' you."

Conan laughs. "Yeah. Stanford and Ohio State."

"Keep it up! You got it made!"

Larry glances at me again.

"Hey. Gotta go. Great game," he says.

The parking lot is nearly empty now — just the coaches and a few players are left. Well, and security. I'm glad Larry decided to ignore me. Maybe when Conan's around I don't seem like such a danger to the campus.

Conan gets in the car, leans over, and gives me a big, long kiss.

"Love you," he says.

"Love you, too," I say — a sense of well-being creeping back into my discouraged soul.

"Big recruiters here tonight," he says, beaming. "My interception and touchdown run — they liked it. And clearing the way for Brian's two touchdowns — they liked that, too. Two major recruiters out watching me and Brian. My dad's jazzed."

"Sounds like you're jazzed, too," I say, smiling.

"I am! Aren't you? Aren't you jazzed for me?"

"I love you *so* much. If *you're* jazzed, *I* want to be jazzed."

Conan's beaming smile fades.

"But?"

"But . . . I don't want you to move far away. And I thought, you know, you might not want to be totally involved in football. Like you want a real education. Remember?"

"Yeah. I know what I said. But I'm *good* at football. Really good. Better than anything else I know of. And these recruiters . . . this is the top! You saw me, you know how good I am."

"I didn't actually see you out there tonight. At least not the second half."

"You didn't see the interception and touchdown?"

I shake my head.

"Why not?"

I catch him up on the continuing saga of my life as an enemy of Hamilton High, including being escorted from the bleachers and off school property.

"That sucks. How can *you* be suspended when you didn't do anything wrong?"

"It's like — there was this thing that happened, and *someone* had to be suspended, and it couldn't be football players because of this big deal game. That's what I think."

Conan shakes his head, frowning.

"Well . . . at least you got to see the first half of the game," he says, as if that's the main thing.

He starts the engine.

"Victory party at Robert's," he says.

"I suppose Brian and Justin and Anthony will be there."

"Well, yeah. It's a VICTORY celebration. The whole team'll be there."

"I can't go."

"Why not?"

"After what those guys did to Kit today? You think I'd go hang out with them, like nothing happened?"

"Come on. There'll be so many people there you probably won't even see those guys. Holly'll be there, and probably Nicole. All of our friends will be there."

"Sure. Kit, and Star, and Frankie. How about Nora and Caitlin?"

Conan sighs. "I know you're upset, and I'm sorry. But this was probably the best game of my whole life. I want to celebrate it with the team."

I'm remembering the ugly plastic penis, the ugly words, the crude gestures . . .

"This party's important to me, Lynn."

. . . the crude chants.

"I go places you want to go sometimes, even if I don't want to," Conan says.

"This is different! I don't ask you to go with me to a KKK meeting!"

"It's not like that! They weren't lynching anyone! They meant it as a joke!"

"Joke!"

"I know. It was stupid, but they were just trying to be funny."

"Conan . . . "

I don't know what else to say. It's like I'm talking to a stranger. I can't believe Conan thinks any of that locker business was just a joke.

Cars line both sides of the street near Robert's house. Robert and some other guys are standing in the driveway, drinking sodas, or beers, I'm not sure which. Conan pulls over to the curb.

"I'm not going in," I tell him. "I can't."

"Have it your way," he says, all quiet and calm.

He pulls away from the curb and drives me home. He leaves the engine running while I get out of the car, then backs down the driveway. Wilma comes running to greet me. Only the lamp by the front window is lit, meaning no one is home. I'm relieved.

I try again to read the Alice Walker book. I skip around in it, trying to find something of interest. So far, all that holds my attention is the title, *The Way Forward Is with a Broken Heart*. Am I on the verge of a broken heart? Conan and I have never before raised our voices to one another. I never once, until tonight, felt as if we were on opposite sides. How could he pretend such nasty harassment of Kit was only a joke? And there's a nagging thought in the back of my mind—like why was his family so cold to me. Maybe they've never even heard of me. Maybe he doesn't care enough to bother telling his parents about me. Maybe I don't know Conan as well as I thought I did.

I call Kit. Check e-mail. Nothing. I'm channel surfing, mindless, when the phone rings. I jump for it, hoping it's Conan.

"Lynn?"

The warm, deep voice I hoped to hear isn't there. Instead it's the light, whispery voice of Frankie.

"Oh, hi Frankie," I say, trying not to sound disappointed.

"Is Kit there?"

"No."

"Well, she's not with Star."

"I called her house just a few minutes ago. No one's there. Maybe she went somewhere with her parents," I say.

"I'm worried about her," Frankie says.

"Why?"

"I just know how hard it can be, everyone laughing and saying mean things."

"Well, maybe she's at that coffee place in Pasadena," I say.

"We looked."

"Who?"

"Me, and Star, and Jerry . . . Can you think of anywhere else she might be?"

"Barb 'n Edie's?"

Frankie laughs. Well, it's not exactly a laugh. It's more like a sarcastic snort.

"I'm sure she wants to hang out with the rah-rah crowd tonight."

"I don't know where else . . . "

"If I come get you, will you help me look for her?"

It's not like I have anything else to do tonight so I agree to go. I give him directions to my house and then change out of my gold sweatshirt. School colors on game night no longer appeal to me.

I'm watching out the window when Frankie pulls up in a VW bug. The old kind. I grab my purse and meet him in the driveway.

"My chariot," he says, reaching across and opening the passenger door for me. The upholstery's torn and there is no headliner.

"Some chariot," I say.

"A diamond in the rough."

"Whatever . . . I don't even know why we're doing this."

"Because she's our friend, and we're worried. At least I am."

We drive by her house to see if anyone's there, but it's dark. We go to the big park, up in the ritzy section. The gates are all locked, but we climb over the lowest one and look around. No sign of Kit, but the shadows of trees reminds me that there's one place we haven't looked. We drive back to my house and walk through the gate in my backyard. There she is, sitting cross-legged at the base of the walnut tree.

"Oh, my God!" Frankie says, running across the yard to her.

He leans down and grabs her arms, runs his hands across her wrists and inner arms, then sinks down beside her. He rests his head back against the tree, eyes closed. I sit across from them.

"What is *with* you?" Kit says to Frankie.

"I've been worried. Are you okay?" Frankie asks, looking intently at her face.

"Yeah. I'm pissed, but I'm okay."

"Good," Frankie says. "Pissed is good . . . When no one knew where you were I started thinking . . .worrying that . . ."

"What?"

"I just thought you could be really depressed, or . . . "

"Or?"

"Or, you know . . . want to . . . hurt yourself."

"You don't need to worry about me getting all stupid and suicidal."

"It's not like it doesn't happen," Frankie says.

"Yeah, well it'll take a lot more than those little pricks to make me want to off myself."

I laugh, glad to hear Kit talking strong again. Kit laughs, too.

"Oh, sure. It's funny now, in your backyard. But once those guys start in on you, they may not let up. It can get depressing. Just promise me you'll always talk things through. Even if you feel alone, you're not alone," Frankie says. He scoots over next to Kit and gives her a big hug. She leans her head on his shoulder.

"Thanks," she says. "Thank you, too," she says to me, as I scoot over next to her on the other side.

The three of us sit talking about all that's happened. Kit says her dad and my mom are going in to see Mr. Maxwell first thing Monday morning. They're going to demand an apology for us, and a five-day suspension for Brian, Justin and Anthony.

"That'll mess up next week's football game," I tell her.

"So?"

"I'm just saying."

"I've been really hoping we'll get to the championship play-offs," Frankie says.

"Like you care about football?" Kit says.

"I care about half-time."

"I don't want my dad to make a big deal out of this," Kit says. "For once I'm on my mom's side."

"I'm with your dad. They *should* be suspended and we should have an apology. It's so *unfair* that we got punished and they're big heroes!"

We talk about tonight's game, how jazzed those guys were. I tell them about being escorted out of the game, and how I refused to go to the party, and how important the party was to Conan. I don't tell them about trying to introduce myself to Conan's family, and how weird that was. I guess I'm hoping Conan can help me make sense of it all.

I wonder what Conan's doing. Is he still at the party? Is he paying attention to any of those girls that always flirt with him? Will he end up taking someone else home? Maybe he's called.

It's cold, which gives me an excuse to go back to my house and get beach blankets for us to wrap up in. Kit and Frankie go into her house to make hot chocolate.

I rush through the door, see the blinking answering machine light, and make a lunge for it. It's for Mom.

I get the blankets and leave a note telling Mom I'm at Kit's. Wilma's all hyper from being alone in the house for so long, so I take her back to Kit's with me. She drags her frisbee along. Kit's brought a thermos of hot chocolate and three cups back to the tree. Frankie tosses the frisbee for Wilma. I swear she shows off whenever there's anyone new around, catching high throws, running circles around the yard with the frisbee in her mouth, then dropping it right at Frankie's feet. Finally I call her to me, thinking Frankie may be tiring of the game. She lies beside me on the blanket, her head resting on her paws.

We warm our hands on our cups of steaming chocolate. Take little sips. Savor the warmth. Frankie breaks the silence.

"Have you ever thought about it?"

"Thought about what?" Kit says.

"Suicide."

19

$\mathbf{I}$t is late now. The streets are quiet. Frankie talks in a low, steady voice.

"I'd always been hassled, all through elementary school. I didn't understand why. I wanted to be friends with everybody. The girls would let me jump rope with them at recess. I was good at it, but the boys teased me all the more when they saw me doing 'Double Dutch' and 'Ice Cream Soda Delaware Punch.' Sometimes I'd make friends with another boy, maybe even play with him after school. Then the others would start teasing him too, and he'd stop being my friend."

I try to remember Frankie from elementary school, but I can't. He probably went to a different school. The thing is, I *can* remember a boy named Timmy, how he got teased all the time, and how I hardly ever thought about it, one way or the other.

"They used to call me names, like Sissy-boy, and Girly-boy and Fag, and sometimes someone would give me a push. But by the time I was in seventh grade, the names were worse and so was the physical stuff."

"Was it everyone? *All* the boys?" Kit asks.

"No. But it seemed like it at the time. Once some guys grabbed me and shoved me into a trash can. I was fag-trash, they said, and they kicked the can over with me in it. A custodian came and helped me out, but kids were standing around, laughing."

"That sucks," Kit says.

"Yeah, well, most people didn't think so," Frankie says.

He goes on talking about his experiences, but my mind is wandering. I'm remembering something I don't want to remember. In the sixth grade, Timmy and I worked on a project together, one of those papier-mâché maps that shows mountain ranges. We painted in streams and desert areas. We weren't exactly friends, but we turned out the best map in the class and we had fun doing it.

One day at recess some of the boys were taunting Timmy. There were five of them, with Timmy in the middle. They were yelling and laughing and they wouldn't let him get away. I stood watching, not liking it, but not doing anything either. Timmy looked at me, like can't you help? But I just stood there. Pretty soon a teacher came and broke it up.

I wonder why I didn't try to help? I could at least have said something. But I didn't. Then the map project was over, and Timmy and I didn't sit together anymore, and we hardly ever talked after that. Thinking back on it now, I feel sort of sick, and ashamed. I wonder whatever happened to Timmy?

"**. . . E**very day before I left the house, I armored myself against both pain and joy . . . I transformed myself into stone."

Because of my wandering mind, it takes me a while to figure out that Frankie is now talking about his freshman year at Hamilton High, but finally I get it.

" . . . older guys who lived to hassle me. Fudge-packer, queenie, that stuff. I was stone. My armor was strong. Even so, they kept it up. One day they caught me after school. They shoved me behind a big dumpster, took my shoes off and threw them in the dumpster, took my pants off and . . . stuff . . . "

"What stuff?" Kit says.

"Just stuff . . . stuff that crushed my armor."

"Like rape?"

"Not exactly. But . . . it wasn't nice. Let's skip the details, okay?"

Frankie's talking so softly that Kit and I have to lean in to hear him.

"I ran home. No shoes. No pants. Trying to stay in the shadows. I hid in the garage for a long time, cold and shivering. I had to wait until all the lights went off in my house and I knew my parents were in bed. I couldn't let my dad see me like that . . ."

His voice trailed off and we sat silent, breathing in the peace of earth and grass and the thinking tree.

Frankie told us that after the pants and shoes incident, he quit going to school. He left in the morning as *if* he were going to school and then walked around in different neighborhoods every day.

"When you're just standing on a street corner, that's when the truancy cops get you. As long as you keep walking, they don't pay much attention."

He'd walk for an hour or so, then sneak back into his house after his parents had both gone to work. He watched old movies on cable — Gene Kelly, Fred Astaire, and other big Hollywood musicals. He rented videos of his favorites, so he could watch certain dance routines, over and over again, mimicking their steps until he knew exactly how it all went together.

"I was happier than I'd ever been. I was lonely, but that was nothing new. I'd been lonely for as long as I could remember. At least I felt safe.

"The school would call home. I'd erase the message and go back to my dance routine. The mail would come, I'd rip up anything from school and throw it away. It was great, while it lasted."

"How long did it last?" I ask.

"About two months. Then someone finally got hold of my dad

at work."

"It took two months? If I'm home for a *day* someone calls my mom at work."

"Yeah, well, I'd started cutting class fairly often back in the seventh grade. It was hard, you know — some days I just couldn't make myself go to school. So when I got to high school, I knew to put down phony numbers on my emergency information. They'd call, get a wrong number, and forget about it for a while."

"But two months . . . "

"Someone in the office got smart and looked up my old records from elementary school, before I'd learned to lie."

"Then what?" Kit asked.

"Then my dad went crazy, yelling and screaming. My mom went on a two week crying jag. The three of us went to school for a conference. It was with Mr. Cordova. That was back when he was still a counselor, before he became a Vice Principal. My parents kept asking why, why, why, hadn't I been attending school. I couldn't tell them. Mexican boys don't tell their Mexican dads guess what — I'm getting beat up because I'm gay. I mean I'm the son my dad waited for, after three girls. He's this macho construction crew boss and I'm going to tell him I'm too cowardly to go to school?"

"You weren't a coward. You were being ganged up on," I say.

Frankie shakes his head. "Even if there'd only been one little guy, I still would have been afraid. That's how I am. I'll never fight. And if I'd run away from TEN guys, my dad would still have thought I was a coward.

"Mr. Cordova was cool, though. Maybe he had an idea why I'd quit going to school. He advised that I go to Sojourner. God! With all those hoodlums? I wanted to do Independent Studies, but my dad wouldn't hear of it. He jumped at the Sojourner idea. Thought it might toughen me up."

Like I said earlier, Sojourner has this reputation for being overrun with gangs, druggies, delinquents and tramps. Now that I've been on the campus a few times, I know that's not true. But it must have been a horrible prospect for Frankie to face.

"My parents were acting like they'd spawned a Charles Manson. Like I was the scum of the earth for opting out of school. My dad kept stomping around and spouting off about what a stupid little twerp I was, and how could he have ended up with me. Maybe they'd made a mistake in the hospital because he couldn't believe I was really his son.

My mom just cried. I wanted to run away, but I didn't have anywhere to run to. I was *not* going to go to a place where I'd be picked on even more than I had been at Hamilton High. I thought about it a long time. It needed to be fast and sure. I didn't have access to a gun. I didn't trust pills. I ended up going to the drugstore and buying a pack of old fashioned straight edge razors."

"You were going to kill yourself?" Kit says.

Frankie nods.

"But why?" I ask, knowing as soon as the words are out of my mouth I've asked a stupid question. Like he hasn't been talking non-stop for hours about how miserable his life was.

Frankie doesn't act like I'm stupid, though. He just tells me he couldn't see any way out but death. Then he starts laughing.

"What's so funny?" Kit says. "This isn't funny!"

"But it is funny, sort of, how one little thing can change everything."

"Like what?"

"Like I've got this thing all planned out. I know to slit my wrists deep up the vein, not across, the way you see in old movies."

"I don't watch that many old movies," Kit says.

"Yeah, well I do. Trust me on this one, they don't show the right way to slit your wrists."

"This is morbid," I say.

"But it has a happy ending," Frankie says.

"So anyway . . . " Kit prompts.

"So anyway, I've got it all planned. I've thought a lot about my mom. I really love my mom, but she was always crying and it always had to do with me. I thought, I'll do this and she'll have one big long cry, and then there won't be anything to cry about anymore. But I didn't want to do it in the house, where she'd be cleaning up the mess. The bathtub would have worked — just rinse the blood down the drain, but then maybe she'd never want to take a bath in the tub again. A hot bath is one of her few pleasures."

"Enough with the details!" I say.

"I'm a detail guy. That's why I'm good at choreography."

"Whatever," I say.

"So ANYWAY . . ." Kit prompts again.

"So ANYWAY, I decided to do it in the backyard. The yard is my dad's responsibility. He could clean up my dead, bloody mess. I liked that idea. So it's after dinner — fried chicken which, if I'd been ordering my last meal wasn't my favorite, but it wasn't bad.

"The folks are watching TV, the one thing they do together without my dad yelling and my mom crying. I get the bag with my package of razors, go into the backyard and assume a cross-legged yoga position. I take the package of razors out, crumple the bag, and toss it on the ground. I rip the cellophane wrapping off and toss it in the other direction. Dad can clean that up, too. I take the razors from the package and line them up on my pants leg.

"I'm sitting there thinking about death, how peaceful it will be, free of worry. I've picked up a razor and lowered it to my wrist, searching in the dim light for exactly the right spot, when my dad yells out the door that I have a phone call. This is weird, because I have no friends. No one, I mean NO ONE ever called me. I ask who it is. He doesn't know, just get my butt in there and answer it. So now I'm stuck. If I cut right then, he'd be out before I could die, demanding that I answer the phone. So I picked up my razors and very carefully placed them in that little watch pocket thing in my jeans, and went to the phone."

"So was it an angel, calling to save your life?" I ask.

He laughs. "It was Guy, from Sojourner."

"Really?"

"Really," Frankie says. "He said he was a teacher from Sojourner, and he wanted to remind me of my enrollment appointment. I kept running my thumb over that small pocket, feeling the outline of the waiting razors. He told me he'd see me in the morning. I said 'okay' but I thought 'Right. Drop by the morgue.' But then he said he wanted me to know I would be safe at Sojourner — that they were the safest school in the whole county, in spite of what people thought about them. He said people were treated with respect at Sojourner. I kept feeling the razors in my pocket. I hung up and went back outside, assumed the position and lined up the razors. But I kept thinking about what Guy had said. A tiny voice within me said, 'What's another day? Try it.' So I did."

"If Guy had waited five more minutes to call . . ." I say.

"I wouldn't be here."

"How did he know to tell you you'd be safe there? He didn't even know you then," Kit says.

"I asked him about that once, after I got to know him. He said Mr. Cordova had called and said he suspected I was afraid to come there, and that I'd probably had some bad experiences at Hamilton High. So Guy called to reassure me."

Frankie gives Kit a long look.

"When I heard what those assholes had done to you today . . . it brought back so many memories. When nobody knew where you were . . . I got scared. Then when I saw you sitting against the tree in that kind of yoga position, I thought . . . "

Kit nods, like she understands, then asks, "Do you think you would really have made the cut?"

"Absolutely."

"Have you ever thought about it since then?" I ask.

"Some," he says.

He takes a package of razors from his pocket, sits in a yoga position, and takes the cellophane off the package.

I jump up, grab the package, and throw it on the dirt. Kit's on her feet too, stomping and grinding the package into the ground.

"Hey! I wasn't going to do anything!" Frankie says.

"That's sick, carrying those around with you!" I say.

"It's security," he says.

"What's that mean?" Kit says.

"It means if things get unbearable, there's always somewhere else to go."

"How unbearable *are* things?" I ask.

"They're not. I got stronger at Sojourner. GSA helped a lot. Before that, I had no idea anyone else had some of the same problems. It was hard coming back to Hamilton High, but I wanted to be involved in music and drama, and there was none of that at Sojourner."

"Were those same guys at Hamilton when you came back?"

"The worst of them, the ones that got me after school that day, were two years older, so they'd gone. Some of my old tormentors are still here, but mostly it's just words. And I have friends now. Things are pretty cool. Except I never, ever go to the bathroom at school. Why press my luck?"

I figure Frankie has to go more than seven hours without a bathroom break if he never uses the facilities at school.

"That's not even healthy," I tell him.

"Says the nurse," Kit smiles.

"For me it's healthier than being caught in the boys' room," Frankie says.

"But how can you even stand it?"

"No liquids from midnight until I get home from school. No breakfast. A small container of yogurt for lunch."

"That sucks!" Kit says.

"As long as it doesn't poop . . ." Frankie answers.

We laugh.

"Enough of my bathroom practices," Frankie says, "You want to know the end of the almost suicide story?"

Kit and I both nod.

"The next evening, after I was home from my first day at Sojourner, I'm sitting at the table with a glass of milk. Guy'd already talked with me about the GSA group, and the kids were cool. It's like, everybody's weird there, so nobody's weird. So I'm sitting there, feeling pretty good, and my dad comes stomping into the kitchen. He slams the paper bag and the cellophane wrapper down on the table, hard enough to make my glass jump. He yells 'What's this? You think I've got nothing to do but clean up your shit?'"

Frankie laughs. "He didn't know how lucky he was. Think about what he *almost* had to clean up."

We all laugh then. Laugh and laugh, silly with relief. Then, slowly, our laughter fades and we become quiet and thoughtful.

After a while, Kit says, "I promised I'd talk things through with you if I ever got really down."

Frankie nods.

"I want a promise in return."

"What is it?"

"I want you to promise not to replace the razor blades."

Frankie is silent for a long time, looking at the bent up stomped package that sits half-buried in the dirt.

"I don't take promises lightly," Frankie says.

"Neither do I," Kit says. "Promise?"

Frankie looks from Kit to me and back to Kit again.

"Yeah. Okay. I promise."

"Link hands," Kit says, reaching for my hand on one side and Frankie's on the other.

Frankie and I grab hands, too, so we make a circle of three.

"I promise to talk things through," Kit says.

"I promise not to replace the razor blades," Frankie says.

They both look at me. "I promise not to stand silently by while people are being mistreated, or picked on, or called names."

We stay connected, no one wanting to be the first to let go. Finally, Wilma pushes her way into the circle and drops her frisbee in the center, breaking the spell.

We laugh then, and drop hands. Kit throws the frisbee one more time, then gathers up the thermos and cups. I get the blankets and Frankie and Wilma and I walk back through my gate to his car. I watch as he backs out my driveway, then take Wilma and the blankets inside. There is still only the one message on the machine. I wonder about Conan. I wonder about the title of Alice Walker's book. I hope there's another way forward, besides with a broken heart.

20

Conan is waiting for me when I get out of my Saturday morning medical careers class. He's smiling, like everything's okay with us. Maybe it is.

His eye is even more swollen this morning.

"Have you been icing your eye?"

"Umm. I did last night."

"This morning?"

"No. It's okay."

"You should ice it every two or three hours. That'll help with the swelling."

"Thank you, nurse," Conan says.

I sock him, lightly, playfully, on his arm.

"Watch it," he says, grabbing my hand and making me hit myself in the belly. That, too, is light and playful.

We walk to his car, laughing, lightly poking at one another along the way. It's as if we've gone back to the time before we knew we loved each other, when we wanted to touch but couldn't admit it.

We continue this slapstick kind of stuff in the car, until I tell

Conan we need to talk.

"Yeah," he says, without enthusiasm.

"You know last night . . . "

"Yeah . . . I'm starved," he says. "Let's get a bite to eat."

"Okay," I say, "but we still need to talk."

"We will. How about Barb 'n Edie's?"

So that's where we go. We order two garbage burritos. I eat half of one and Conan eats the rest. Then he gets a large order of fries. Some old guy who I guess is a Hamilton High football fan comes up to Conan and congratulates him on last night's game. He wants to go through it play by play and I guess Conan doesn't mind because he gets all involved in the conversation. I open my medical careers textbook and begin highlighting terms I need to learn for next week.

Having talked the game all the way through to a fumble during the last seconds, Conan's fan finally leaves. When we go to pay our bill, Edie says it's on her. She thanks Conan for putting Hamilton High's football team back on the map.

"It's good for business," she tells him. "The more wins, the more the community comes out for games. The more people come out for games, the more people stop here after. We were bulging at the seams last night — wall to wall people."

"Thanks," he says.

After running errands for his mom and stopping by Robert's to pick up the jacket he forgot last night, Conan asks, "Anyone home at your house today?"

"Just Wilma."

"Where's your mom?"

"Some training deal at Microdyne. She'll be home about six."

We go to my house. Conan puts on some music. We stretch out on the carpet, side by side, touching. Conan moves to kiss me, but I move away. "We really have to talk," I say.

"We will. We will," he says, kissing my neck, pulling me closer to him. "Just know I love you," he whispers.

For a while I forget about talking.

We lie together, still sticky, but relaxed and close. I'm on my side, one leg thrown across Conan's tree-trunk thigh, my head resting on his outstretched arm.

"Conan."

"Ummm."

"I saw your family at the football game last night."

"Yeah. They were sitting down there with Antoine and Derek's parents."

"They wouldn't even talk to me."

Conan leans up on his elbow, jostling my head.

"You talked to them?"

"I *tried* to. Sabina was the only one who even noticed I was there, though."

Conan sits up, fastening his pants and pulling his shirt on over his head. We're not so relaxed now. I fasten my bra, button my top and pull my pants back up, wondering what's the big hurry. Usually we lie close together for a long time, after we've had our fun.

"What did Sabina say?"

"She came running to see me at half-time. Your mom acted like I was, I don't know, trying to kidnap Sabina or something."

"So that was it?"

Conan sits on the couch, putting on his size fourteen shoes.

"Sabina was being sweet. You know, telling your mom that I have fingernails, and I have soft cheeks."

Conan groans.

I'm sitting next to him on the couch, putting my shoes on, too. I look at his worried face and start getting a really uneasy feeling. I remember how, as soon as it became a regular thing, he started waiting for me down at the corner when I'd pick him up for school. And how I offered to take Sabina home for him after they'd been at my house one day. Even though he was late for a doctor's appointment and I could have easily saved him some time, he insisted on taking her himself.

"They don't even know about me, do they?" I ask.

He shakes his head no.

"That's cold," I tell him, moving across the room to the other chair.

"Come back over here beside me," he says. I don't move.

"You're practically part of my family! My mom's always telling her friends how great you are, she knows all your favorite foods, and your favorite TV shows and *your* mom doesn't even know I EXIST! You don't even care enough about me to *mention* me to anyone in your family!"

I hate that I cry when I get angry, but I'm crying. Conan comes and sits on the arm of the chair, trying to pull me toward him.

"It's not like that, Lynnie. I love you. How can you say I don't care about you?"

I move back over to the couch.

"Right. You love me, but I'm not good enough to meet your family."

"No. Just listen for a minute."

He comes back over to the couch and sits next to me again.

"I've just been waiting for the right time to talk to them . . ."

"What's so hard about saying you've got a girlfriend and you're really happy about it?"

"It's just not that simple with my family. I *did* try to talk to my dad a month or so ago. I told him how you gave Sabina a dog license for Fluffy, and how much Sabina liked you."

"Sabina?? What about you???"

"I was just warming up to it. That's all. And then Sabina comes in and starts on that she has fingernails and soft cheeks business."

Even though I'm mad, I have to laugh at that. It's like Sabina is *obsessed* with my fingernails and soft cheeks.

"So then my dad says, this Lynn girl. She must be white."

"Oh, my gosh! That's *so* stupid! Like only white people have fingernails and soft cheeks?"

"No, it's just, I think Sabina is figuring out how we're the same. We all have soft cheeks and fingernails. It's not like she's been around many white people up close."

"That's weird."

"How many black people had you touched when you were four years old?"

He's got me there. I have to admit it wasn't until I started school that I was around all different kinds of people.

"We lived in the 'hood,' you know? And she's not in school yet. You're probably the first white person she's ever touched."

"So did your dad think Sabina got cooties from me or what?"

Conan gives me this patient, don't be stupid look.

"My dad went into this whole rage about how black boys who hang around with white girls are suicidal, and how there's never, ever been any white blood in our family, and how it'd kill my mom if she thought I was with a white girl and I'd better not be bringing any half-breeds home so I'd better get that white meat off my mind."

"White *meat*?"

"I'm only telling you what he said."

"What about you? What did you say?"

"I didn't say anything. When my dad gets like that there's no talking to him."

"It sounds like your family is as racist as any KKK fool running around in a white sheet."

Conan bristles. "No, they are *not* racist," he says.

"Right. They don't like me because of my color. I call that racist."

"Call it what you want. But my parents are not trying to keep you from voting, or attending school, or getting a job. They're all for equal rights. They just don't want to mix it up — which is about black pride, not racism."

"Well it feels racist to me," I say. I go into the bathroom and clean up, taking my time.

When I come back out Conan's still sitting in the same place, staring off into space. I sit next to him, but not touching.

"I'm *not* ashamed of you. God, I feel so lucky to be with you.

I've never been close to anyone like this before. I couldn't wait to see you, last night, after the game. And I missed you so much at the party . . . "

"I thought you were mad."

"I was, at first. But then, after I got to the party . . . I could see why you wouldn't want to be there . . . Once the beer started flowing some of the guys were all hyped, talkin' mess . . ."

"I don't see why you even want to hang around with them."

"We're a team, that's all."

The phone rings. It's Mom, saying she's going to dinner with friends and won't be home until ten or so. Conan and I decide to call out for pizza and watch videos.

Mom's a little nervous about me and Conan hanging out in the house when she's not home. She says she doesn't want us making babies. I tell her we never do anything that could make a baby, which is true. I'm not sure she believes me, though. She's always leaving Planned Parenthood pamphlets sitting around — stuff about the pill, and condoms, and depo shots, and cervical caps. She says it's good to be informed.

Conan calls for pizza, then calls his mom to say he won't be home for dinner. I can't help hearing his side of the conversation.

"Oh, sorry," he says. "Can you save it for tomorrow night?"

"Just with some friends . . . yeah, I'll be home by midnight . . . probably pizza . . . yeah, I know your steak'll be better . . . maybe a movie, or video games, I'm not sure . . ."

He hangs up and I get all sarcastic with him. "Oh, yeah, Mom, I'm having dinner with the love of my life. Her cheeks are soft and she has fingernails."

"Get over it. Okay?"

"It's just so stupid!"

"It's stupid for you to want to meet them. I can tell you right now, you won't like them and they won't like you. Why should I be fighting with them all the time about you? It wouldn't do any good."

Conan walks out the door. I hear Wilma's short bark and then the whoosh of the frisbee. I stay inside, thinking. I hate that Conan's pretending I don't exist as far as his family's concerned. Then I start thinking about my dad. He's on a month long business trip, setting up computers for a new company. But if he were coming over to visit me, I wouldn't tell him about Conan, either. He'd get all upset over nothing, and probably be rude. So I guess I understand why I'm the mystery woman at Conan's house.

Maybe it shouldn't matter. Except I can't get over the unfairness of it all, that they're judging me by the color of my skin, not by the kind of person I am. Just like my dad would do to Conan. Why are people like that?

I go outside and join in the frisbee toss. Conan gives me a tentative smile. I smile back.

He says, "It's not about you. It's about my family. I've got my own ideas. Their way isn't my way. But for now, it's best if I lay low with them."

The Pizza Man comes tearing up our driveway, jumps out of the car, opens the hot box and hands the giant pizza to Conan. Wilma acts like he's a big threat, barking, growling, running up to him with her bristles up.

"Wilma! Get over here!"

I grab her by the collar while Conan pays for the pizza. We go back inside and set it out on the coffee table in front of the TV. I get sodas and we settle in to watch "Chicken Run."

During the previews Conan says, "About my family. I don't want you to think I don't love them. Or respect them. I do. I just see things differently is all."

I scoot over close to Conan. He puts his arm around me. I know everything's going to be all right between us, no matter what other people think.

We laugh 'til we're weak over the chickens, but it's not just a comedy. It gives us a lot to think about. And I don't know about Conan, but for me, it'll be a long time before I eat another Clucker's.

21

Kit and I, plus my mom and her dad, show up at Mr. Maxwell's office at 7:45 Monday morning. Kit's dad wears his sheriff's uniform, which I think is a nice touch.

Kit is wearing gray cargo pants, a gray turtleneck tee shirt, and her Monarchs sports jacket. She has a rainbow headband around her shaved head. Silver studs line the edges of her left ear, from top to lobe. Besides rainbow Pride bracelets on each wrist, she's wearing two heavy, metal-studded leather bracelets.

Mom's in her usual business attire, a tailored skirt and jacket, silk blouse, and stylishly sensible shoes. I'm wearing nondescript.

Yesterday, Mom, David, and Jessie met to talk through their "strategy." Jessie's strategy is to wish Kit would blend into the woodwork. For a Cherokee, she sure isn't much of a fighter. (Oh-my-gosh. Why do stereotypes keep invading my brain? I make a silent apology to Jessie, and to the Cherokee Nation.)

Anyway, Mom and David decided that since Woodsy was the only faculty person who witnessed the ugly scene at Kit's locker, it would be good if she could be at the meeting with us. Mom left a message on Woodsy's voice mail. She's waiting, roll book open on her lap, reading student papers. The adults do the introduction thing. Woodsy's brought copies of our witness statements, in case we don't have our own copies with us. We don't.

Mr. Maxwell comes out to greet us, then ushers us into his office.

As soon as everyone is seated, he says, "What we have here is a difficult situation."

"And it's been made more difficult by the way in which it was handled," David says.

There's a lot of back and forth banter and then Mom asks Mr. Maxwell to show her, in the education code, what grounds he has for my suspension. He talks about principal discretion, and Kit's defiance of authority.

David says Kit, and everyone else, has a right to be safe at school.

"I'm sure you're aware, Mr. Maxwell, that harassment of anyone based on race, sex, gender or sexual orientation is a criminal act," David says, sounding more like a lawyer than a cop. "Schools are legally required to protect students from such harassment."

Manly Max sputters around about making mountains out of molehills. Then he gets all heated about how Kit should do her part by dressing appropriately.

We're in Maxwell's office for over thirty minutes. He suspends our suspension, but when David demands that the worst of the boys, Brian, Anthony, and Justin, be suspended, he gets nowhere.

"I'll handle the boys in an appropriate manner," Mr. Maxwell says.

"What they've done *is* grounds for suspension, Mr. Maxwell," David says.

Mr. Maxwell stands, walks around his desk and opens the door.

"Thank you for coming in, Mrs. Wright, and Mr. Dandridge. I always appreciate talking with parents who care. Teachers, too," he says, giving a nod toward Woodsy.

He shakes hands with Mom and David on the way out. Woodsy rushes off to class. Kit and I get tardy excuses from Miss Ramirez and head toward our first period classes. Only a few latecomers are in the halls now, and Kit and I amble along, talking.

"I like that your dad came in his uniform," I tell Kit. "He's so cool with you."

"In some ways. But we got in a huge fight this morning. My mom, too."

"About what?"

"About the way I dress. Underneath it all, Dad agrees with Mr. Maxwell that I shouldn't be calling attention to myself. And Mom . . . she'd actually laid clothes out for me to wear this morning, like I was five years old and she could still be my fashion boss. I told her those days were over.

"Then she started crying about how hard she tried to be a good mother, and where did she go wrong. That's *all* I hear from her anymore."

"But your dad?"

"He'd like me to 'be more subtle.' Keep a lid on it until I'm in college, then it might not be such a big deal."

When I don't say anything more, Kit accuses me of thinking the same thing.

"That's not fair," I tell her.

"When I first told you, you even said . . ."

"Don't start throwing stuff in my face that I said months ago. I'm standing by you now, all the way, and you know it!"

I don't mean to be yelling but my *gosh* she pisses me off sometimes. *I'm* going to her damn group, *I'm* taking shit from Manly Max, right along with her . . .

"Sorry. SORRY!" she says, then lowers her voice. "I was so freaked Friday, in your kitchen — and you were totally there for me . . ."

We turn the corner into the main hall and stop. The display case is shattered. One of the custodians is sweeping up glass while a campus supervisor directs straggling students around the mess.

Kit and I check it out. Nothing in the case is disturbed, except Frankie's poster. **FLATTEN FAGGOT FILTH** is written across it, in large, heavy black strokes. In the corner is a stick figure hanging from a gallows, like in the hangman game. Underneath are seven separate lines, with three letters filled in. *F R _ _K _ _.*

Kit wants an emergency GSA meeting at lunchtime. We get an okay from Emmy to meet in the library, then let people know, word of mouth.

In peer communications, I start telling Conan about the broken display case, but he already knows.

"Who did it?" I ask.

"Round up the usual suspects," he says, glancing across the room toward Brian and Eric.

Conan won't name anyone, but I think he could if he wanted to.

I tell him I'll be in the library during lunch.

"Leaving me to eat alone?" he says.

"Like you don't always have a mob of hero worshipers wanting to hang around with you."

"But there's only one hero worshiper I want to eat lunch with," he says, smiling at me in that way he has — the way that still warms my soul and kicks up my heart rate.

"Come with me to the meeting," I say.

It looks as if he's thinking about it. Then he shakes his head.

"I'll be at the usual table if you change your mind about the meeting," he says. "Otherwise, I'll meet you outside the library after lunch."

Woodsy gives us the same assignment she gave to her afternoon class on Friday — write about homophobia. She offers a brief definition of homophobia — fear of homosexuals — and tells us to write our opinions, observations, and experiences.

Brian puts pencil to paper and acts like he's spelling out a title.

"F-a-g-o-p-h-o-b-i-a. Fagophobia," he calls out.

Eric laughs the loudest, but others laugh, too.

"Brian, please step into my office," Woodsy says. Her manner is stern.

She opens the door and stands waiting for Brian to enter. She walks in behind him, but is only gone a moment. Returning, she closes the door behind her.

"Please write freely, fully, and from your hearts," Woodsy says. "When you've finished writing, reread your paper and be sure it says what you want it to. After you've given me your papers you may use whatever time is left for study or free reading."

I have a hard time getting started. What can I say? I don't think I can relate to homophobia. I mean, what's to be afraid of just because a person is only attracted to people of the same sex? I don't get it. It's not like I ever see anyone standing back, quivering in fear when Frankie walks down the hall. It's more like they're laughing, or putting him down — like they're so much better than he is.

I'm still mulling this stuff over when I remember what Raymond said about how gay bashers are on shaky ground with their own sexual orientation. I don't exactly understand it, but what if some of the guys who pick on Frankie are afraid they're like him in some way? And by picking on him they're trying to prove they're not like him at all. But then, what does it mean when they pick on Kit? Are they afraid they might be like a lesbian? I've got to start writing. I'm only confusing myself. That's a start: "Homophobia is confusing to me . . ."

After we've both turned in our papers, Conan and I talk quietly.

"What did you write?" he asks me.

"I mostly wrote about how I don't understand homophobia. I know some people hate homosexuals — like it's immoral and against God. Like they hate evil. The fear part, though — what's that about?"

Conan says fear and hatred are part of the same thing. I still don't get it.

"What did you write?" I ask him.

"I didn't write about fear of homosexuals. I wrote about fear of Homo Sapiens."

"Fear of people???"

Conan nods.

"I don't think that's what Woodsy meant."

"Look at the word. Homophobia. It *could* mean that, couldn't it?"

"I guess. But it doesn't."

"Well, it does to me. I wrote about how fear of people messes up the whole world. Think about it. If that cop hadn't been afraid of Mark, then Mark'd still be alive today. And if white people hadn't been afraid of black people, we'd have been free of all that segregation shit a hundred years ago. We'd never even have had it in the first place."

"And if black people weren't afraid of white people, I wouldn't have to pick you up at the corner on the days I drive. I could pull right into your driveway, instead."

Conan gives me a look. There's a long pause. Then he says, "Maybe." That's all he says, but I can see my remark got to him.

22

All of the GSA members show up in the library for the lunch-time meeting. I see the Sojourner group got the word. There's Jerry, and Dawn, all Harleyed-out in her leathers. Even Susan, Conan's neighbor who eats Rice Krispies Treats with peanut butter and jelly for dinner. I haven't seen her since that first meeting at Sojourner High.

Mr. Cordova's here, too, and so is Woodsy.

"Sorry I didn't have time to make cookies," Guy says, as he passes out store bought cookies.

"At least they're not those dry old Mother's things."

"I *like* those cookies," I say, wanting to be supportive of Emmy.

Jerry says he wishes we could have macaroons sometime.

"So bring some," Star says.

Frankie stands. "We have more important things to talk about today than cookies," he says.

We go over the ground rules, like we do at the beginning of each meeting.

"Anything to add to the ground rules before we get started?" Frankie asks.

Mr. Cordova stands. "Not all of you know me, since I don't usually get to your meetings. But I want to assure you I'm here as a GSA supporter. I will adhere to your ground rules. EXCEPT . . ." he pauses to be sure we're all paying attention. "EXCEPT that I am compelled by law to report anything that would indicate you might be a threat to yourself or to others, or that your life is in any way endangered."

This is not exactly news to us. Emmy and Guy tell us the same thing at every meeting.

Frankie suggests we get caught up with what's been going on. He asks that Kit or I tell about the penis on the locker incident. Kit nods to me from across the room, where she's sitting next to Star. I guess she'd rather not be put on the spot. I start talking about seeing a group near our lockers. When I get to the part about the plastic penis and the white glue, the meeting comes undone, everyone talking at once.

"Those assholes!"

"That sucks!"

"Jock jerks! . . ."

Frankie finally makes himself heard over the angry roar.

"Can we please calm down? Let's get through this without interruption, then we'll open discussion."

There are a few more grumbles.

"Listen and reflect," Frankie says, which is what he always says when things get out of hand.

I continue then, telling the rest of the details, even though my face is burning with embarrassment. Our group is mainly student run, with advisors in the background, but it's a huge relief to me when Woodsy offers to tell the part about meeting with Mr. Maxwell. She takes notes from a folder, then stands and tells about our session with Mr. Maxwell.

"We should get caught up on the display case incident, too," she says to Frankie, then sits down.

Frankie sits looking at the floor.

"Who saw it?" Emmy asks.

Caitlin is, as usual, sitting off to one side, with Nora. In a voice that is barely audible, she says, "I saw it."

Everyone gets real quiet.

"So tell us," Jerry says.

Caitlin talks in a quiet monotone, as if she were a beginning reader, reading out loud for the first time. Weird. Her speaking voice is as weak as her singing voice is strong. Those of us on the other side of the room stretch forward across library tables, straining to hear. When she gets to the part about the hangman business she pauses. Tears well in her eyes. Nora fishes around in her backpack for a packet of tissues and hands it to Caitlin. Caitlin takes one, wipes her eyes, takes a deep breath, and finishes her account.

Frankie's still looking at the floor. He's slumped down in his chair, as if drained of all energy. I hope he's kept his promise, about not replacing the razor blades.

In the silence that follows, Mr. Cordova says "I know something about the display case incident."

"What?" Jerry asks.

"I have to trust that you'll hold to that ground rule — what's said here stays here."

Everyone nods, except Star, who says "Yeah. Unless it's information that says you're a threat to your own life . . ."

Guy shoots her such a look she stops mid-sentence. I've never seen such a nasty look on such a nice face.

"Only kidding," Star says to Mr. Cordova.

He waits, looking into her eyes as if he's trying to read her sincerity.

"Really," Star says. "I was out of line."

Another pause, then Mr. Cordova says, "There's a witness to the breaking of the display case, and the defacing of the poster. But the witness is afraid to come forward, so all we can get is an anonymous report. It's better than nothing because it offers important information, but we can't discipline anyone based on it."

Jerry says, "So nothing's going to happen to whoever did it?"

"Without real evidence, our hands are tied."

"Frankie's life's been threatened, and the school's just going to drop it?" Kit says.

There's a frenzy of outrage.

"If the school won't protect us, we better freakin' protect ourselves!" Star says, slamming her fist down on the table for emphasis.

Finally, Frankie looks up. "We need to stay united and come up with some workable strategies — not just vent."

"I'll strategize those guys if they come after Kit again," Star says.

Dawn stands. "And I'll give them a little extra strategy for you too, Frankie! I've got friends. You all know that!"

"C'mon, Dawn," Jerry says. "Now you're threatening the threateners?"

"Yeah, well I'm not one of those turn the other cheek chicks. Any more of this shit . . ."

"Dawn," Frankie says, pointing to the "share the air" ground rule. "Let's hear from everybody. Okay?"

Dawn takes her time sitting down. "I mean it," she says.

Star nods in agreement.

Jerry asks Frankie, "Are you and Kit the only ones taking shit?"

"I don't know," Frankie says.

"Maybe a place to start is to try to get an idea of the extent of harassment here at Hamilton High, or at Sojourner, for that matter," Guy says.

Emmy goes to the dry erase board with markers.

"C'mon. We've put our stories out there," Frankie says, showing more life now. "Anyone else being harassed? Put down? Pushed around? Think about it. Is this *our* school, too, or are we in enemy territory?"

Woodsy suggests we hand out cards for people who don't want to speak out. Even though it doesn't deal with the gay/lesbian stuff, I have a put-down that's been bugging me. On my card I write: "White meat." Then I fold the card and put it in my pocket.

Students begin talking, hesitantly at first, but soon the room is buzzing with the need to speak and be heard. Emmy writes shortened accounts of abuse, both verbal and physical.

In an amazingly short time, the board is filled.

"Let's read these back," Frankie says to Emmy.

"Name calling, as in dyke, faggot, queer, fudge-packer, carpet muncher, pervert, anti-Christ, girly boy, butt-fucker . . ." she goes through the list as if she were reading off a list of innocuous spelling words for a coming test — perfectly calm, except for the slightest quiver of her lower lip.

"A teacher laughing when one student calls another a faggot. Another teacher using the term 'that's so gay' — like gay is a synonym for dumb, or stupid. Lots of anti-gay stuff in the boys gym. Graffiti — fuck dykes 'til they're straight," she says, the quiver more noticeable now. Silently, she hands her marker to Guy and sits down. He continues reading from the board.

"Shoving gay, or thought to be gay, students in the halls, pretending it's accidental. Threatening remarks — See you tonight, Fag-bo, then yelling out the person's address or place of work. In gym, girls refusing to dress anywhere near someone they say is a 'clit-licker.'"

No one says anything for a long time after Guy finishes reading from the board. I don't know about the others, but I feel sick.

Caitlin has her head down on the desk, resting on her arms. Her eyes are closed. Frankie pulls a chair up next to her, on the other side of Nora. He whispers something and Caitlin nods, still with her head down.

Woodsy stands and looks around the room.

"The bell's going to ring in about five minutes," she says. "I don't want us to leave here on such a discouraging note. Look around the room and remember that we are here for one another." She pauses, following her own advice to look around the room.

"Close your eyes for a moment and envision all of the supportive people in your lives." Another pause.

"Love is stronger than hate."

"I hope so," Frankie says, "but we still need strategies."

We decide to meet again, after school.

Conan is waiting for me as I leave the library.

"Why so glum?" he says, falling in step beside me.

"Sorry."

I'm on the verge of telling him about everything that went up on the board, but the confidentiality thing stops me.

"I wish you'd been there," I tell him.

He smiles, shaking his head. "I get enough hassle from the team as it is, just for eating lunch with you at the same table as Kit and Frankie and some of your other friends."

"They're your friends, too," I remind him.

"I guess. Kit is, anyway."

"What about Frankie? You guys talk. Can't you say *he's* your friend?"

Pause.

"C'mon. Lighten up, Lynnie."

I try to. I really do. But I keep thinking about how hard it must be, to be insulted and pushed around because you're somehow different than what people think you should be. I can't get it off my mind.

At the door to the choir room, Conan kisses my forehead.

"See you after school. No practice today," he says.

"I'm going back to the library after school," I tell him.

"Why?"

"To finish the GSA meeting."

"Lynnie. Sweets," he says with that smile. "This is my only non-practice day for a week. I thought you'd want to spend it with me."

"I do, but . . ."

"No buts," Conan says.

"Come with me. It won't last too long."

Conan gets that stiff look on his face.

"I don't know why you're so caught up in this thing anyway. It's not like it's a club for people like you!"

"Gay *Straight* Alliance," I remind him. "Not everyone in there is gay, or lesbian, or whatever."

"Practically," he says.

"You don't know that."

"It doesn't take a genius . . ."

"There are plenty of straight people in the group," I say.

"Name them."

"No! What's said in the group stays in the group! Besides, most people don't even divulge whether they're gay, or straight, or whatever."

"Then how do you know there are plenty of straight people there?"

"I just do! This is a stupid conversation," I say.

I turn away and walk into the classroom. Then I get all scared and go running back out after Conan.

"I'm sorry. I'm just upset," I tell him.

"Meet me in the parking lot after school," he says.

Why shouldn't I? I ask myself, what's my top priority here? The answer is Conan.

"Okay," I say.

In the choir room, Frankie has the boys lined up in the back, practicing a basic step they'll be using in the silly Christmas songs section of our winter concert — "Rudolph the Red Nosed Reindeer," "All I Want for Christmas is My Two Front Teeth," — you get the idea. The girls are standing around the piano, working with Mr. Michaels on a few rough spots in "Dona Nobis Pacim." Caitlin has a short solo. She's been singing it perfectly for weeks, but today she starts off all wrong. She tries again, then stops. She wipes her eyes and shakes her head sadly.

Mr. Michaels motions for the rest of us to take a short break, and moves closer to Caitlin.

"What is it?" he asks softly.

She shakes her head. Nora comes over to them and says something to Mr. Michaels, who nods. Nora and Caitlin gather up their things and leave the classroom, Nora opening the door for Caitlin as if she were incapable of doing it for herself.

"What's wrong with Caitlin?" I ask Kit.

"I guess that whole business about Frankie and the hangman thing really got to her."

"Are they really good friends?"

Kit gives me one of those looks of disgust that she saves for special occasions.

"We *all* care about each other in GSA."

"Well, yeah. I mean that stuff's upsetting to all of us. But Caitlin . . ."

"Star said she'd heard some rumor that Caitlin's older brother was gay, and that he had some kind of tragic death."

"Where'd she hear that?"

"Gigi — this woman who hangs out at the coffee bar. But Star says you can only believe about half of what Gigi says."

Mr. Michaels calls the group back together.

"We'll start with the medley of carols," he says.

He waits a moment for us to find the music in our folders, then takes his little round pitch pipe from his jacket pocket, gives the pitch, and for the rest of the period we turn our total attention to singing. About half way through class our alto section becomes stronger and brighter, and I know that Caitlin's come back.

23

It's after ten o'clock when the phone rings.

"Where were you?" Kit demands, not even saying hello.

"What do you mean?"

"The meeting this afternoon?"

"I went with Conan instead. No football practice today."

Silence.

"How *was* the meeting?"

"You should have been there to see for yourself," Kit says.

"Hey. I have a life, too. You go to GSA meetings, you get to sit with Star, all up close and personal. I go to meetings and miss being with the one *I* love. So don't start."

More silence. Wilma is stretched out across my feet, her eyes half closed. I scratch behind her ears. She turns on her back, exposing her soft underside, wanting a belly rub.

"C'mon Kit. How'd it go?"

"Confidentiality," Kit says.

"I'm not asking for gossipy details. I'm wondering what strategies you came up with?"

Another silence. Then, finally, "We didn't do well with strategies. It was like, should we bake cookies and be more involved with other campus clubs, try to broaden our social base, or should we just bomb the boys' gym and get it over with."

"Let me guess whose suggestion that was."

Kit laughs. "I thought you didn't want gossipy details."

"Dawn better not be saying that stuff. She'll get the SWAT team on her butt."

"Right," Kit says, all sarcastic. "It's nothing for Frankie's life to be threatened, but stay away from the jocks."

"So anyway . . . the meeting."

"So anyway, it was frustrating. But Emmy told us about a national gay rights organization. We're arranging for a speaker to come talk to us."

"Sounds good," I say.

"Yeah. I can only hope it will be at a time when Conan has football practice," Kit says.

"Get over it! . . . "

Kit sighs. More silence.

"SO ANYWAY . . ."

Wilma stirs, opens one eye and looks up at me, as if asking me to quiet down.

"Yeah. Okay. I looked that organization up on the Internet."

"And . . ."

"There's this stuff about what's going on all over the country," she says, finally loosening up with me.

"Check out the website. It's awesome!"

In the middle of telling me how to find the website, though, Kit gets a call waiting beep. She flashes off, then comes back to let me know it is Star.

"Gotta go. See you in the morning," she says.

Kit has priorities, too.

After her shower, Mom comes to my room to say goodnight. She's in her old terrycloth robe, with a towel wrapped around her sopping hair.

"How'd the rest of your day go, after our conference?" she asks.

I tell her about the broken display case, and Frankie's poster.

"Do you think things are getting worse?"

"Maybe. Or maybe I never noticed how bad they were before."
She gives me a long, thoughtful look. "It's good that you're
standing up for Kit," she says.

"I guess. But sometimes I want all this stuff to go away, and for
things to be like they were before she started letting it be known that
she was a lesbian."

"Really?"

I consider her question.

"Really, I guess not," I say. "People should be able to be
themselves without taking a lot of . . ." I can't quite say the word.

"Shit?" Mom asks.

"Yeah. People shouldn't have to take shit just for being themselves."

Another thoughtful look from my pajama clad Mom, only now
she looks sad.

"I've been thinking about how I grew up, and how I'm afraid I've
fallen down on the job with you."

"What do you mean?"

"You know how Gramma and Grampa were, always trying to
make things better for other people. Or fighting what they thought
was wrong."

"Civil rights marches?"

"And anti-Vietnam war marches. They were even on some FBI
list of suspected communists."

"Gramma and Grampa?" I say, looking at their sweet, gentle
faces smiling at me from the collage over my desk.

"They took a stand. They thought the war was unjust, a terrible
mistake — so much death and destruction. They refused to pay their
telephone taxes, because that money went directly to finance the
war."

"Did they get in trouble?"

Mom laughs. "No. I think they just made it onto a list of very
good people."

She walks over to the collage and looks closely at their picture.

When she turns back to me there are tears in her eyes.

"Remember when we saw them on the six o'clock news? They were at a demonstration at the Federal Building. Remember that?"

I nod.

"That was only six months before Gramma died," Mom says, again looking at their picture.

"I remember seeing them on TV, but I don't remember what the demonstration was about."

"They wanted amnesty for illegal immigrants. 'Those people grow our food, tend our gardens, clean our houses! They have inalienable rights, too!' Gramma told me."

"What happened?" I ask. "Did it work?"

"Well . . . things got better, then the other side fought harder . . . it's that pendulum thing. But Grampa always said that even if the road to justice is two steps forward, one step back, there is still forward movement. I like to believe he was right."

Mom looks at the other pictures in my collage, like she's seeing them fresh.

"I'm proud of you," she says.

Then she unwraps the towel from around her head and uses it to vigorously rub small sections of hair from the ends to the scalp, working her way from side to back to side. She is so intent upon her task, that I'm afraid she will forget to tell me why she is proud of me.

When no hair is left untouched, she takes her brush from the pocket of her robe and brushes her hair — about eighty strokes short of the recommended one hundred. Like mine, Mom's hair is wiry — a nondescript brown. I try not to hold it against her, that she passed her hair on to me. But why couldn't she have hair like Jessie Dandridge's? THAT would have been an inheritance. You can be sure I wouldn't have wasted it, like Kit did. I'd let it grow down to the middle of my back. It would glimmer in the sunlight. Conan would run his fingers through it slowly, lifting it, letting it fall, caught by the beauty . . .

" . . . thinking about how they showed me it was important to stand up for what's right . . ."

Oops. Unruly thoughts.

"... but I get so caught up in my work, and keeping things going around here, I forget to look beyond us, at the broader world ... Gramma used to have a sign on her refrigerator that said, 'All that is necessary for evil to triumph is for good people to do nothing.' Something like that, anyway ... I wonder whatever happened to that sign?"

Mom's getting a faraway look in her eye. I'm pretty sure I got my tendency for unruly thoughts from her.

Right now, I'm worried that Mom's already past the part where she's proud of me, and I missed it during my hair thoughts. And now *her* thoughts are all wandering, and I may never know what she first came to tell me. I'll have to ask straight out.

"Why are you proud of me?"

She does this mom kind of thing — intent eye contact.

"Because you have the courage to stand up for what's right, even if I haven't been a very good example for you."

I feel a twinge of guilt, knowing how I just blew off the afternoon's GSA meeting. On the other hand, I know what Mom's saying is at least partly true.

She gives me a long hug. "You're a good person, and I'm glad you're my daughter," she says. Then she's off to bed.

All the while I'm doing homework, I have this thing in the back of my mind that says my mom's proud of me. I like it.

In the morning, Conan gets to my house earlier than usual. We sit in the car, talking, waiting for Kit. After a few minutes, she comes rushing through the gate, her backpack thrown over one shoulder, a bunch of papers in her hand. She's talking before she even closes the car door behind her.

"You won't believe what I found on the Internet last night! It is so vicious! Are people born cruel, or what? And half of these ... "

"What are you *talking* about?" Conan says, glancing at Kit in the rearview mirror as he pauses at the end of our driveway.

"This!" Kit says, waving around several sheets of paper. "This is from a website I found last night. It lists crimes, thousands of them, against people who are homosexual, or trans, or whatever —

it's sick! But here's the really awful part. Listen to this!"

Kit reads from what I now see is a printout from a website.

Vincent Ratchford, twenty-four, Chico, California. Found dead in his off-campus apartment. Apparent cause of death, blunt force trauma to the head. Unsolved.

"**R**atchford, like in Caitlin Ratchford?" I ask.

"Yeah, so then I clicked on his name and found more information. It's got to be her brother."

"Are you sure?" Conan asks.

"Listen," she says, and reads more details from the printout.

"Born in Los Angeles. Grew up in Running Springs, California. Survivors include grandparents, parents, younger sister. That's got to be Caitlin. It's not exactly like their last name is Smith."

"But Running Springs . . ."

"Right. I did the math. This thing happened six years ago. I bet they moved here shortly after."

"God," Conan says. "No wonder she's the way she is."

"One of the news reports said DEATH TO PERVERTS was written in big letters all across the wall — in lavender paint."

The rest of the way to school, we ride in heavy silence, then sit, immobilized, in the parking lot. Finally, Conan says, "Homo Sapiens. Freakin' Homo Sapiens."

Kit looks at him, puzzled. He turns to me, kisses me, gets his stuff out of the car and walks slowly toward the gym. Kit and I head off in the opposite direction toward the main building.

"What'd he mean by that?" Kit asks.

I tell her about Conan's response to the "homophobia" assignment we had in Woodsy's class. How he wrote about people fearing people, and how that's the cause of a lot of messed up stuff. Kit's quiet. Thinking, I suppose.

"Conan's smarter than he seems," Kit says.

"What's *that* supposed to mean?"

"Just . . . you know, that stupid jock thing . . . and he's so big, and sort of sweet, like that big dumb guy in *Of Mice and Men* . . ."

"And black!" I say. "That's what you really mean, isn't it?"

I know a bright red is creeping from my neck upward. So what? I'm angry, and I don't care who sees it.

"No! Oh, my gosh! You know I didn't mean it like that!"

We're both stopped in the middle of the hall, facing one another, with a stream of students hurrying around us.

"I'd never dis Conan. I totally respect him."

I stand looking at her, projecting my bright red color in her direction.

"Look! I'm half Cherokee! I know better than to believe any of that racist trash."

I sigh. Why did I jump to the conclusion that my liberty-and-justice-for-all friend would suddenly turn racist? It doesn't even make sense.

"Sorry," I say . . . "It's just . . . "

"You've only got one nerve left, and I just stepped on it," she says, quoting from a poster of a harried woman that hangs over Woodsy's desk.

I laugh.

"Spirit sisters?"

We grasp hands for a moment, long enough to remember our spirits come from the same source. Then we go to our separate first period classes.

During physiology we go over terms and functions of the alimentary canal. Just thinking about the gunk that's hanging out in my gastronomic tract is enough to make me want to reverse peristalsis and barf my breakfast. I've got to get tougher or change career plans.

Conan is waiting for me at the end of first period, so we can walk together to PC.

"Do you think Kit's right, and it was really Caitlin's brother who was killed?"

"Sure sounds like it," Conan says.

"That's just so sad. I feel awful about it. Poor Caitlin."

"Even if it's not Caitlin's brother, it's someone's brother,"

Conan says.

The first thing I notice when I enter Woodsy's class is a bright, multicolored, rainbow sign over the chalkboard. It's about four feet long and a foot high. Printed across the colorful background, in silver letters, is "NO ROOM FOR HOMOPHOBIA."

"What happened to 'Make Lemonade'?" Eric asks.

"It was time for a change," Woodsy says.

"I like the lemonade poster better," Eric says.

"Fine. When you're the teacher in this classroom, you can put it back up."

I can tell this will be a no nonsense day in PC. Woodsy hands out a list of what's required for the next notebook check. In the front of our notebooks we keep a laminated copy of our PC contract — the one we all signed at the beginning of the semester, promising to maintain confidentiality, and to treat one another, and guests, with respect. The next notebook section contains a daily activity log, telling what we did, and rating that period on a scale of one to ten. Then we have sections for speakers, group projects, class discussion, individual reading and other comments.

"What do you have in your log for November 3?" Conan asks.

I turn to my log sheet. "That was the day we did the role play thing, remember? You were the mean dad, and Tiffany was out way past her curfew?"

Conan laughs. "And you were the pesty little sister, and Kendra was trying to talk you out of tattling," he says, filling in the 11/3 blank in his log sheet.

"What about 10/30?" I ask.

"Individual reading," he says.

We go through the rest of the period, working back and forth to fill in the blanks.

Nora is at our lunch table today, but Caitlin is not. I don't think I've ever seen one without the other before.

Conan and I sit side by side, sharing lunches. Well . . . mostly I share mine.

"Mom sent extra brownies for you," I say, passing a couple of brownies his way.

He takes a bite and rolls his eyes skyward, chewing slowly, appreciating every last crumb.

"I love your mom."

"And . . .?"

"And what?"

"And what about ME?" I ask, acting all jealous.

"Ummm. You, too," he says, then takes another bite of brownie.

At the other end of the table, I see Kit showing Nora the printout she'd read to us earlier. Nora nods her head and looks away. Frankie, looking over Kit's shoulder, doesn't seem surprised. I wonder if he's known all along.

In the choir room, Mr. Michaels has a NO ROOM FOR HOMOPHOBIA sign exactly like Woodsy's. His is prominently displayed across the top of the choir bulletin board.

We rehearse the Christmas music again, but we don't sound as good as when Caitlin's here.

Before we start volleyball practice, Coach Terry calls us together.

"I think by now everyone's heard of a couple of malicious incidents that have taken place on our campus, but just in case . . ."

She relates the details of the locker incident, and also of the vandalized display case and the hate message left on the GSA poster.

"These are serious, disturbing events," Coach Terry says, "and they must not be tolerated. Anyone who thinks this kind of behavior is a joke needs to adjust her attitudes."

I glance over at Nicole, who is staring at the ground.

"Women athletes often are the targets of dyke jokes," Coach Terry says, looking at each of us individually before she continues. "This is unacceptable. No one . . . NO ONE! . . . has the right to ridicule another person."

Gail, great spiker, slow thinker, says "But what if the person really is a . . ."

"Dyke? Lesbian? Woman who is attracted to women?" Coach Terry prompts.

Gail nods.

"Is it acceptable for a straight male to be taunted and harassed because he is attracted to women?"

All eyes are on Terry, who looks directly at Gail.

"Is it?" she asks.

Gail shakes her head no.

"Listen. We are all creatures of the earth, and as such we are entitled to the utmost respect. On this team, such respect is *mandated*."

Terry puts us through a tough workout, calls us back together, and talks about our coming game.

"Franklin's the toughest team we've played. But we're the toughest team they've played. Tomorrow afternoon's game will either take us to the playoffs, or be our last of the season. You're awesome," she says. "It's an honor to work with you." She reminds us of the respect mandate and sends us off to shower.

In the gym, after showers, we towel off and dress, all of us near the middle of the room, instead of me and Kit at one end and the whole rest of the team at the other. I guess Coach Terry's talk helped close the great divide.

When I stop by the library after practice, I notice there are three NO ROOM FOR HOMOPHOBIA signs posted at various places in the main room. I guess Frankie's been busy printing signs.

We *are* an awesome volleyball team. But so is Franklin. In spite of all the conditioning, Kit's amazing serve, my set-ups, Gail's spikes, we lose by two points. The season is over for us. When I realize I've played my last high school volleyball game . . . I don't want to get all blubbery about it, but it's been a big part of my life, and it's a strange feeling to know it's over.

24

W e've posted flyers in all of the English classrooms —
everyone has an English class.

7:00 PM TUESDAY
SAFE SCHOOLS:
EVERYONE'S RIGHT. EVERYONE'S RESPONSIBILITY
Bring parents and other concerned adults.
Refreshments will include delicious homemade cookies.
Sponsored by: **H.H.S. GAY STRAIGHT ALLIANCE**

T hree days after posting flyers in English classes, probably less
than half still remain in classrooms. When I ask Miss Banks what
happened to hers, she gives me a blank look.

"What flyer, dear?"

"The one that announced the special GSA meeting."

She looks around the room. "Well, I don't know. Someone must
have taken it down when I wasn't looking."

It's not until later in the period that I wonder about Miss Banks'
explanation for the missing poster. Someone must have taken it
when she wasn't looking? She's *always* looking.

Tuesday evening Kit, Frankie, Star, Emmy and I get to the library early to set things up. We're arranging chairs in a circle when Frankie points to the NO ROOM FOR HOMOPHOBIA sign at the far end of the library. Emmy groans.

"How could that have happened without me seeing it?"

PHOBIA has been blacked out, and in its place there is a big, glittery, silver S. So now the sign reads NO ROOM FOR HOMOS.

Emmy pulls a chair over next to the wall, climbs up on it, and tears the defaced sign down.

"I'm sure it wasn't like this when I left for lunch."

She rips the sign into little pieces and shoves the pieces into the trash.

"There are more where that came from," Frankie says, grinning. "They mess them up, we replace them."

"You must be spending a fortune on printing costs," Emmy says.

"It's cool," he says. "I'm doing some design work for Kinkos, and they're letting me use their stuff."

"Great, Frankie!" Emmy says. "A job where you get to use your talent!"

Frankie does a Fred Astaire shuffle and turn, bows low, and says, "*One* of my talents."

We all laugh, then the ever-practical Star reminds us of the time, and we get back to rearranging the room. Guy shows up with dozens of cookies and china plates and cups. Jerry is right behind him, carrying a huge coffee maker.

"Let's put this table over to the side, where it will be easy for people to serve themselves," Guy says.

Kit and I move the table while Guy shakes out a tablecloth. He covers the table, then sets out china cups and saucers and two large, matching plates.

"Hey, Guy — We've got plenty of plastic plates and cups," Emmy says, walking toward the back where she keeps such supplies. "We've even got a paper tablecloth . . ."

"Stop! Do *not* take another step! I do *not* drink from plastic and my cookies will *not* be displayed on plastic . . ."

"I'm only thinking about clean up," Emmy says.

"And *I'm* thinking about the whole experience," Guy says, reaching into a large paper bag and carefully arranging cookies on the plates.

"Try this," he says to Jerry, handing him a cookie.

Jerry looks at the cookie with suspicion, then takes a small bite.

"Wow! Macaroons!" he says.

At that moment, Jerry looks like he's about five years old, all innocent, and caring only about a cookie. I know that sounds strange — Jerry with his green Mohawk and piercings, his eye make-up, spiked collar and wristband. It's true, though. The macaroon moment flashed an image of an earlier Jerry.

"Hey, man. Thanks," he says, giving Guy a quick hug.

Guy passes the plate to the rest of us. "Anyone else want a pre-meeting cookie?"

Of course, we all do. Guy replenishes the plate and takes a long look at the table, then rearranges the coffee cups. I stack extra chairs back by the computers, so people will have to sit in the circle. Star cleans the dry erase board and makes sure the markers are good. Kit's wandering through the stacks.

"Hey, Emmy. You should have that *Our Bodies Ourselves* book in here."

"I do," Emmy says.

"Where?"

"Look in reference."

A large woman comes in carrying a khaki shoulder bag and a clipboard.

"Emmy?" she says, looking around the room.

Emmy walks over to her and shakes hands.

"Benny Foster, from GLSEN."

"I'm Emmy Saunders, and this is Guy Reyes. We're the GSA co-advisors. This is Star, and . . ."

Emmy introduces each of us, except Kit, who's still hidden somewhere in the stacks.

Benny unloads her bag, putting various books and flyers on a table near the back of the room. I guess she's probably about my mom's age. Her hair is cropped short and her face is plain and weathered. She's wearing jeans, a heavy flannel shirt, and industrial style boots. Maybe she just got off lumberjack duties and didn't have time to change her clothes? Maybe I was expecting the GLSEN version of Barbie? Maybe I should get a grip?

"You know you've got picketers out there?" Benny asks, continuing to set out materials.

"Who are they?" Guy says.

"The 'God made Adam and Eve, Not Adam and Steve,' bunch."

Emmy picks up the school phone and calls for security. No answer.

"There's got to be someone around here," she says. "We've got Adult Ed classes, and ROP, and . . . "

Mr. Cordova comes in, accompanied by a student I've seen around but don't really know.

"Oh, Victor. I'm glad you're here. We have picketers . . ."

"I know, I've been out there."

Mr. Cordova motions me over.

"Lynn, this is Felicia. I talked her into coming, but she's reluctant. Watch out for her, will you?"

"Sure," I say.

"Do we need security out front?" Guy asks Mr. Cordova.

"I've got Larry coming up, and the new woman, Kelly. Just a precaution, though."

"How many are there?" Frankie asks.

"Umm, maybe about twenty. I warned them against blocking the entrance."

A few more people come in and now there's a buzz of voices as people talk and help themselves to coffee and cookies.

"Do you want a cookie?" I ask Felicia.

She shakes her head no.

"Are you a sophomore?" I ask, making a wild guess — well, except how wild can you be, when you've only got four choices?

This time, Felicia nods her head yes. I wonder if our whole means of communication will be me talking, she nodding. She's quite thin, and pale — birdlike, in a graceful, fragile way. She's wearing a necklace with a cross, like the ones Eric and Tiffany wear.

"The cookies are really good. Guy made them."

She shakes her head again, but this time utters a faint no thank you.

Kit finally emerges from her exploration of the stacks.

"There's some good ten percenter stuff in here," she says.

Emmy looks Kit's way. "And that surprises you?"

"Well . . . I just never found it before."

"And you never asked . . ."

"I bet there are plenty of others around who aren't asking, either," Kit says.

"But *you* finally asked."

"Because it was safe. It may not have felt safe during school hours."

From the expression on Emmy's face, it's as if Kit just sent a news flash her way. She walks toward us, but is interrupted by a couple of parent types who've just entered.

I introduce Kit to Felicia. Kit sits with us for a few minutes, but then Star motions her to sit by her, across the room. That's cool. If Conan were here, I'd want to sit with him, too.

It is nearly seven now, and the place is filling up. Nora and Caitlin come in with someone I think must be Caitlin's parents, because Caitlin and the woman look like they could be clones.

Frankie's mom is here, looking nervous. Star's "adopted" mom is here, too. Both of Kit's parents and my mom come in together and sit over near the Ratchfords. Kit's mom looks about as comfortable here as Mrs. Sanchez does. Kit goes over to talk to them, then returns to her place next to Star. Mom gives me a quick wave, and a smile. I smile back, glad she's come.

Frankie and Dawn take a few more chairs from the stack to enlarge the circle. Emmy introduces herself, welcomes people to the library, then introduces Benny, who will be offering strategies meant to achieve a safe school environment for all students. I catch Kit's mom staring at Jerry, then at Benny, as if she's never seen anyone like them. She gives Dawn an appraising look, too. The one person she doesn't seem to notice is Kit, sitting close to Star, with Star's arm around her shoulders.

We introduce ourselves around the circle, each telling our name, and something we like — an activity, food, color, any one thing.

Jerry says he likes macaroons, holding one out for all to see, then popping the whole thing in his mouth. Everyone laughs, even Jessie. That can't hurt. When it's David's turn, he says he likes his daughter. Kit smiles, but it's an embarrassed kind of smile. When it's Star's turn, she says she likes David's daughter, too. That brings another laugh, although this time Jessie's laugh is less than hearty.

Mr. Harper and Woodsy come in just after introductions, but we pause for them each to say who they are and what they like.

Guy explains that GSA is a student run organization, and suggests that adults listen first, then talk if there's something new to be said. Frankie goes over the ground rules, asks if there are any additions, or objections, and then Benny hauls her big lumberjack body out of her chair. She starts with national statistics regarding experiences of LGBT youth. (No — LGBT is not a sandwich. It's an acronym for lesbian, gay, bisexual and transsexual.)

Benny reads from a pamphlet. "Ninety percent of LGBT youth hear homophobic remarks in their schools — words such as faggot, dyke, or queer. Thirty-six percent hear such remarks from faculty or school staff. Sixty-one percent experience verbal harassment. Forty-six percent experience sexual harassment — including comments and touching. Twenty-seven percent experience physical harassment. Fourteen percent experience physical assault. Forty-one percent do not feel safe in their school because of their sexual orientation. Thirty percent of all teen suicides come from LGBT youth, which make up only ten percent of the teen population. LGBT youth are four times more likely to skip school because they feel unsafe."

Pause.

Jessie says, "Then why are they like that if it's so awful?"

Benny waits a moment, seemingly gathering her thoughts. Then she asks, "When you woke up this morning, did you decide to be heterosexual?"

"No," Jessie says.

"When you wake up tomorrow morning, will you decide to be

homosexual?"

"No! Why would I?"

"Could you, if you wanted to?"

"No!"

"Well then, does it make sense to you that *I*, or others like me, could wake up in the morning and decide to be *heterosexual*?"

Benny and Jessie maintain eye contact for a long time. Finally, Jessie looks away.

"I suppose not," Jessie says, but I'm not sure she believes it.

Kit slides down in her seat. Are we off to a good start here, or what?

Frankie says to Benny, "The statistics you just read scare me. They're my friends, they're me."

"Our son is a statistic," Mr. Ratchford says.

Pause.

He has our attention.

"Dead six years now."

Another pause.

"I'm terrified that my daughter could become a statistic, too, if we can't somehow deal with the tragedy of Vincent's murder."

Pin drop silence. And more silence. Mr. Ratchford puts his arm around Caitlin. Mrs. Ratchford sits looking straight ahead, at nothing, tears streaming down her cheeks.

The door opens and a tall woman in a red wool suit, silk blouse and red leather shoes stands frozen, taking in the scene. Her nails are manicured and her soft brown hair, complete with highlights, is neatly styled. "Classic" would be the advertising term if she were a featured model.

Jerry eases out of his chair and walks over to her.

"It's okay, Mom. Come on in," he says in a whisper. He leads her to his chair, then pulls up another and sits directly behind her.

As caught as I am by the Ratchford drama unfolding before me, I can't help also being caught by the contrast between Jerry and his mom. She looks as if she's just stepped out of a high-powered executive meeting, and he looks as if he's the cover child for *Beyond Bizarre*.

As far as the meeting goes, it's too late to make a long story short. I can at least try to condense a few things for you, though.

It turns out that the Ratchfords came to Hamilton Heights for a fresh start, after their son, Caitlin's brother, was murdered. For Caitlin's sake, they didn't want to dwell on their sorrow, so no one ever talked about Vincent, or his death. But for days, ever since the threat to Frankie, Caitlin's been begging her parents to stop acting as if nothing happened. She loved her brother, loves him still. She misses him every day. She wants to be able to talk about him with her parents. She wants pictures of him back up in the house. She wants to keep him alive in her heart and in her memory. If she can't even have that much of him . . .

That's why they came to the meeting tonight. For Caitlin, and for Vincent. They decided that the best way to honor Vincent's life was to work against the terror of homophobia. Part of their work will be to talk about Vincent, and to share their experiences with others.

When the whole story finally was told, we sat like lumps, drained. Then Frankie stepped between Mrs. Ratchford and Nora, and took their hands, and then we all joined hands.

"We'll work together," Frankie said.

Does this sound like a daytime soap, or what? But I tell you, it was real life, and I'll never forget it. I doubt that anyone else will, either.

After the intensity of the Ratchford story, things were somewhat subdued. Jerry's mom and Star's "adopted" mom told about their experiences with PFLAG, and encouraged others to come to the next meeting. We took a short "cookie" break, during which time people chatted and browsed around the library. I saw Kit lead a reluctant Star over to David and Jessie and make introductions. That was brave of Kit. I hope Conan will be that brave some day.

Here's some of what we learned from Benny Foster during the second part of our meeting: The education code protects students from discrimination and harassment because of gender and sexual orientation, in the same way that it protects against discrimination based on religion, race or sex. Crimes against people for those reasons are classified as hate crimes, and they're punished more severely.

Cool.

She outlined specific steps to follow if a school doesn't work to protect students. Go to the school board, which has an obligation to follow certain procedures to protect students, and to resolve complaints. If the school board doesn't follow through, the State Department of Education is obligated to take over. If *that* doesn't get anywhere, Benny's advice is to sue the school district. Sounds extreme. But when you think about it, what Frankie experiences, and Kit, and lots of others, is pretty extreme, too.

Benny told us of a case about a hundred miles north of here in which a student filed a lawsuit against his school district, and won. The guy had experienced constant verbal harassment, some even from teachers. He was spat upon in the halls, threatened, pushed, and his complaints were ignored.

"Believe me, your school district does not want any such lawsuit. Your principal may be reluctant to do the right thing, but you've got the law behind you and eventually he'll realize that."

By the time Benny leaves, I see that she's a very nice person, who knows a whole lot about how GSA groups can fight discrimination, and who's working hard to spread the word.

It was late by the time we washed Guy's dishes and set the library back in order. The picketers were gone. I'd hoped to see them, but I suppose if I keep hanging around GSA groups, I'll have other chances. The thing is, until tonight, I've thought I was going to GSA mainly for Kit, and maybe a little for Frankie. But now I know it's for me. I want to stand up for what's right, like my gramma and grampa did. I don't want to be one of those good people who do nothing, and allow evil to triumph. Not that I expect to change the world and everyone in it. I'll just work on this little H.H.S. piece of the world.

25

At the beginning of second period, in PC, a bunch of students are crowded around a table looking at the newspaper. I squeeze in beside Conan. **UPHOLD FAMILY VALUES PLEA** is the headline on the front page of the *Hamilton Heights Daily News*. Pictured below are thirty or so picketers gathered in front of the school's main entrance. Conan reads aloud:

A group calling itself Americans for Family Values (AFV) gathered at Hamilton High School to demand that the school's Gay Straight Alliance (GSA) be immediately and permanently banned. AFV claims that GSA is a major factor in the "rising tide of perversion" on our city's high school campus.

The demonstration was prompted by last night's GSA meeting, which included club members, school advisors, and other concerned adults. Stanley Weiss, father of a Hamilton High School senior . . .

"**C**ool!" Brian says, giving Eric a high five. "Your dad hit the front page!"

Eric laughs. "I know. He sent me out to Kinko's to get a hundred copies at 5:30 this morning."

. . . and spokesperson for the demonstrators, stated that "GSA's inclusion of a GLSEN (Gay Lesbian and Straight Education Network) representative at tonight's meeting shows their contempt for the values Americans hold dear." Weiss also claimed that GLSEN blatantly promotes aberrant lifestyles, and recruits innocent youth into a life of sexual perversion.

"Oh my gosh! That's so stupid!" I say.

Woodsy comes out of her office just as the bell rings.

"I swear, if any of those butt fuckers comes near me . . ."

"Eric!"

"Sorry, Ms. W. I meant to say hom-o-sex-u-al," he says, dragging the word out in a sing-songy tone.

Brian and a few others, mostly boys, laugh.

"And I meant to say go see Mr. Cordova," Woodsy says, scribbling out a referral and handing it to Eric.

"Class hadn't even started!" he whines.

"Go."

Eric crumples the referral into his pocket and slams out the door.

"That's cold," Brian says.

"Read that sign, please," Woodsy says, pointing to the rainbow sign.

Long pause.

Finally he reads, "NO ROOM FOR HOMOPHOBIA."

"And this, too," Woodsy says, pointing to the red and white sign over the other end of the chalkboard.

"NO PUT-DOWNS," Brian reads.

"Thank you," Woodsy says. "I want to remind you all of your promise to maintain confidentiality and to treat one another with respect. Are we together on this?" Woodsy asks.

There is a general murmur of assent.

"Conan?"

"I'm cool."

"Steven?"

He nods.

"Tiffany?"

"Sure."

"Brian?"

"Whatever."

"Not good enough, Brian. Respect. Confidentiality. Got it?"

"Yeah. Okay," he says, doodling in his notebook

Woodsy picks up the paper, shows the headline and picture, then reads the article. The part Conan didn't get to, before the bell rang, says:

GSA advisors Guy Reyes and Emily Saunders say the special meeting was called to explore ways of ensuring school safety for all students. Benny Foster, the GLSEN representative, labeled Mr. Weiss' charges of recruitment "ludicrous." As for upholding traditional American values, Ms. Foster stated, "Maybe AFV should go back to school and brush up on American traditions. Have they forgotten the right to freedom of assembly? Maybe they could revisit the First Amendment. Is the right to free speech not an American tradition?"

"**W**here's the truth?" Woodsy asks.

"The part about recruitment into sexual perversion's a total lie," I say.

"It is not!" Brian says, flashing an angry look my way. "Eric's dad showed me a web site that . . ."

"Let's stick to the article," Woodsy says. "What are the major issues here? How does any of this affect life at Hamilton High?"

In spite of Woodsy's call for respect and no put-downs, the discussion doesn't quite live up to her guidelines. Here are some comments from period two PC:

GSA is cool.

Homosexuality is a sin.

Homosexuality is the perfect means of birth control.

GSA sucks.

There should be one school for homosexuals, so they won't be trying to hit on normal people.

Homos breed AIDS.

GSA clubs shouldn't be allowed.

Everyone has a right to be who they want to be.

Any pervert tries to touch me, he's dead (this remark was brought to us courtesy of Brian Marsters).

What's the big deal?

I've only mentioned a few of the comments, but that's enough for you to see that people are pretty opinionated when it comes to the whole gender identity thing.

At the jock table, Eric's passed around copies of the morning's newspaper article.

"Hey Eric. Your ol' man's right. That pervert club should be banned!"

Justin supposedly yells his comment to Eric, but he's looking at our table the whole time.

"My dad says it's up to all of us normal people to stem the rising tide of perversion!" Eric yells.

"I'll do my part!" Brian says.

They laugh their mean laughs.

"How about you, Robert?" Justin calls over to our table, where Robert and Holly sit eating their lunch.

Robert smiles nervously, and keeps eating. We *all* try to ignore the other table, but it's not easy. Before the bell rings, the jocks gather up their trash and walk past our table. As Brian and Eric walk past Frankie, they "accidentally" spill stuff on his head and neck — leftover milk, from Eric, and bits of catsup soaked lettuce from Brian.

"Oooooh, I'm tho thorry," Brian lisps in a phony high-pitched voice. He strikes a limp-wristed pose, then licks his pinky and runs it across an eyebrow, all to the great amusement of Justin, Eric and Anthony. The four of them strut across the quad, laughing, showing off. Hardly anyone else is laughing, but no one is saying what jerks they are, either.

Frankie sits, unmoving, and I remember what he told us that night under the tree — about how when things were really awful for him, he turned himself to stone.

Kit stands and starts picking pieces of lettuce from Frankie's hair, wiping the catsup off, one strand of hair at a time.

Conan brings a bottle of water and a handful of fresh napkins back from the lunch counter.

"They're pond scum," Kit says. "Don't let them get to you."

She takes a dampened napkin from Conan and wipes carefully around Frankie's ears and at the back of his neck. Conan gives her a fresh napkin and she works on his hair again. All of this time, Frankie looks straight ahead, stony.

Across from Frankie, Caitlin watches, teary eyed. Dr. Kit thinks Frankie reminds Caitlin of her brother. That's why it's doubly upsetting to her when anyone picks on him.

The bell rings. We all gather our stuff to go to class, but Frankie sits there, immobile.

Caitlin and Nora stand waiting. So do the rest of us. My guess is that none of us wants to leave Frankie out here alone.

"C'mon, man," Conan says. "I'll walk with you."

Pause.

Finally, Frankie looks up at Conan. "It's okay," he says. "They've had their fun for the day."

"We'll walk together anyway," Conan says.

Conan, Kit, Nora, Caitlin, Holly, Nicole and I, with Frankie in the very middle, walk to choir. Douglas and Brian are talking near the door to the choir room. Brian points to Frankie and says something to Douglas that gets a big laugh. Brian and Conan, the saviors of the Hamilton High football team, exchange angry glances.

Once inside the door, Frankie becomes his old, pre-trashed self. He gets the girls lined up to practice a new piece of choreography, and Mr. Michaels works on specific sections with the boys. I'm leaning against the back wall, waiting for my turn to practice with Frankie, when I get a glimpse of movement from Douglas, down close to the piano. He's standing out of Mr. Michaels' line of vision, but where the other singers can see him. He nods in Frankie's direction, then does the pinky licking, eyebrow smoothing thing that pond scum use as a gay stereotype.

Mr. Michaels turns his head just in time to see Douglas's gesture. Practice stops.

"Mr. West, show us that again, please," Mr. Michaels says.

Douglas turns red.

"Lost your nerve, have you?"

Mr. Michaels is an awesome choir teacher. But he's not what you'd call big on anger control. And when he starts addressing students as Mr. or Miss . . . watch out. We're all attentive now, eagerly anticipating the coming drama.

"Sneakiness does not become you, Mr. West."

Douglas says nothing.

Mr. Michaels makes a theatrical sweep of his arm, pointing to *the* sign, which I suppose means we're getting *another* impromptu lesson on the homophobia theme. Cool.

"DO YOU SEE THAT?" Mr. Michaels yells out in his best, operatic style.

Douglas nods, the red of his face now nearly purple.

"BELIEVE IT, MR. WEST! THERE IS NO ROOM FOR HOMOPHOBIA IN CHOIR! GET OUT!"

Mr. Michaels turns so that his outstretched arm now points to the door. Douglas gathers his things and leaves. Any other teacher would write up a referral, but Mr. Michaels never bothers with paper work when the need to banish a student arises. Once he sent a girl out for chewing gum. Where shall I go, she'd asked. To the fiery place for all I care had been his answer.

"Anyone else suffering from an incapacity to control their homophobic impulses?"

He makes eye contact with everyone in the room, one at a time.

"Choir is about making music together, from our purest hearts and from our purest souls. If disrespect exists among us, then we can't do justice to music."

Pause.

"All right. Boys."

He raises his arms, gives the downbeat, and proceeds with the rehearsal.

Since there is no rainbow-homophobia sign in Miss Banks room, we should be free of that particular focus.

I mean, I appreciate that Woodsy and Mr. Michaels are paying attention, and demanding respect. But right now, I'm sort of tired of the subject.

After school I make a quick trip to the library, to return *The Way Forward Is with a Broken Heart*. It was okay, but I didn't love it the way I loved *The Color Purple*.

Kit is standing at a table with books spread out all over it. She's putting little rainbow triangle stickers on the spines.

"What's that for?" I ask.

"Emmy's idea. Now it will be easy to find books that relate to sexual orientation and related stuff . . ."

I pick up a book and browse through it, then another.

"There's a lot here," I say, taking a sticker and putting it on the spine of the book I'm holding.

"Yeah, but it doesn't do any good if people like me can't find it."

"Nobody's going to know what these stickers mean," I say.

"Yeah they will. Frankie's making a flyer that'll go on the check-out counter, and Emmy's going to put an announcement in the bulletin."

"I'm meeting Conan in about fifteen minutes," I tell Kit. "Want a ride?"

"If I can get these books finished," she says.

I take a sheet of stickers and start applying them to book spines. Kit picks up her pace and we finish with time to spare.

We get to the parking lot just as Conan is leaving the gym. The first thing I notice is how badly he's limping. Then I see he's holding an ice pack to his forehead. I walk to meet him.

"What happened?"

"Practice got a little rough today," he says.

"Brian and Justin?"

"Yeah. And Anthony. And your old friend, Eric." Conan laughs. "Having Eric attack you would be like Wilma fighting off burglars. Except that Eric wears cleats."

Conan pulls up his pant leg and I see that his shin is scraped and raw.

"He kicked you?"

"More like jumped up and down on my leg."

Kit walks over and takes a look.

"What'd Coach Ruggles say?"

"At one point Coach yelled at Justin to remember they wanted to save me for playoffs, but mostly he didn't notice what they were doing."

We get into Conan's car for the ride home.

"I can't drive holding this thing," he says, handing me the ice pack. His forehead looks worse than his leg.

"What's with them, anyway?" I ask.

"Like you can't guess," Kit says.

Conan nods. "It's what I get for not laying low."

"You mean because you eat lunch with us?"

"Yep. I eat lunch at the queer table," he says. "And it got them riled when I walked to class with Frankie and everyone today."

"Football players suck!" Kit says.

Conan stops the car.

"Want out?" he asks Kit. He's smiling when he says it, though.

"Not you. I didn't mean you!"

"So, who?"

"The rest of those guys," she says.

"Who?"

"Aye! Get over it!" Kit says.

Conan's still not moving.

"Okay! I get your point! Anthony, Brian, Eric, Justin, those football players suck. I don't know for sure about the rest of them. Maybe not Robert."

Conan puts the car back in gear and starts up again.

"How about, *most* football players suck?"

He stops.

"How about innocent before proven guilty?"

"I just get so *mad*. That thing with Frankie today was so stupid, and cruel! And the stuff at my locker? If there were an Academy

Award for assholes, they'd all have statues on their mantles!"

"*But* you can't think that just because there are a few idiots in a group, everyone in the group is an idiot," Conan says.

Kit sighs. "I know."

Conan eases out into traffic.

I laugh. The psychologist just got a lesson in psychology. Or was it logic? I don't know. Right now, my nursing impulses are taking over and I'm worried that Conan's cuts and scrapes could get infected.

When we get to my house, I suggest Conan come in and let me work on his wounds.

He gets out of the car. "Work on *me*," he smiles. "Never mind my wounds."

Kit groans. "I'll leave you two perverted *heteros* alone."

Inside, I lead Conan to the bathroom. He sits on the edge of the bathtub and I gently wash his leg and forehead with warm, soapy water. I use sterile cotton balls to swab all of the messed up areas with disinfectant.

"Aw! AWW! YOU'RE KILLING ME!!" he screams.

"WHOA! ENOUGH! UNCLE! UNCLE!!"

Mom bursts through the door, looking as if she expects to see a murder in progress. She stops, takes in the scene, then sits beside Conan on the bathtub, laughing.

Later though, when we talk about the day, she warns us to take care, to stay alert.

"There are some very angry people out there. There's a man at work who's part of that Americans for Family Values group. He says they'll do whatever it takes to rid schools of 'perversion'."

"What does he mean — whatever it takes?" I ask.

"I don't know. But what you did today, walking to class as a group, is probably a good thing to do *all* of the time."

"Don't worry, Claire. I'll watch out for Lynn," Conan says, draping his arm around my shoulder.

"Small comfort," Mom says, pointing to the ice pack Conan is holding against his forehead. "Look at the mess *you're* in."

It is dark when I walk with Conan out to his car. I sit beside him in the front seat. We kiss and argue playfully about which one of us loves the other the most.

"I'm happiest when I'm with you," I tell him.

"I want us to last, Lynnie. Forever."

"Me, too," I say. But I can't help thinking forever is a long time to keep my existence a secret from his parents.

"Conan?"

"Ummmm," he murmurs, contented.

"Oh, just . . . nothing," I say. Why spoil a beautiful moment by asking why his family still doesn't know we're together?

26

Holly and Nicole show up at our Thursday GSA meeting, complete with brown bags.

"There's no one to eat lunch with on Thursdays," Nicole says.

"Besides, we hate what those guys did to Frankie," Holly says.

"And to Kit," Nicole says.

They stand back near the door, away from the circle of chairs.

"C'mon," I say. "Meet the rest of the group."

They follow about ten paces behind me, as if they're being led to their own executions.

"This is Dawn. She's from Sojourner High."

Dawn reaches out to shake Nicole's hand. Nicole hesitates, then extends her hand. Same thing with Holly.

As I lead them over to Jerry I remember the first time I met him — how I judged him to be an absolute weirdo because of his outlandish looks. Leaf is sitting near Jerry and the two of them . . . well, let's just say I can understand why Nicole and Holly are holding back.

"They're really nice guys," I tell them. "You'll see."

"Let's get started," Frankie says.

I lead our two newcomers back to a spot where they know people. They sit next to Caitlin.

We hand out 3 x 5 cards. Kit explains to Holly and Nicole that everyone writes something good from their past week, and something not so good.

Emmy starts a bag of Mother's Cookies around while we're writing on the cards. Jerry takes a cookie and makes a face. Emmy walks over, takes the cookie from Jerry, pops it in her mouth, and takes the bag from his hand. Those of us who are in on the cookie controversy laugh.

Jerry gives Emmy a long look. "May I please have one of those delicious cookies?" he pleads.

"That's better," Emmy says, handing the cookie bag back to him.

Felicia comes in — slinks in, really. She sits next to Kit, who hands her two cards and explains what we're doing.

Kit collects the cards and hands them to Emmy, who reads them out loud. Several say the best part of their week was the GLSEN meeting.

Another card, which I know is Kit's, says that the best part of her week was that her parents came to the meeting, and that her mom met another mom she liked.

Jerry, who never keeps what he's written a secret, says that the worst part of his week was leaving the GLSEN meeting with his mother, and being taunted by picketers. He pulls yesterday's *Hamilton Heights Daily News* article from his notebook and holds it up, pointing to a picture of a picketer.

"My dad," he says. "I gave up on him a long time ago — no big deal anymore. But my mom — I felt bad for her."

Jerry looks down at his desk, trying, I think, to hide his sadness.

A bunch of the cards say the worst part of the week was the football jerks dumping trash on Frankie.

Guy says, "Moving GSA meetings to this campus has really cranked up the stakes for the homophobes."

"But why?" Kit asks.

"They've been in control, free to say what they want and to

believe their way is the only way, pretty much without being challenged. Now they're faced with a group that supports what they hate — tolerance and acceptance of diversity. They're angry, and they're scared. The more visible GSA becomes, the more the Americans for Family Values types will try to put a stop to it."

"They don't scare me," Kit says.

Looking around, I'm not sure everyone else is as confident as Kit.

After all the cards have been read, Guy asks Frankie if he reported yesterday's incident with the "spilled" milk and garbage in his hair.

"What's the point?" Frankie says. "Nothing will happen."

"Nothing *can* happen, if it doesn't get reported."

"Look what happened to Kit and Lynn when *they* reported that incident. *They* got suspended and the guys who did it got to be football heroes."

"Frankie's right," Star says. "This place isn't like Sojourner, where people respect each other. Here, if you don't fit the mold, you're shit. It's okay to insult you. Even teachers think it's your own fault if you're harassed. You've asked for it, because you're different."

"Not fair," Guy says. "Look at Emmy."

"She's a librarian. Librarians are different," Star says.

"Two of my teachers kicked students out of class for anti-gay stuff," I say.

"Well, *I* got kicked out of this rat hole because of anti-gay stuff, too," Star says.

"You were doing anti-gay stuff?" Kit asks, wide eyed.

"No. But, when I got sick of hearing dyke, and homo, and *lots* worse, and complained, *I* was the one who was kicked out."

Holly nods her head. "In econ Mr.Rini called a guy a fag. And he's always saying stuff to the Vietnamese students, like 'eaten any tender dogs lately?'"

"Good old Rini," Guy says.

Emmy sighs and shakes her head.

"What about the stickers?" Nora says.

"What stickers?" Kit asks.

"You know, those anti-gay things . . ."

No one seems to have any idea what Nora's talking about.

"Where are they?" Emmy asks.

"One is on Ms. Woods' door, and two are on the boarded up display case outside the administrative offices."

"Describe them."

Nora takes out a sheet of paper and starts drawing. Then she holds it up for us to see.

It is a circle, about the size of a hamburger bun, I guess. Inside it says HOMOS, and there's a diagonal line drawn through it.

"HOMOS is in lavender and the circle has a broad, black border. The background is white, and the line is bright red."

Frankie groans. "Those people know *nothing* about how to use color!"

Ah — welcome laughter.

Kit gets us back on topic.

"The stickers, and what they did to Frankie — that proves Guy's point — about anti-gay stuff getting worse."

"You should report that thing yesterday," Jerry says to Frankie. "They can't keep getting away with that shit."

"Sure they can," Frankie says. "They've been doing it for years . . . Look, I've only got six months left and I'm out of here."

"What about the two hundred or so others, the rest of the ten percenters, who'll be left behind?" Guy asks.

"Two hundred? We've only got fourteen here today, and this is the biggest group we've ever had."

"I'm talking about other students who have a different sexual orientation than most people consider to be normal. And who are afraid to come to a meeting. They need to know that *someone* cares about their safety."

I sit chewing on my pencil, remembering something from one of Benny Foster's handouts.

"If Frankie doesn't want to file a complaint, can I?"

Emmy and Guy exchange looks.

"Good question. I'm not sure," Emmy says.

I rummage through my notebook and find the flyer that tells, among other things, the official, legal definition of harassment.

"Dumping stuff on Frankie? That was conduct that created a hostile educational environment. That stuff affects all of us," I say.

Emmy nods, thoughtfully.

"We should make official complaints about every little homophobic incident," Kit says. "Document everything. If Manly Max doesn't take action, we should go to the school board, like Benny said."

Frankie nods. "Okay. I'll fill out an official complaint, but I want you to fill one out, too, Lynn."

Me and my big mouth, I think. "No problem," I say.

"I'll do one, too," Caitlin says, in a voice loud enough to be heard.

"Let's sum up," Emmy says.

"Report. Document. If nothing happens, take it to the next step," Kit says.

Star stands and raises her arm over her head, closed fisted.

"No more shit for dinner," she says.

I stifle a gag reflex.

Just before the bell, Conan walks in.

"Let's get Frankie and Kit in the middle," he says, "and we'll all walk them to choir."

Guy walks to the door and looks out into the hallway, then says to Emmy, "You might want to call security."

It's the guys from the jock table, plus Douglas, and about ten other students.

"Christ First," Felicia mutters.

I wonder if she's trying to tell me something about how to live my life, but then I realize that the non-jocks are members of the campus Christian group. They are standing just outside the door, holding hands, heads bowed. As soon as we walk through the door, they start chanting in unison, "No to perversion! Yes to Jesus!" We walk past them, quickly, and then gather around Frankie and Kit. The jocks are standing a short distance down the hall, blocking our way. Emmy rushes ahead of us.

"Please move along," she says to them. "It's time for class."

No one moves. Emmy walks over to Brian and looks up at him, her face inches from his.

"I said MOVE ALONG," she says.

We are nearly up to them now, Conan in front. He keeps walking at a steady pace. Brian takes one baby step to the side, as does Justin, to the other side. Conan walks through the opening. Emmy stays close to Brian, who first yells "carpet muncher" at Kit, then slowly turns away and walks down the hall. The others follow Brian, except for Robert, who walks away from the jocks and over to Holly. He takes her hand and walks with us.

We stay grouped together, down to the end of the hall and down the stairs. Once on the first floor, the jocks turn to the left. We turn to the right and stop outside the choir room. Frankie, Kit, Caitlin, Nora and I go inside, and the others go on to their own classes.

"Something else to document," Kit says.

Douglas comes into the room just as the bell rings. Mr. Michaels tells us what music to have ready, then calls Douglas into his office. A few minutes later he calls Frankie in.

Caitlin, who is sitting behind me, leans forward and asks, "What does he want with Frankie?"

"I don't know," I say. "But I don't think it's to dump garbage on his head."

Caitlin actually laughs! I turn to be sure it came from Caitlin. It did. It's so surprising, I laugh, too. Nora, Kit, and the rest of the sopranos join in. Caitlin laughs harder. It's a pretty laugh, in her singing voice.

Mr. Michaels, Douglas, and Frankie come back into the room. Frankie sits down. Douglas stands next to Mr. Michaels in the front of the classroom.

"Please give Douglas your attention," Mr. Michaels says.

"I'm sorry . . ."

"Speak up Douglas, so everyone can hear you."

"I'm sorry if I offended anyone yesterday," he says, looking way embarrassed. "I was only trying to be funny. I didn't mean it to be disrespectful to anyone."

Mr. Michaels looks at Douglas for what seems like a long time, then asks the class, "Apology accepted?"

There's a murmer of agreement. Douglas takes his seat in the tenor section, and for the rest of the period we work on making music from our purest hearts, and our purest souls. No unruly thoughts enter my mind, and Douglas' short solo sounds sweeter than ever.

After school, Frankie, Kit, Caitlin, and I go to the library to get official complaint forms. Stuck on the door is one of the anti-gay signs that Nora told us about. I try to scrape it off, but it's got the sticking strength of a bumper sticker.

We decide that even though Mr. Michaels followed through on the incident with Douglas, it should still be reported — more evidence of harassment at Hamilton High. Caitlin fills out a form stating that Douglas' gesture in class yesterday was demeaning to gays, and that it disrupted her work, and the work of the class.

Frankie and I fill out separate reports about the jocks dumping trash on him, and Kit reports the incident in the hall after GSA, including Brian's "carpet muncher" remark. Emmy has already reported that scene to Mr. Cordova, and she's filing a vandalism report about the sign on her door. We'll see what happens.

It is nearly five when I join Dr. Kit under the tree. She gives me her theory on why Caitlin now can talk and laugh, after she's been silent for so long.

"If she couldn't talk about the most important thing in her life, her brother's murder, then why talk at all? But now that things are out in the open, she's free to express herself about other things, too."

I lean back against the trunk.

"Are you going to start charging me for your theories, after you get a license to practice psychology?"

"Not unless you're going to charge me for your advice about icing strained muscles."

"Let's just agree right now that spirit sisters don't charge for advice or information."

"Deal," Kit says.

"It's the end of volleyball for us," I say.

"Yeah," Kit says. "I think about that, too."

"Now it only lives in our memory banks," I say.

We sit quietly, until Wilma's bark breaks the silence. I go home for a few frisbee tosses and Kit goes inside. Events of the day wash over me as I fall into the thoughtless rhythm of frisbee play with Wilma. I'm saddened by intolerance and hateful judgments. I wonder what my grandparents would say, if I could talk with them about all that's been going on. Could they advise me?

You won't believe this. I barely believe it myself. But moments after I've thought about my grandparents, Grampa is standing at my left side. Gramma is next to me, on the right. Their love envelops me. I want the moment to last forever, but as soon as I think that, their presence fades. Was it only my wishful imagination? Were they really with me? All I know is that my sadness is replaced with hope, and I feel a lightness of heart which I've not really felt since the first day of Kit's new image, when friends kept their quiet distance.

In the house I take thirty dollars from the money I'm saving for Christmas.

"Can I borrow the car for about an hour?" I ask Mom.

"The keys are by the phone," she says.

I drive to Free Expressions in Pasadena — a place Kit has told me about. I buy ten large rainbow stickers with "embrace diversity" printed across them, and fifteen of those beaded Pride bracelets. Even small steps are important, I think, wondering if the thought came from me, or from the visit with my grandparents.

In the morning, as we wait for Conan to pick us up, Kit notices the bracelet I'm wearing.

"Cool," she says.

I show her the big rainbow stickers. She looks at me questioningly.

"To cover the anti-gay signs," I tell her.

She laughs. "Let me take two for the signs on the display case boards."

At lunch the kids at the table notice my bracelet.

"Out and proud?" Holly asks, looking from me to Conan and back again.

"For solidarity," I say. "Want one?"

Nora, Caitlin, Holly and Nicole each take one. Frankie already has several of his own. Conan and Robert politely decline.

Everyone thinks the rainbow stickers are a great idea, and by the end of the day "embrace diversity" has covered the anti-gay signs. The colors are better, too.

27

Friday night. The first of the play-offs for state championship.
Even though we're playing clear over at Pacific Hills, the visitors'
side is filled with Hamilton High fans. On the football field, you'd
never guess that Brian and Conan were at odds. They play beauti-
fully, each backing the other, neither competing for glory. It's an
easy win. As we stand to sing the alma mater, Mr. Maxwell holds
his arms up, signaling to the band not to start the song. Then he gets
on the microphone and thanks everyone for their school spirit. He
has never seen such a fine team in all of his years as an educator, and
he's proud and humbled to be a part of Hamilton High. He praises
the coaches and names all of the starting players, asks that we
remember them in our prayers, and then, finally, nods to the band
to play.

"I'd rather pray to end world hunger," Nicole says.

"It wouldn't hurt you to add something for the team, too," Holly
says.

Time for my mind to wander. I look down to where Sabina is
sitting on her dad's shoulders. As if she feels me looking at her, she
turns around and smiles. I wave, then watch as the Parkers all stand

and move down the bleachers to the field below. They're talking and laughing, proud of Conan, I'm sure.

Monday morning, in peer communications, Woodsy's aide, Janet, reads the daily bulletin to the class. Woodsy sits at her desk marking attendance in her roll book.

The bulletin is full of praise for Hamilton High's football team, and for the great display of school spirit shown at Friday's game. There are announcements of coming events, scholarship applications, and club meetings. This week's GSA announcement says the club is open to everyone, and invites students to come show their support for a safe school environment for *all* students. The Christ First club invites students to "join them in their fight against the rising tide of perversion at Hamilton High School."

Woodsy looks up from her desk, obviously surprised.

"May I see that?" she asks.

Brian and Eric exchange quick, barely noticeable thumbs-ups.

Janet hands Woodsy the bulletin. She reads it silently, shakes her head, then hands out information outlining the week's schedule and related assignments. There are a bunch of magazines, books, pamphlets, and newspaper articles spread out on a table in the front of the room. The topic is eating disorders, and we're to read and take notes on two or three articles, in preparation for Thursday's panel of speakers.

About halfway through class, when I go to the table to get another article, I notice one of those anti-gay signs stuck to the front of Woodsy's desk. I'm sure it wasn't there when we came in. How could it just suddenly appear? Then I remember seeing Eric and Brian hovering around Woodsy's desk, like they were waiting to use the pencil sharpener. I pass a note back to Conan, telling him to look at Woodsy's desk.

I remove one of my three remaining "embrace diversity" signs and show it to Conan. We laugh.

"Let me," he says, taking the sticker from me.

Near the end of the period, Emmy comes into the classroom.

Woodsy glances at the clock. We have less than ten minutes left until the bell rings.

"Continue your reading. Be sure to put the materials back up on the table and write in your activity log before you leave."

She and Emmy walk into her office and close the door. Through the large window that allows her to look out on the classroom, I see Emmy hand Woodsy some papers. They both look angry. I wish I could hear what they're saying.

At lunch, Frankie tells us that Emmy called Mr. Cordova to see how such obviously inflammatory language as "the rising tide of perversion" could possibly have been okayed for the bulletin.

"Cordova told her he was no longer the person who gives final approval on the bulletin. Mr. Maxwell is. But get this, she talked with a student from the Christ First club, and found out that some of the Americans for Family Values people are helping them organize against GSA."

Frankie glances over at the jock table and lowers his voice. "Eric's father is one of the main people behind all of this, and I guess Jerry's dad's involved, too."

"Did Emmy say anything about the complaints we filed?"

"Just that Mr. Cordova will be calling people in."

"Maybe he already has," Conan says. "Our friends at the other table are pretty quiet today."

They *are* quiet, but I notice that when they leave, there are two of the anti-gay stickers on the table. That takes care of the last of my 'embrace diversity' stickers.

Those of us who filed complaints stop in the library after school to see if Emmy has heard anything.

"I think Mr. Cordova will probably be calling you to his office tomorrow. He talked with the other side today."

"What'd they say?"

"Mr. Cordova didn't reveal any conversation. All he told me was that he'd given them each very strong warnings. He let them know that their behavior was very serious and could be categorized as hate crimes."

By the time we've finished talking about the complaints, and the new hate signs, and things in general, it's nearly time for football practice to be over.

Since I drove today, I offer to take everyone home. We walk out to the parking lot to wait for Conan. It's nice outside. Brisk and clear, but not cold. The field is empty and all the equipment has been brought in, so I know it's only a matter of minutes before Conan comes out. We stand outside the gym, talking and waiting.

Frankie is all excited about play-offs, and the band's half-time performance.

"We're going to look *so* much better than Serrano," he says. "The play-offs aren't *only* about football."

He puts an imaginary flute up to his lips, draws himself up to his full height, and high-steps out, humming the first bars of "Seventy-six Trombones." We're doubled over with laughter at Frankie's act when suddenly, a bunch of football players burst through the gym doors. It's the wrong bunch. Justin, Brian, Anthony and Eric are around Frankie in a flash. Justin grabs Frankie's head and forces it downward.

"You want something to blow on? Blow on this!" Justin says, thrusting his crotch in Frankie's face.

We rush at them, trying to pull Justin off. He pushes me back, but loses his grip on Frankie. Brian pushes Frankie to the cement and Kit and Caitlin shove him away from Frankie. Anthony shoulders Caitlin away. Brian turns on Kit.

"Wanna play, Squaw?"

Kit pushes at him. He grabs her butt and pulls her into him, thrusting toward her. He shoves her to the pavement, pins her arms back and straddles her.

"I'll show you what you need," he says, ripping her jeans open.

Frankie struggles to get to his feet but Eric kicks him down. Justin gives him another kick. I shove Justin away. Frankie jumps up, lunges at Brian. Pulling. Kicking. Biting. Frantic to get Brian off Kit.

Eric runs toward Frankie and I shoulder him aside.

Frankie has Brian around the neck, from behind, yelling. "Leave her alone! LEAVE HER ALONE!! WHAT KINDA SHIT *IS* THIS?"

As if out of nowhere, Conan jumps in. He grabs Brian by the arm and yanks him aside, momentarily throwing him off balance. Brian turns back to Kit, ripping at her shirt. Conan pulls Brian off. Kit gets to her feet. Brian stands facing her, his face distorted with anger. He reaches for her. She kicks him, hard, in the groin, and he's down on the pavement, doubled in pain. Mr. Cordova runs up to us, panting hard from what must have been a sprint clear across the length of the parking lot. Larry is right behind him as Coach Ruggles rushes out of the gym.

Justin spits at Frankie. "Freakin' faggot!" he screams. "Stay outa my space!"

Conan steps between them, nose to nose with Justin.

"NO MORE!" he says.

"This is not your business," Justin says.

Conan stands, still and solid.

Larry takes Justin by the arm and guides him over to the steps.

"Sit here. Cool down," he says. "You, too," he motions to Eric. "Keep your distance, Conan."

Coach Ruggles is bending over Brian, telling him to take deep breaths, try to relax, move a little. Brian is groaning, curled into himself.

Mr. Cordova tells the coach and Larry to walk Brian, Eric, Justin, and Anthony up to the office, and motions for the rest of us to walk with him.

"I've got an injured player here," Coach Ruggles says. "I don't think he can walk to your office."

"Then call 911 and get him out of the parking lot," Mr. Cordova says. "Ambulance, or my office. That's it."

Brian rolls over on his hands and knees and Coach Ruggles helps him straighten up.

According to Mr. Cordova's instructions, the football players are seated in his office, and the GSA kids are on a bench on the other side of the room. Larry takes something that looks like baby wipes from a big first aid kit and hands them out for us to clean up with. Mr. Cordova comes out of his office.

"Are you okay?" he asks, first turning his attention to Kit.

"Maybe a little bruised," she says, rubbing the back of her head.

"How about you, Frankie?"

"Okay."

"Any other damage?" he says, looking from me to Caitlin and back again.

We both shake our heads no.

"Okay, so we need written reports."

He gives us each a clipboard with paper and pen and tells us to include specifics, who did what to whom, what was said, as many details as possible.

"What about them!" Kit says, pointing in the direction of Mr. Cordova's office.

"Coach Ruggles is in there with them. They're writing statements, too."

My hands are shaky and I'm having trouble thinking, so it takes a while to write what happened.

When we've finally all stopped writing, Mr. Cordova collects our statements and reads through them, occasionally asking for clarification, mostly nodding his head.

"Okay. Thank you. You can go now."

"What's going to happen to *them*?" Kit asks, motioning toward Mr. Cordova's office.

"You don't need to worry about seeing them at school tomorrow, if that's what you mean."

"Why? Are you going to suspend us?" Kit says, in her most sarcastic tone.

Mr. Cordova gives her a long, hard look, finally staring her down.

"*They* won't be at school tomorrow."

"What if Mr. Maxwell . . ."

"Kit. Trust me on this one. They won't be at school . . . now go home, take long showers, and get a good night's sleep. I'll probably be here until nine or so, if any of your parents want to call. I'll see you tomorrow."

He turns toward his office.

"Wait," I say. "What about Conan?"

"What about him?"

"He's one of the good guys," Frankie says.

"Hold on," Mr. Cordova says, going into his office and closing the door.

After a few minutes, Conan comes out. I know what Cordova advised, home and a shower. But none of us is ready to go home yet. We're all still buzzed on adrenaline. We go straight to Barb 'n Edie's. We each get sodas, then order three garbage burritos to share. Caitlin calls Nora from her cell phone, and Nora shows up about the same time as the burritos. Star comes in a few minutes later.

"Whoa," she says, looking us over. "Was there a war or something, and I didn't know it?"

I see what she means. Frankie's forehead and cheek are scraped up. Kit's shirt is torn. My lip is swollen. We've all got something to show for our struggle.

We tell Nora and Star the whole story, complete with details of Conan's timely arrival and Kit's well-placed kick to Brian's groin.

Star puts her arm around Kit.

"You okay, Kit-Kat?"

Kit nods her head.

"Wish *I'd* been there," Star says.

"Coach Ruggles was demanding suspension for you," Conan says to Kit. "He said you'd be better off at Sojourner, with the other misfits."

"He *said* that?"

"Yep. Said any girl who was hostile enough to kick a guy you know where was too dangerous to have on campus."

Star snorts. "Told you. That's how they are."

"What'd Cordova say?" Kit asks.

"He said you were acting in self-defense — appropriate behavior considering the situation."

"What else did they say?" Kit asks.

"It was hella weird. Cordova was talking about suspension pending expulsion and Ruggles was talking about tomorrow night's game. It's like they weren't even in the same conversation."

"Can we beat Serrano if those guys are suspended?" Frankie asks.

Conan shakes his head. "No way."

"But we've still got you," Frankie whines. "Can't the barbarian make it happen?"

"We'll get trounced! The only thing that could save us would be if a bunch of their main players were as stupid as ours and got themselves suspended."

"Who cares about a freakin' football game, anyway," Star says.

"Lots of people do," Frankie says.

"Do you think Frankie and Kit'll get blamed if we lose the championship?" Nora asks.

"Of course," Frankie says. "Even though *they're* the ones who messed up."

Later, when Conan and I are parked down the street from his house, he tells me he knew something was going on in the parking lot. He could hear angry yelling but he took his time leaving the gym.

"That laying low thing," he said. "No need to get involved."

"But . . ."

"I didn't know *you* were there . . . I was dressed and leaning up against the wall, waiting for things to get quiet, when I heard . . . "

He swallows, like there's something in his throat that's keeping him from going on. I snuggle closer to him, resting my hand on the back of his thick neck.

"When you heard what?"

"When I heard . . . "

He shakes his head, takes a deep breath, and tries again.

"When I heard Frankie yelling 'What kinda shit *is* this' it was like Mark all over again. I don't even remember how I got from the gym to where he and Brian and Kit were piled up, but I knew I had to stop it before things got worse than they already were . . . "

"I was so glad to see you . . . I thought Brian was really going to hurt Kit . . . and everyone else was . . . Frankie . . ."

I don't want to cry, but I can't help it. Conan strokes my hair and kisses me, very gently, on my swollen lip.

"It's over," he says. "Everything's okay."

"I just . . . thank you . . . "

When Conan finally gets out of the car to walk to his house, I tell him I can drive again tomorrow. I'll meet him at the corner.

"See you here, then," he says.

I watch him walk away, watch his long, sturdy strides, his broad back — just seeing Conan walk makes me feel safe.

When he rounds the corner, I start the car and drive home.

28

My mom and I talk for a long time about all that's been happening. I want so much to tell her about the visit from Gramma and Grampa, but it sounds so weird . . . Just as I'm getting my nerve up, we're interrupted by the telephone. It's Conan.

"About tomorrow morning," he says. "Just pull into my driveway. I'll wait for you on the porch."

"But . . ."

"Don't worry about it," he says.

Even though it's a quick conversation with Conan, when I get back to Mom, the sense of closeness has faded. I'll tell her about my visit from Gramma and Grampa some other time.

When I check e-mail before bed, there's a message there from Kit.

I won't be riding with you in the morning. My parents set up a meeting with Mr. Cordova, to talk about Brian's attack yesterday. My dad wants to file charges against him.

Also, this awesome thing happened. My mom went to a PFLAG meeting with Star's "mom" and it's like my mom's had a major attitude adjustment. Can you believe it?

It feels strange, driving into Conan's driveway. But he's there, waiting for me. Sabina is inside, at the window, where she waves and throws kisses as we back out, like the first time I ever picked Conan up for school — back before he got weird about having his parents see me.

At the first stop sign, Conan gives me a big kiss, then backs away.

"Your lip's not so swollen this morning," he says.

"I'm back in kissing condition," I tell him.

"We should take advantage of that right now," he says. "If those guys are suspended, who knows *what* condition I'll be in after the game."

"If? I thought for sure they were being suspended."

"Yeah. That's what Cordova said. But Coach kept saying he wanted Mr. Maxwell to deal with his players."

"That shouldn't change anything," I say.

"Shouldn't," Conan says.

"On the other hand . . ."

Conan nods.

"Mr. Maxwell is *totally* into Hamilton High winning the championship."

"What do *you* think should happen?" I ask Conan.

He is quiet for a long time.

"I want to be on the championship team. I want to play the big game and win. That'd be awesome. But . . . if you ask me what *should* happen — they shouldn't get away with the kind of stuff they've been doing."

I park as far away from the boys' gym as I can, not wanting to go *near* that place. I turn toward Conan for one last kiss before we go to class, and I see rainbow-beaded bracelets lined up on both arms.

"Cool, huh?" he says, grinning.

"Way cool," I say, counting ten on one arm and seven on the other.

"Makes your three look a little weak," he teases.

He reaches into his backpack and pulls another handful of bracelets out.

"In case anyone else wants one."

"Did you go out for those last night? After I left you off?"

He nods.

"You didn't even want *one* yesterday," I remind him.

"That was yesterday. Lunchtime, to be exact. But then all that stuff with Frankie and Kit — it hit me right in the gut — seeing them ganged up on, for no reason except for who they are. Harassed in the halls, beaten up in the parking lot, spit on, Kit practically raped . . . the way *my* brothers and sisters have been treated . . ."

"So . . . the bracelets?"

He takes a deep breath.

"I don't know if I can explain it. I wouldn't even try with anyone but you."

I wait.

Another deep breath.

"When I got home last night, I went to my room, closed the door, and tried to read the econ assignment."

"Like reading the phone book," I say.

Conan smiles in agreement.

"But it could have been the most interesting story in the world and I still couldn't have read it last night. I kept hearing Frankie yelling at Brian, asking 'what kinda shit *is* this.' And Frankie's voice turned to Mark's. Those were the very last words Mark ever said to me. And I kept hearing them over, and over, and over . . ."

Long pause. I'm aware that only a few stragglers are left in the parking lot, that we should be getting to first period, but I want to hear what it is Conan is struggling to tell me.

"So I . . . I talked with Mark, and he . . ."

Conan looks at me, trying to decide whether or not to go on.

"You're probably thinking Looney Tunes . . ."

I shake my head.

Another pause. Then . . .

"So I kept hearing Mark asking that question and then it was like he was really in the room. 'I couldn't help it,' I told him, 'I tried to get you to calm down.' And then, this strange thing . . ."

I wait. And wait.

Conan's voice is a whisper when he continues.

"I got all warm inside, like I do sometimes with you. Not sexy, I don't mean that, but . . . full of love. And for the first time I knew without a doubt that Mark's death was inevitable. That there truly was nothing I could have done to change things."

I reach over and rub Conan's back. "You must feel so . . . relieved . . ."

Conan nods. "But that's not all. Mark . . . I don't know how, and I know it sounds weird, but he told me . . . well, not exactly in words, but he let me know. . . the way I can honor his memory is to pay attention to the 'what kinda shit *is* this' question. There's more to life than laying low."

Larry is walking toward us.

"Do you think I'm all whacked?" Conan asks.

I shake my head. "Do you feel whacked?"

"No. I feel good. Like a huge stone's been lifted from my shoulders."

"And the bracelets?"

Larry comes to Conan's side of the car and bends down, hands on his knees, so he can be at eye-level with us. With Conan, really. As usual, he doesn't look at me.

"You've got to get to class, man."

"Give us a minute," Conan says.

Larry looks sort of beat this morning. Maybe the meeting with the football players went on for a long time last night.

"Nah. C'mon," he says, opening the door.

"What happened after I left last night?" Conan says.

"You know that's all confidential."

"We won't tell anyone," Conan says.

"No man, I can't be givin' out privileged information. I need this job."

"Well . . . Are we starting tonight with the usual players?"

"I don't know . . . Maxwell's . . ."

Larry's on the verge of opening up when he sees Conan's bracelets.

"What're these? Whose side are you on anyway?" He gives me a dirty look. I mean a DIRTY look, then turns back to Conan for an answer.

"I'm on the side of tolerance," Conan says. "Whose side are you on?"

"I'm on the side of decency," Larry says. "Now get to class."

We get out of the car, lock up, and walk slowly in the direction of the main building. Larry watches.

"So, the bracelets . . . " Conan says, glancing down at his colorfully arrayed arm. "When you brought some to lunch yesterday, I thought it was a great idea, for everyone else. But now that I'm no longer laying low . . ."

We walk past Kit's parents' car, parked in the first row next to the main building. They must have been here since sunrise to get that spot.

"Conan?"

"Ummm?"

"I want to tell you about this thing that happened to me the other night — sort of like with you and Mark, only for me it was my grandparents."

Conan slows his pace even more. He looks at me intently, attentive. I'm about to tell him of my own strange and precious experience when Larry catches up to us.

"You *really* need to move faster," he says, walking along beside us, making further private conversation impossible.

Inside the main building, Larry still hovering, Conan gives me a quick kiss. "Tell me later," Conan says.

We go to our separate first period classes. I wish I'd get lucky and have a sub, so maybe I'd get away with coming in late. No such luck.

Neither Eric nor Brian is in second period, but Tiffany is. Unlike Larry, Tiffany is more than happy to tell all she knows.

"Cordova suspended them, but they'll play tonight," she says.

"They can't play if they're suspended," Conan says.

"Mr. Maxwell's going to fix things," she says. "He was *steaming* when he found out Cordova suspended them. They can be suspended *next* week. Like Monday through Thursday, then play again on Friday. That's what Eric's dad says."

Tiffany's wearing her cheerleader outfit, as they all do on game days. "Why should the whole school suffer?" she whines.

I notice that Woodsy, who usually starts class as soon as the bell rings, is more interested in what Tiffany is saying than in getting started. When her office phone rings, she goes back to answer it, rather than asking Janet to take a message.

Steve says, "I don't even know what this is about. Why'd they get suspended anyway?"

"They were joking around after school, and that gay guy, Frankie, made a big deal of it. And Kit, you know?"

Steve nods. "Shaved head, flannel shirt, bracelets?"

"Yeah, she was way tweeked — acting like Brian'd practically raped her. I mean, why would Brian even want to get near *that*, when he can get all the *normal* girls he wants."

"So what exactly happened?" Steve says.

"Well . . . that Frankie guy was *dancing* and *prancing* . . ."

I jump in. "Brian, Anthony, Justin, and Eric *attacked* Frankie — big brave football players four on one, then Brian went after Kit . . ."

Tiffany interrupts, "That's not true . . ."

"You weren't there!" I yell. "They kicked Frankie, spit on him, Brian had Kit down on the pavement. He ripped her jeans open . . ."

Woodsy comes out of her office. She glances at the videotape on her desk, then says maybe we should save the eating disorders film for Monday. Maybe we need to work on rumor control today.

"Let's go around the room and get each person's insight on this situation, one by one, before we get into a free for all. Okay?"

Kids nod. We move the desks into a circle, like we always do for discussion.

Woodsy starts out by telling what she's heard — that there was an incident in the parking lot, between some of the football players and some of the GSA students, that the football players were the ones who attacked, and that their actions were cause for suspension, if not for expulsion.

"Was anyone hurt?" Steven asks.

"I understand that no one needed medical treatment," Woodsy says.

"Brian was hurt *really* bad," Tiffany says. "That Kit girl did about the worst thing a girl can do to a guy . . . she kicked him in his . . . you know . . ."

"Nuts?" Steven asks.

Laughter.

"It's not funny!" Tiffany says, on the verge of tears.

Woodsy asks if anyone in the class was there, and if so, would they be willing to give an eyewitness account.

I tell what I saw and experienced.

Then Conan raises his bracelet-ringed arm and Woodsy calls on him to tell his story. I can tell that his bracelets have caught everyone's attention, but he doesn't mention them. He tells how he heard Frankie yelling, and then what he saw when he ran out.

Tiffany again tries to convince people that it was all only a joke, but I'm not sure anyone believes her. Conan has a lot of credibility.

Everyone agrees that the boys should be suspended, but about half think their suspension should be arranged so it won't interfere with the football game.

By the end of class, people are much less heated in their opinions, except for Tiffany. She sits fingering her gold cross, fuming.

Just before the bell rings, Conan holds both arms up and shakes his bracelets.

"I want that justice for all deal we say in the pledge of allegiance every morning. For the whole rainbow bunch of us. If you agree, and want to let it be known — I've got a bracelet for you."

He stands outside the classroom door, bracelets in hand. Steven takes one.

"Thanks man. Those guys suck," he says.

Two girls also take bracelets. We're about to walk away when Woodsy walks up to us. She holds out her right arm and Conan slips a bracelet over it.

"Thank you," she says. Then, "I didn't want to announce it to the class, things are so tense right now. But Emmy asked me to tell you there'll be a quick GSA meeting in the library after school today."

"Thanks," I say, and then rush off to English.

I notice a few kids in there with rainbow bracelets. They smile at me, even though we hardly know one another. I also notice some guys looking my way in a not so friendly manner.

At lunch, Robert is wearing a bracelet. "Cool," I tell him.

The jock table is empty, except for a couple of B-team players and Tiffany and Tammy.

Kit fills us in on the details of the morning.

"My parents and I met with Mr. Cordova early this morning. They told him they were concerned for my safety and they wanted to know who was suspended and for how long. He said he couldn't discuss another student's discipline matters with them — private information and all. But he could assure them that none of the boys involved in yesterday's incident . . ."

"Incident!" Frankie says. "It wasn't an incident, it was an *attack*!"

". . . anyway, none of them will be at school today."

Tammy and Tiffany are both looking our way — another of those "if looks could kill" situations.

Kit continues talking about the meeting. "My mom was upset . . . how could that have happened, broad daylight, supervised campus, etc., etc., and my dad talked about my legal rights, and hate crimes. Mr. Cordova just kept saying we didn't need to worry about any of those boys being on campus today."

"So does that mean they're suspended?" Nora asks.

"Wait'll you hear the rest. Maxwell came storming into the room, yelling about how Cordova was way out of bounds, suspending the guys who would take us to the championship, and how they were going to 'fix' things. He was in such a temper it was like we were invisible. At least until my dad stood up."

Kit laughs. "And how will you 'fix' this, Mr. Maxwell?" my dad says all quiet like, the way he talks to people when he's ready to slap the handcuffs on. Old Manly looks confused to the max — discombobulated, was the way my mom put it. But then he switched to his smooth educator talk — how it would all be taken care of in a just and timely manner. You bet it will, my dad told him, and we left the office."

"So, will they play tonight?" Conan says.

Robert laughs. "Or, by the end of the game, will the rest of us be all maimed and left in pieces on the field?"

Holly looks worried. "Maybe the game should just be called off."

"No can do," Frankie says. "We need that half-time extravaganza."

29

Conan and Robert both show up after school at GSA. None of the kids from Sojourner are here, or Guy, either, since it's not a regular lunchtime meeting. Emmy and Woodsy both look worn. Emmy starts the meeting off.

"Here's what's happening," she says. "Mr. Cordova suspended all four boys for two weeks, pending expulsion."

Conan lets out a low whistle. "That takes care of football season," he says.

"*If* the suspension holds," Emmy says. "Mr. Maxwell and the parents of the players are putting tremendous pressure on Mr. Cordova to rescind his decision."

"Can Maxwell make him back down?" Kit asks.

"Not officially," Emmy says.

"But . . . ?"

Emmy looks over at Woodsy, who looks grim.

"This is all confidential," Emmy says. "My telling you any of this . . . well . . . it's the kind of thing teachers are never supposed to do. But I think you have a right to know what's going on . . . If it's a matter of Mr. Cordova's job, or going back on the suspension . . ."

"His job?" Kit says.

"Look. We don't know how any of this is going to turn out," Woodsy says. "What we do know is there is a lot of emotion and controversy over how things should be handled right now. Seeing the added bracelets on campus is wonderful. GSA is gaining support. But . . ."

Woodsy points to another anti-gay sticker on a table in the reference section, and on a shelf that contains a number of books with rainbow triangle stickers.

"Those four boys aren't the only ones who are hateful and intolerant."

We spend some time reviewing the information Benny Foster gave us. Then we parcel out assignments — all to be completed at least an hour before game time.

Woodsy will call the legal advisor at the district office and tell him, or her, of the situation here.

Conan and Robert will present information to Coach Ruggles regarding his legal responsibility to maintain an environment that is safe for *all* students.

Emmy will confront Mr. Rini with his alleged non-compliance of the education code in accepting and promoting anti-gay harassment.

Kit, Nora, Caitlin, Felicia and I will each contact a board member and notify them of a possibility of a lawsuit if they are not compliant with procedures designated by the State Department of Education.

Holly and Nicole will go to Pasadena and buy more bracelets, "embrace diversity" stickers, and some smaller rectangular rainbow stickers that are made by a company called Pride, not Prejudice. We all contribute whatever is in our backpacks or pockets, so they'll have money to buy plenty of materials.

"We should blanket this place with rainbow symbols," Caitlin says, showing the smile we're just now beginning to get used to.

"Run it up the flagpole," Kit says.

"Maybe not," Woodsy says. "Messing with what goes up the flagpole is a sure way to enrage the Americans for Family Values group."

"So?" Kit says.

"So . . . we're about trying to pull people together, not push them further apart."

By six o'clock it is clear that our work has paid off. The district legal advisor, Brenda Lester, had a heart-to-heart with Manly and Coach Ruggles. She told them they were leaving themselves *and* the school district wide open for a lawsuit if they didn't take strong measures against *any* human rights violations. I guess she got through, because none of the gay-bashing four are on the field when I climb the bleachers to take my place next to Holly and Nicole.

Manly sits down on the bench, next to Coach Howard. Conan, Robert, and the second string players make a valiant effort to beat Serrano. At half-time we are six points behind, and it is obvious that our guys are outranked. Still, the Hamilton High half-time display is glorious, with precision marching sprinkled with swing.

In the end, we lose by six points to a team we should have beaten by at least twelve points. That means we're probably out of the play-offs. If Piedmont and Fruitridge *both* lost their games tonight, we'd still have a chance. Not likely, though.

Manly gives his usual pep talk, before the alma mater.

"We're not out of the game, yet. We must keep our spirits high," he says, but anyone can see even he's not convinced there's a chance. The alma mater is not so heart-felt as it was last week. Our guys drag off the field, defeated. Watching the Parker family walk down the steps, I see that they're dragging, too. Well, except for Sabina, who's as energetic as ever, still yelling the Barbarian cheer.

Tonight, for the first time in many weeks, I go to the after-game party with Conan. It is at a place in the Heights — big, with a swimming pool and spa in the back, a huge den that's set up with iced sodas and snacks. Tim, whose house we're at, is one of the second stringers who was trying to hold things together in the game. He seems pretty happy that he finally got to play a full game.

There is, of course, plenty of talk about the suspensions. Conan and Robert, still wearing their rainbow bracelets, say there are more important things than winning the championship. They may be the only two who believe that. Conan offers rainbow bracelets to some of the others. No takers.

An hour or so into the party, Coach Ruggles calls and asks to talk to Conan.

"No way!" I hear Conan say.

We gather around the phone, waiting impatiently for whatever news it is that Conan has just heard.

He laughs, says good-bye, and hangs up.

"We're still in the game," he says. "They both lost."

Laughter and the slap of high fives fill the air. Then Conan says, "We're not *really* still in the game. Muir will THRASH us next week."

"Maybe the rest of the team will play next week," Tim says.

"Ten day suspension, pending expulsion," I tell them. It's not like I've revealed any secret information. Tiffany's already spread the news to the whole student body.

"That could change," Tim says.

I don't think so, but I keep *that* thought to myself.

It is nearly midnight when the four suspended players make their entrance, drunk and rowdy. Conan guides me out the back door and around the garage. We squeeze through a narrow passage between houses to get to where his car is parked.

"Laying low?" I ask him.

"Fighting with drunks is always stupid, and that's what would have happened if we'd stayed there."

We drive to the darkest place on my block, not far from where we were stopped on that night a couple of months ago.

Conan pulls me close to him. We kiss, and fondle, and hold one another, skin to skin, making our own kind of no-babies love. After, he tells me, "I can live without being on a championship team."

"You're so close, though."

"Yeah, but we can't pull it out of the bag without the full team."

I pull Conan's jacket across my half-open blouse and snuggle closer to him.

I tell him about how my Gramma and Grampa came to me, night before last, and how they gave me hope and reassurance, kind of like Mark had given him.

"We're soul mates, Lynnie," Conan says.

We're warm and comfortable together. Conan's worn out from being the barbarian, plus covering for the missing players. I can tell by his steady breathing that he's asleep. I let myself drift off, too. Then, I don't know how long we've been sleeping, but we're shocked awake by blaring horns, and flashlights, and laughter.

"Get these heteros out of the car. We'll teach them a lesson!"

Frankie opens the door, laughing his maniacal laugh.

Conan stiffens awake, then relaxes when he sees who it is. Caitlin and Nora open the door on my side of the car and start dragging me out.

Holly, Nicole, and Robert are bouncing on the car bumpers, yelling "Earthquake!"

We stumble out, laughing.

Conan and I get our jackets from the car and follow our rag-tag group back to Kit's. She gets blankets from her house, and sets up a little short-legged barbeque that we can warm our hands on. Star comes out of Kit's house with cups and a big thermos of hot chocolate. Pretty soon Jerry shows up, and then Leaf. Wilma's barking her head off, so Conan opens the gate for her. She's dragging her half-eaten frisbee with her.

"No, no, Sweet Willy," Frankie says, as she drops the frisbee at his feet.

He runs to his "chariot" and retrieves a brand new frisbee. He throws it upward, where it makes a graceful arc and then descends. Wilma grabs it, somehow smiling but keeping it secure in her mouth at the same time. She drops it at Frankie's feet.

He throws it again, higher and farther. Wilma leaps, twists, grabs, descends.

"Anyone can dance, with a little guidance," he says.

We laugh — an appreciative laugh.

"Maybe anyone can dance with a little of *your* guidance," Caitlin says.

"Really," I say to Frankie. "I can't believe you got those tuba guys to actually be light on their feet!"

More laughter.

"I *wish* we could march in the championship game. Why did those guys have to be such screw-ups?"

"Because they're *total* assholes," Kit says.

Conan shakes his head. "Not total," he says.

"Right," Star says. "The whole bunch of them combined don't have even one redeeming social quality."

"You're wrong," Conan says. "All four of those guys — they're great team players. I've never been on a team where guys worked so well together, nobody hogging the glory, or getting miffed about whatever play was being called . . ."

Robert agrees. "Yeah. It's like everyone was working for everyone else . . ."

Conan says, "Too bad their idea of a team is so small. If they could just think of the whole school as one big team . . ."

"Yeah. Or the whole human race," Caitlin says.

I'm glad Caitlin's finally talking. I like what she has to say.

"Remember what that gay dude said in PC?" Conan asks. "The worst gay bashers are guys who're afraid *they* could be gay . . ."

"So they do all that stuff because they're fearful?" Caitlin asks.

"I'm only repeating what the guy told us in PC," Conan says.

"The Fearful Four," Nicole says.

"The Asshole Four," Star says. "That's the only way to describe them."

Kit starts quoting Freud, or Jung, or whoever, saying how we hate in others what we're afraid to look at in ourselves.

"Does it work the opposite way?" Star asks. "Do I love in you what I love in myself?"

We bat those ideas around until my head is spinning. I have to relax with a few frisbee throws, which makes Wilma happy.

Kit passes the thermos around again. Robert adds coals to the barbecue.

"We should get some marshmallows," Holly says.

We all nod in agreement, but nobody leaves to buy marshmallows.

After a while, Star says, "Confession?"

"Not if it's going to hurt," Kit says.

"I don't think so," Star says, moving closer to Kit.

"Let's hear it then."

Star tells about the first time she ever talked to Kit, at the beach, when Kit and Conan and I had managed that perfect after school getaway.

"I'd seen you before. Even noticed you a year ago, when I was still at Hamilton High."

"Really?" Kit says.

"Really," Star says. "You were so . . . oblivious."

"So what's to confess?" Frankie prods.

"So, I'd talked to Kit, and I wanted to get to know her better . . . *Lots* better," Star smiles.

"Confession!" Frankie says.

Star looks at Kit. "Well . . . in the late afternoon I kind of . . . watched you."

"Like from where?" Kit asks.

"Ummm. From behind the restrooms. From inside my car. Just places."

"You never told me this before!"

"I'm telling you now."

"Telling it very slowly, too," Frankie complains.

"Anyway, after it was dark, and the three of you were huddled together, I decided to see if I could sit with you. So I kind of snuck up behind you, but before I could make myself known, you all started singing . . ."

"Blue Moon," Kit says.

"Yeah. And it was so beautiful . . . I couldn't interrupt, or think of a way to join in. I snuck back to my car, where I sat crying."

"Why crying?" Kit asks.

"Just . . . I guess I was lonely for something the three of you had."

Kit starts the song. "Blue moon, you saw me standing alone . . ."

Conan and I join Kit, "without a dream in my heart, without a love of my own."

Nora, Caitlin and Frankie chime in. Maybe it's the night, and the moon, the new frisbee, or the old harassments, but something's working right. We sound good. Then Kit's dad comes out with his guitar. Amazing! He sits next to Kit, picks the melody line, and sings along with us in his low, coarse voice. "Blue moon, now I'm no longer alone, without a dream in my heart, without a love of my own."

We sound so good, we do the last verse again, then sit huddled in a circle, knowing it's true, we're not alone. David looks at each of us around the circle, then leans over and kisses Kit on the forehead.

"Goodnight, sweet Katherine," he says.

Then he leans in the other direction and kisses Star.

"Goodnight, sweet Star," he says.

He takes his guitar and goes back into the house. Star puts her head on Kit's shoulder. Happy tears stream down her cheeks. Others of us have our own tears, wishing a dad would appear to gently kiss us, too, on our deserving foreheads.

We sit in our loose circle, close, talking of lost football championships, and symbolic bracelets, the family values group and what it all means. We talk about how fast things are moving — nearly the end of the first semester now. Caitlin says she doesn't think she'd still be here, if it weren't for us, and GSA. We scrunch in a little closer. We're so quiet our breathing becomes obvious. Then Star breaks the mood by starting her stupid joke routine — actually, it's stupid advice this time. Like:

Never test the depth of the water with both feet.

If you drink, don't park. Accidents cause people.

If at first you don't succeed, skydiving is not for you.

Before you criticize someone, you should walk a mile in their shoes. That way, when you criticize them, you're a mile away and you have their shoes.

That's the one that gets us all up and saying good-bye.

"Group hug, group hug," Frankie pleads.

We gather close, arms around one another. "Love you, babes," Frankie says.

He throws the frisbee in the direction of my gate. Wilma chases it, catching it just before it hits the ground. Conan and I follow her, open the gate, and let her inside. One more kiss, and he goes to his car. I watch, then join Wilma in the house. She's already waiting at the foot of my bed, ready for sleep.

EPILOGUE

Mom adjusts my cap, carefully draping the gold tassel to the left. Tonight, after I walk across the stage and shake hands with Mr. Maxwell, I'll move it to the right, showing I'm a graduate.

Mom hugs me, teary eyed. She stifles a sob.

"Mom. Mom! Get a grip," I tell her.

She wipes her eyes, laughing.

"I'll feed Wilma, and then we'd better go," Mom says.

I won't admit this to Mom, but when I think about leaving high school, *I* feel like crying, too. Everything changes now. Friends scatter, responsibilities increase, life gets serious. Not that it hasn't been plenty serious already.

Here's what happened where we left off — back in December.

Mr. Maxwell and Coach Ruggles were determined to reinstate Brian, Eric, Anthony and Justin in time for them to play the next game. Mr. Maxwell called the Fearful Fours' parents early Saturday morning, after we got trounced by Serrano. He said Mr. Cordova had overreacted — they'd get the boys back in school in time for the next game. They had a championship to win.

Monday morning, after Mr. Cordova refused to back down on the suspensions, Brian's dad came stomping into the office, yelling that Mr. Cordova was ruining Brian's life — said the suspension meant Brian'd lose his scholarship. Mr. Cordova said the only one ruining Brian's life was Brian.

Things got heated. Mr. Marsters threatened to sue the school. Mr. Cordova called the district's legal advisor, a representative from the local teacher's organization, and the newspaper.

In the middle of the turmoil, Felicia marched into Mr. Cordova's office. She was still wearing her necklace, except that the gold cross had been replaced by a slightly larger enameled cross, bright with the colors of the rainbow. She said she wanted to make a statement regarding the destruction of the school's display case. Once the charge of vandalism and destruction of school property was added to Brian and Eric's crimes, it was out of the question even for Manly Max to maneuver them back to school in time for the next game.

The family values group became even more irate. Eric's dad and the picketers were at school every day for two weeks, from ten until two. They walked back and forth across the main entrance. Besides the usual "Americans for Family Values" signs, others said:

DON'T LET PERVERTS RULE OUR SCHOOL
GOD IS CRYING
REINSTATE DECENCY
BRIAN, ANTHONY, ERIC, JUSTIN
   WE'RE WITH YOU!
FAGGOTS BURN IN HELL

Another group of picketers gathered across the street each day — people from PFLAG, and the Episcopal and Methodist churches, and other organizations I'd never even heard of. When my mom could get away from work, she joined them. Kit's parents and Caitlin's parents were usually there, too. Their signs said:

SAFE SCHOOLS FOR ALL
HATE IS NOT A FAMILY VALUE
RESPECT ALL GOD'S CHILDREN

At lunchtime, students from the Christ First club stood near the picketers, heads bowed, in what the newspaper described as a prayer vigil.

On walls and classroom doors, more anti-gay stickers appeared, covered quickly by embrace diversity stickers. PFLAG members contributed to a sticker/bracelet fund, and Free Expressions placed a rush order to replenish their dwindling supply.

When Kit and I handed out Pride bracelets in choir, all but two students took them.

While the picketers and pray-ers did their thing at the school's entrance, GSA held open forums every lunchtime in the library. Some students came because they were truly interested, others came to harass. Some showed up because they were angry that our football team was bound to lose the next game.

Usually Mr. Harper and Woodsy were there, along with Emmy and Mr. Cordova.

Our message was that *all* students have a right to be educated in a safe environment — that we're dealing with basic human rights issues.

"How about the right not to have faggots and fairies hittin' on you?" one guy yelled.

"Exactly," Emmy said. "If someone keeps asking you to have sex with him, or her, and they persist after being told no, that's sexual harassment, and you should file a complaint."

A lot of students didn't know the difference between a hate crime and shoplifting. At every forum we focused on the seriousness of hate crimes — we put up posters, and handed out flyers defining hate crimes as those that are committed against people because of their particular race, color, national origin, sex, disability, sexual orientation (or perceived sexual orientation) or religion.

At every forum we asked students to help us make Hamilton High School a place where all students could be safe and feel welcome.

"How can anyone who's gay feel safe and welcome here with picketers who're talking about how faggots burn in hell?" one kid asked.

"Those people shouldn't be allowed out there," the girl sitting next to him said.

"But see, we have freedom of speech, and freedom of assembly in this country," Mr. Cordova said. "That was our stand when we pushed to have GSA meetings on this campus. It works for everybody, not just the people we agree with."

Conan was right in his prediction that Muir would thrash us. We lost forty-seven to six. At the end of the game, Mr. Maxwell got on the microphone and said what a great season we'd had, and what a great school Hamilton High was. He looked tired. His blue suit was rumpled. Honestly, I felt sorry for him.

I'd heard that Brenda Lester and the superintendent had examined the school's complaint file, and they'd been shocked at Maxwell's lack of attention to certain situations. His "boys will be boys" dismissal of serious infractions is exactly the sort of thing that got a neighboring school district slapped with a very costly and embarrassing lawsuit. The superintendent warned Maxwell he'd better get his practices and attitudes in line with recent legislation or start thinking about an early retirement.

At the end of their ten-day suspension, all four of the guys who'd attacked Frankie and Kit in the parking lot were expelled from Hamilton High. They were reassigned to Sojourner. Star was delighted. "For once, the bash*ers* get banished and the bash*ees* get justice."

Once the championship was lost, and the fate of the Fearful Four was set, the picketers stopped demonstrating. The Christ First group went back to whatever it was they did when they weren't holding prayer vigils on the sidewalk. And once all of *that* died down, there was no longer a need for a GSA daily forum, so we went back to our usual weekly meetings.

Basketball players gradually took over the designated jock table, and they were mellow, even friendly to our group. Of course, with Conan and Robert wearing Pride bracelets, the whole bunch of us gained credibility.

When we went back to school after Winter Break, it seemed that the whole anti-gay thing had faded. No one was plastering insulting stickers all over, or making crude remarks to Frankie or Kit. There'd been this super intense time, and now things were on the verge of boring.

Not that everything was perfect. Emmy noticed that books with rainbow stickers on them were missing from the shelves. How could they get past the library's new and supposedly foolproof security system? When she did a computer search, she found that fifteen of those titles had been checked out during one week's time. Most had gone to members of the Christ First group. Two had been checked out by Eric's younger sister. There was nothing wrong with that, except we all doubted those particular students were trying to educate themselves regarding lesbian, gay, bi, and trans issues. It wasn't until March that Emmy realized that *all* of the rainbow stickered books were missing from the shelves. They were all legally checked out, but not one had been returned. When Emmy called homes about the books, she would always be answered politely and get a promise that the book would be returned the next day, but they never were.

Nicole wrote an editorial for the school newspaper, saying such tactics were dishonest — the sneakiest form of censorship. We took turns writing letters to the editor of the *Hamilton Heights Daily News*, so there would be at least one a week. We pointed to the hypocrisy of so-called Christians who stole school property. We questioned where theft fit into the ideals of "Americans for Family Values."

I haven't told you this part yet, but Conan accepted the football scholarship to Ohio State. I know why I haven't mentioned it. I don't like to think about it. Speaking of football scholarships, when the college coaches learned of Brian's expulsion from Hamilton High, they withdrew their offers. Conan says it's sad, because Brian is such a good player. I say it's karma.

Anyway, because of Conan's scholarship deal, he had some extra money. He rented a limo for the prom, and he and I, Kit and Star, Holly and Robert, and Caitlin and Frankie all rode in the limo. Nora came with Douglas, from choir. Can you believe it? She says he's turned nice. I thought Douglas was a lifetime member of the idiot club, but then, when I think about how uptight I was with Kit . . . well . . . thank *gosh* idiots can get smarter.

Get this. Kit and Star both dressed in tuxedos. Star's was a dark purple, and Kit's was sky blue. Kit's hair was about four inches long by then, and she had it twisted in narrow strands which were held together by beads, like the rainbow beads in her Pride bracelets. When I think about what my fantasy of this night was, and the reality I've ended up with — all I can say is that reality is way more interesting.

I don't know about proms, anyway. There's all of this big deal about them, and money, and then you go, and you stand in line forever to get your pictures taken, and then, after about two dances, it's time to go. The most fun was after the prom, when we all went to Kit and Star's favorite place in Pasadena. Everyone there knew them, so even if the rest of us were like misfits in that place, it was okay, because we were friends with Kit and Star. We danced, and laughed, and played darts, and pool, and stayed until closing time. I guess you could say we embraced diversity.

"LYNN!"

Mom's standing in the doorway, purse in hand.

I shake my head, trying to bring my wandering mind back to the present. "I swear, you'd better never be an emergency room nurse the way you lose track of the here and now," she says.

We both laugh. I take one more look in the mirror and follow Mom out to the car.

When we turn the corner, we're right behind Kit and her parents. Her mom is in the front seat, but turned toward Kit, talking animatedly. When I think how things were with them, when Kit first came out . . . it's a minor miracle. And Kit . . . she hasn't exactly changed through all of this, she's just become, I don't know, more

Kit. Looking back on all that's happened, it's hard for me to believe I was so uptight about everything when Kit first told me she was a lesbian. It's like what's to worry about?

Something else I've not told you yet — Kit's going to stay with her aunt and attend California State at San Francisco. I'll miss her soooo much. Which is another thing I don't want to think about right now. I really don't want to walk across the stage tonight drowning in tears, with my face all blotchy from crying, and snot running out of my nose. Oh my *gosh!*

What else do you need to know? Conan finally told his family about me. They flipped. But he told them that's who I'm with, that's who I love. Let me know when you want to meet her. So far, no dates are penciled in. Here's the thing though, now that Conan's acknowledged me, I don't care so much what his parents think.

What will I remember about my senior year when I'm thirty? Or forty? Or fifty? I'll still remember Celie, and Shug, from *The Color Purple*, and how Celie finally found love when Shug helped her break the man-made rules. I'll remember how Kit grew strong and happy once she determined to be true to herself. The beach, with Conan and Kit. All of the times under the tree I've told you about, and some I haven't. Pride bracelets. Choir. Emmy and Rosie. Woodsy, Guy and Mr. Cordova.

Of course, I will remember Conan. Again Conan. And more of Conan. I expect we'll be together, years from now, remembering it all. And we'll treasure the strength of our love for one another, knowing we've overcome those crazy rules that say color is more important than spirit.

Besides *The Color Purple*, I'll remember the title of the Alice Walker book I *didn't* read — the one titled *The Way Forward Is with a Broken Heart.* But I'm going to remember it as *The Way Forward Is with an **Open** Heart.* Because it is. And I'll for sure remember that love is stronger than hate. All of that and more is what I learned in my senior year of high school.

Photo : Melanie Mages

ABOUT THE AUTHOR

In addition to *Love Rules,* Marilyn Reynolds is the author of six other young adult novels, *If You Loved Me, Baby Help, But What About Me?, Too Soon for Jeff, Detour for Emmy,* and *Telling,* and a book of short stories, *Beyond Dreams,* all part of the popular **True-to-Life Series from Hamilton High.**

Besides her books for teens, Reynolds has a variety of published personal essays to her credit, and was nominated for an Emmy Award for the **ABC After-School Special** screenplay of "Too Soon for Jeff."

Reynolds is a seasoned educator who has worked for more than twenty-five years with teenagers facing a multitude of crises. Her extensive background with young adults includes teaching reluctant learners and at-risk teens at alternative high school settings in California. She often is a guest speaker and seminar leader for programs and organizations that serve teens, parents, teachers, and writers.

When she is not reading, writing novels, or participating in conferences, Reynolds enjoys walks along the American River, visits from children and grandchildren, and movies and dinners out. She and her husband, Mike, live in northern California.

NOVELS BY MARILYN REYNOLDS
True to Life Series from Hamilton High:

IF YOU LOVED ME — Are love and sex synonymous? Must Lauren break her promise to herself in order to keep Tyler's love? *". . . an engaging, thought-provoking read, recommended for reluctant readers." BookList.*

BABY HELP — Melissa doesn't consider herself abused — after all, Rudy only hits her occasionally when he's drinking . . . until she realizes the effect his abuse is having on their child.

DETOUR FOR EMMY — Novel about Emmy, pregnant at 15. American Library Association Best Books for Young Adults List; South Carolina Young Adult Book Award.

TOO SOON FOR JEFF — The story of Jeff Browning, a senior at Hamilton High School, a nationally ranked debater, and reluctant father of Christy Calderon's unborn baby. Best Books for Young Adults List; Quick Pick Recommendation for Young Adult Reluctant Readers; ABC After-School TV Special.

BUT WHAT ABOUT ME? — Erica pours more and more of her heart and soul into helping boyfriend Danny get his life back on track. But the more she tries to help him, the more she loses sight of her own dreams. It takes a tragic turn of events to show Erica that she can't "save" Danny, and that she is losing herself in the process of trying.

TELLING — When twelve-year-old Cassie is accosted and fondled by the father of the children for whom she babysits, she feels dirty and confused. *"A sad, frightening, ultimately hopeful, and definitely worthwhile purchase." BookList.*

BEYOND DREAMS — Six short stories dealing with situations faced by teenagers — drinking and driving, racism, school failure, abortion, partner abuse, aging relative. *". . . book will hit home with teens." VOYA*

Visit your bookstore — or order directly from Morning Glory Press
6595 San Haroldo Way, Buena Park, CA 90620. 714.828.1998.

Free catalog on request.

Visit our web site at www.morningglorypress.com

ORDER FORM
Morning Glory Press
6595 San Haroldo Way, Buena Park, CA 90620
714.828.1998; 1.888.612.8254   Fax 714.828.2049

			Price	Total
Novels by Marilyn Reynolds:				
__	*Love Rules*	1-885356-76-5	9.95	_____
__	Hardcover 1-885356-75-7		18.95	_____
__	*If You Loved Me*	1-885356-55-2	8.95	
__	*Baby Help*	1-885356-27-7	8.95	_____
__	Hardcover 1-885356-26-9		15.95	_____
__	*But What About Me?*	1-885356-10-2	8.95	
__	*Too Soon for Jeff*	0-930934-91-1	8.95	_____
__	Hardcover 0-930934-90-3		15.95	_____
__	*Detour for Emmy*	0-930934-76-8	8.95	_____
__	*Telling*	1-885356-03-x	8.95	_____
__	*Beyond Dreams*	1-885356-00-5	8.95	_____
__	Hardcover 1-885356-01-3		15.95	_____
	Breaking Free from Partner Abuse			
__		1-885356-53-6	8.95	_____
	Your Pregnancy and Newborn Journey			
__		1-885356-30-7	12.95	_____
__	*Your Baby's First Year*	1-885356-33-1	12.95	_____
__	*The Challenge of Toddlers*	1-885356-39-0	12.95	_____
__	*Discipline from Birth to Three* 1-885356-36-6		12.95	_____
	Teen Dads: Rights, Responsibilities and Joys			
__		1-885356-68-4	12.95	_____
__	*Surviving Teen Pregnancy*	1-885356-06-4	11.95	_____
	School-Age Parents: Three-Generation Living			
__		0-930934-36-9	10.95	_____
__	*Safer Sex: The New Morality* 1-885356-66-8		14.95	_____
	Teen Moms: The Pain and the Promise			
__		1885356-25-0	14.95	_____
__	Hardcover 1-885356-24-2		21.95	_____
	Teenage Couples: Expectations and Reality			
__		0-930934-98-9	14.95	_____
__	— *Caring, Commitment and Change*			
	Paper 0-930934-93-8		9.95	_____
__	— *Coping with Reality* Paper 0-930934-86-5		9.95	_____
__	*Will the Dollars Stretch?* Paper 1-885356-78-1		7.95	_____

TOTAL _____

Add postage: 10% of total—Min., $3.50; 15%, Canada _____
California residents add 7.5% sales tax _____

TOTAL _____

Ask about quantity discounts, Teacher, Student Guides.
Prepayment requested. School/library purchase orders accepted.
If not satisfied, return in 15 days for refund.

NAME _____ PHONE_____
ADDRESS _____
_____